The Things We See In The Light

Amal Awad

16pt

Copyright Page from the Original Book

PANTERA
PRESS

First published in 2021 by Pantera Press Pty Limited
www.PanteraPress.com

Cover Design: Amy Daoud
Publisher: Lex Hirst
Editor: Lucy Bell
Proofreader: Alexandra Nahlous
Typesetting: Kirby Jones
Author Photo: Hoda Afshar
Printed and bound in Australia by McPherson's Printing Group

 This project is supported by the Copyright Agency's
Cultural Fund

TABLE OF CONTENTS

Praise for The Things *We See in the Light*

'A sparkling new voice in Australian fiction.'
Nikki Gemmell

'This book is delicious: sweet, warm and unexpected – the best kind of dessert, but not a guilty pleasure because the characters are so real and their struggles so human that I could not stop thinking about them after the last page.'
Alice Pung

'Awad brings her trademark intelligence and insight to this big-hearted story of a woman building a new life – a cross-cultural delight.'
Toni Jordan

'A woman's journey of self-discovery, the power of enduring female friendships and an unexpected love story. *The Things We See in the Light* ticked all my boxes. Warm, wise, witty, intelligent and insightful, I loved everything about this story. A wonderful

own-voices novel by one of Australia's finest Arab writers.'
Tess Woods

'*The Things We See in the Light* is an emotional journey from heartbreak to wholeness. Awad's new book brings the Australian Arab woman's diaspora front and centre, shining a light on the power of friendship in personal healing and growth. A story woven from the threads of culture, self, community and friendship, examining the intersection of female power and vulnerability.'
Sasha Wasley

'Full of flavour, Amal Awad's *The Things We See in the Light* is a warm, emotive and uplifting story. It's about the power of friendship, facing fears, and being brave enough to find your true self. The perfect book to immerse yourself in, but be sure to keep both tissues and chocolates handy!'
Kaneana May

To Anastasia, Barbs, Cat and Jo – the original childhood crew and the best friends I could ask for

Glossary

As this story includes several Arabic words and phrases, a glossary has been included for the reader's reference.

abaya	Full-length robe
abu	Father of; Arabs generally address each other as 'father of' or 'mother of'
akhi	My brother
alhamdulil-lah	Praise Allah (used in relation to giving thanks)
Allah yirhamo	God rest his soul
Allah yirhama	God rest her soul
ammi	Uncle (but also used as respectful title for father-in-law)
amti	Aunt (but also used as respectful title for mother-in-law)
assalamu alaykum wa rahmatullahi wabarakatuh	May the peace, mercy and blessings of Allah be upon you (an Islamic greeting)
ayb	Inappropriate/shameful/rude
dua	Invocation to God
habibti	My darling, my sweetheart (feminine)
halal	Permissible
haram	Forbidden
hayati	My life

im	Mother of; see 'abu' above
inti horra	You are free (said to a female)
istikhara	Prayer for guidance
keffiyeh	Traditional cotton headscarf worn by Arabs; also a symbol of Palestinian nationalism
mabrook	Congratulations
mahram	Unmarriageable kin
mashallah/masha'Allah	Praise Allah
naseeb	fate/destiny
nikah	Islamic marriage ceremony
o'balik	May it be your turn next (said to someone as a wish for the same event/achievement to happen for them, e.g. marriage, engagement, graduation, pregnancy)
oud	A musky, essential oil fragrance drawn from the agar tree
wajib	An obligatory act; duty
wudu	Ablutions made before prayer
yallah	Come on; let's go

Time doesn't change, time reveals.

–Arabic proverb

home

Chapter 1

The ending of a relationship will always make you question the beginning.

If every group has their archetypes – the cool one, the dreamer, the beauty – I'm the boring one. I have one talent: food. My best friend, Samira, is the imaginative dreamer; her cousin Lara is the life-loving wild one. While my friends had growing pains, I suffered a crushing social phobia. I wrapped it up in piety. But I was never racked with the same worries as my friends. You need to have desires and goals to be anxious about how your life's turning out.

These thoughts flood my mind as I approach the front gate of Lara's apartment block under a blanket of light rain. Uncertainty flows through me, and I suddenly feel self-conscious about my unexpected arrival. If there's anyone likely to appreciate spontaneity, it's Lara, but my body is tense, my nerves tightened like a thousand tiny bows.

Seeing her again feels bigger than the choice I made to return home.

I drop my small piece of luggage onto the concrete, stained wet by the rain. There's a flat number on the brick pillar and I squint at it in the dim light of a crescent moon. On my phone screen is an email Lara sent last year: a promise to send her a package from Jordan. I double-check the address, then look up again. It's the right place.

Before I can further question the wisdom of my arrival, I walk to the front door, pulsing with renewed intention. The apartment block looks weathered but not ancient. It's only four storeys high. The glass door is framed by white wooden panels, the kind that were everywhere in the 1980s. When I discover that the intercom is busted, I'm filled with relief. I wipe my hands down the sides of my thighs, examine them briefly, then grip the thick silver doorknob like it's a lifeline.

It's several flights up to Lara's door. I knock once, then again a few seconds later. Eventually I hear murmurs, then the door swings open and I crane my neck upwards to meet the gaze of a man. He's familiar, but it takes me a moment to place him. Pensive expression. Broad-shouldered and bearded.

'Hakeem?'

The man frowns, concerned. 'Yes?'

He doesn't recognise me. We both look different. Hakeem still bears the markings of the stern, bearded recluse I once knew, but he now has a lighter sprinkling of facial hair, more hipster than 'fundy', as Lara used to call him.

As for me, my headscarf used to fall nearly to my ankles – nothing like the gypsy-style scarf that crowns my head now, exposing my chin and leaving room for small gold earrings and the gold necklace I always wear.

Hakeem and I barely used to interact, both well-versed in lowering our gazes. But now I search his face for clues, or comfort; confirmation, perhaps, that if he has changed, it's not so ridiculous how much I have too.

'I'm Sahar. Lara and Samira's friend?'

Recognition registers on Hakeem's face just as Lara steps into the room behind him, jangling a few coins and asking about dinner. She does a double-take, then covers her mouth in alarm before rushing towards me.

'Bloody hell!'

I want to cry – with relief and anger and shame all at once. I feel like a stranger in a foreign country, although this is my home. But even after everything that's happened, one look at Lara and I feel safe. It's the oddest feeling, and I can't explain it at all.

***

Hakeem commences a quiet exit just as dinner arrives.

'Sorry,' I mutter. 'You don't need to go.' The sentiment isn't reflected in my voice or my words. But Hakeem, a bit awkward and shy, leaves with a smile and a hand to the chest.

Lara pushes me onto the sofa then follows him to the door. My face warms at the thought of the embrace they must be sharing, and I feel the weight of breaking them apart, even if it's only for one evening.

The door closes and Lara yells out, 'Stay where you are.' Then, 'You must be starving,' she continues from another room, and there's the sound of kitchen clattering. I have missed her voice, her hybrid Australian-English accent.

'Not really. I had something on the plane.'

Crackers and cheese. I didn't have the stomach for more.

While I wait, I grow curious about how Lara lives. On the wall beside the hallway entrance is a painting in broad brushstrokes of an Arab woman – a red *keffiyeh* scarf sitting loosely around her shoulders – with voluminous black hair and piercing brown eyes. She stares into the distance, not looking at her audience. The main wall presents a startling portrait of Lara and her band onstage, spotlights spraying white light above them. Lara stands out with her wild mane of hair, tight black pants and sparkly blue top, her eyes closed as she sings into a microphone. Large, dangly earrings complete the look. Below the picture, resting on the floor, is a guitar case.

Lara has grown up. Or perhaps, simply, into a better version of herself. She was never someone who needed a lot of things, only experiences, even if they could be emotionally explosive. That's what she liked – to smash into things.

My face flushes at my silent assessment of Lara as she plods back into the room carrying plates, cutlery and glasses.

'You look so different,' she says, beaming at me, then she indicates to the photograph of her onstage. 'Samira took that; clever thing.' She lays out a floral Mexican oil cloth – the kind our mothers always used to cover our dining tables. 'Wog mat!' She laughs. 'I'm so grown up now. It's disgusting.'

Lara serves up a slice of pizza for me. 'Vegetarian; don't worry.'

I smile gratefully. It's been years since I've had to think about food as *halal* or not. In Jordan, everything was halal, and I long ago stopped worrying about it. 'Anything is fine, thank you.'

A short silence follows as we negotiate plates and napkins. Lara twists open the lid of a bottle of sparkling water and starts to pour.

'So, how long do I have to wait before I ask what you're doing here?' she says. The lightness in her eyes fades as she hands me the glass of water.

'A while longer.'

'But you're all right?'

'I'm fine. I'll tell you everything, but not tonight. Is that OK?'

Lara responds with a smile. 'Of course.' A few moments later, she ventures, 'Is there anything you want to ask me?' Her eyes are bright with the desire to share information.

'How serious is it with Hakeem?'

Lara pours herself a drink. 'He's my person, I guess.'

'Is he your ... *engaged to you* person?'

'We're somewhere between dating and engaged.'

'Between?'

'It's complicated.'

Lara seems uncomfortable with the truth of her connection with Hakeem, like she's wearing the wrong-sized shirt and is puzzled that it doesn't fit.

'Are you disappointed that you fell for a Muslim?' I ask.

'No, just surprised.'

We eat in silence for a moment, then Lara breaks out into a grin. 'So, tell me: when did you get so trendy? I barely recognised you.'

'Hardly trendy, Lara.' I glance down to inspect my clothing. A knit top over black jeans. Fair enough. These clothes hug my body, rather than surround it. This current version of me is the sweet spot my husband, Khaled, favoured – conservative but not religious. Shorter headscarves, some jewellery, a dab of blush and a stroke of eyeliner.

'At least we've moved past the *hajjeh* look,' Lara says. 'You're wearing an actual top over jeans instead of those wraparound dresses that practically went down to your ankles. Lordy.'

'No, please. Tell me what you really think.'

'Frumplestiltskin.'

'OK, OK.' But a smile creeps across my face.

'I think you would have worn an *abaya* everywhere, if you actually went out at all.' Lara covers her mouth as she negotiates a bite of pizza. 'But there's something else, too.'

'I'm a bit thinner,' I say, reaching for a slice of pizza. 'It makes me look taller.'

I try to remember at what stage of my evolution she last saw me. Was my skin already darker from years of exposure to the unforgiving Middle Eastern sun? I'm far from 'cherubic', as Samira used to describe me. Now I'm considered gaunt, with more pronounced cheekbones.

'Not that,' she says, shaking her head. 'Your energy is different. And you're still a shorty.'

I'm starting to feel embarrassed, but Lara is oblivious to my burning cheeks. I take a bite of pizza and close my eyes, allowing my tastebuds to awaken.

'You're calmer,' she says. 'I mean, not that you were ever loud. But you were...'

'Intense. I know.'

'Especially about religious stuff.'

I offer my agreement with a shrug.

'Have you spoken to Samira?' Lara leans closer. 'And your brother! Does he know you're here?'

'No. Not yet.' My whole body shifts as I tense up. I am reminded that this home I return to is incomplete. My parents are gone. My brother, Salim, is the one remaining link.

Seeing Lara's worry, I try to loosen my response. 'Please, just give me a minute to settle in.'

Lara's expression turns swiftly to remorse. 'Oh my God, of course. I'm sorry.' She reaches over and gives my knee a squeeze.

'It's OK. It's just, my husband doesn't even know where I am yet.'

Lara's eyes widen. She openly processes her shock before pinning me with an enquiring look. 'Babe, I know you're not ready to talk right now, but are you OK?'

I nod, relieved when she doesn't press me further.

I left Sydney in search of a happily ever after, but I didn't return home to find one. When I think about it, survival is what has always motivated me. I am a practical person, not a romantic one.

It explains so much now.

***

A couple of hours later, I wrestle with sleep beside Lara in her large bed.

We're sharing tonight; she insisted, and I agreed without argument. Lara embraced me like a favourite teddy bear as she fell easily into slumber. Half an hour later, I extricate myself, reassured by her steady breathing that she is fast asleep, perhaps already travelling in dreams.

I try to get comfortable. The mattress is soft, but it's not mine and my body rebels against the unfamiliar. The trancelike state that brought me home has faded, and the nerves are evolving into full-blown anxiety, plucking at my insides – a warning shot that something terrible is going to happen, even though the worst has already occurred.

I haven't checked my phone since leaving Jordan. Something for tomorrow, not tonight. I close my eyes again and again, and each time, his face appears. Tonight, I'm lucky. It's not the ending but the beginning that comes to me in flashes.

Before the memories plunge me into proper sorrow, I slow my breathing. I need to occupy myself without delay. I need work to busy my hands. I need

to find a place to live, to create my own space.
I need to forget.

Jordan

The first year

I can't get used to the heat. It's thick and suffocating, wrapped around me but also moving through me. Sometimes, it feels like it's burning my skin and I wonder if this is what hell would be like. Not even the cotton of my headscarf brings relief; I can only find that indoors, in the chilled embrace of rooms running the AC twenty-four seven.

It's odd how this is what makes me feel so far from home – not the strangers I must get to know, or the husband who studies me like he is also wondering how I landed here. Khaled is too good-looking for me, far too Arab, and I am too Muslim. I saw this quickly, but we're still finding our rhythm, so I try not to be offended when he laughs at my conservatism or when he is casual about faith. We will get there, I tell myself, even as anxiety crowds my body.

I still myself, but nothing can be done about the weather, the air, the frantic pace of a city throbbing with activity, the cacophony of sounds from the streets outside that dim only in the early hours of the morning. Everything here erupts into life after eight pm.

I could retreat to the kitchen, but even that feels strange and hollow. In Sydney, the kitchen was my work and meeting place; an expansive, sunlit space that held me, that carried the stories of my friends. Here, although the kitchen is large, it's long and narrow, with a small window that only just manages to throw a shard of light into the room. Whenever I use it, I feel like I'm trapped in a maze, and when I turn this way and that, I am met by emptiness in every direction.

One evening, after I complain mildly about how big the villa is for just two people, Khaled mistakes my meaning and offers to get us a maid. The idea mortifies me.

'A lot of people have maids here. It's no big deal,' he says. 'But if you think you can manage without one, *inti horra.'* He says that a lot. *Inti horra.* You are free.

We occupy a handsome villa. Khaled's family has wealth, and great respect. They are classy and kind. The house is Khaled's, the outcome of years spent in the Gulf working at high-end engineering firms. 'I didn't waste any time,' he had told me during our engagement. He has achieved a lot for a thirty-seven-year-old. The villa is no small thing: modern and spacious, it sits below the mountains. No crowded hilltops and big families occupying three-storey flats for Khaled's family.

My in-laws, Im and Abu Naeem fret over me. My father-in-law, whom I address as *ammi,* takes the seat at the end of the table when we dine out in large, noisy restaurants – the quintessential patriarch who enjoys his high status. He never lets me cook for him. I learned not to take this personally. He just likes eating out, to be taken care of by others, for his family to be taken care of by waiters.

I've been here nearly six months. At first, Khaled made it seem like this was a transitional phase of moving on to the next stage, but it's clear this is not temporary.

On a family trip to Jordan two years ago, I knew my parents hoped I would meet someone. I acquiesced to the pressure of our less religious family to attend a wedding. My cousins insisted on making me over. They good-naturedly giggled at my clothing ('Like my mum's aunties!'), and the length of my headscarves (something about bedsheets). When I refused to uncover for the evening, they transformed me into an unknown and uncomfortable – and to my mind, temporary – version of me. I wore make-up, and they didn't overdo the bright colours.

I looked different and so everything else about me shifted. My shyness was interpreted as sly confidence. Arabs love to say '*shayfa halha*'. She's up herself. That's what they thought of me, and that's what attracted Khaled to me. When the aunts told me he was enquiring about me the next day, I felt an unfamiliar flutter.

It was a tentative yet swift courtship, but it is only now that I am getting to know my husband. Somehow, I had believed that our interactions by phone – calls and texts – were a worthy exploration. They weren't. He is different to how I pictured him, even if on the outside he is the same: handsome, masculine, confident. He is a good son, a good brother. He knows how to talk, though I never feel truly connected to him. I am realistic enough to know that love, if it comes at all, must be developed and earned. But too often, I feel as if I am one of his responsibilities.

We have edged into a scalding summer. Everyone jokes about the weather – you can do that when you're used to it. Better than the cutting winter I arrived in. We joked about that, too – how I shouldn't take it as a bad sign that I arrived in Amman the same day as a rare snowstorm.

Now that the weather is better, Khaled's family keep me busy while he travels for work. We sample the famous *felafel* in downtown Amman. We eat sweets at stores bursting with delicacies. They ferry me to ancient sites – the Roman Steps and Jerash. Despite being too old and tired to navigate these places themselves, my in-laws want to show me the beauty of Amman.

The family had gifted me with half a kilo of gold as a dowry; the heavy, yellow kind made up of thick chains and elaborate designs. Some afternoons, I sit with the jewellery, strangely in awe because they don't match me. But they are elegant, and my sister-in-law Zainab expects me to wear them as a new wife. The nicest piece is a thin gold bangle given to me by Khaled's younger sister, Dina, and I don't mind the small hoop earrings from Khaled. But the piece I come to treasure is the pendant with my name in Arabic calligraphy.

'You see, *habibti*,' Khaled says to me, 'everyone has contributed something. You are our family now.'

Chapter 2

Every day I paint my skull with the memories.

In Lara's small kitchen, I search for ingredients. I'm wearing my favourite red, *dishdasha* a long, embroidered dress our Arab mums customarily wore around the house.

The cupboards are poorly stocked, and the fridge contains only a handful of paltry offerings. I locate a bag of bread that has lost its freshness, but on quick inspection, I see it has no green spots. There are some eggs, a tub of hummus, a slab of haloumi cheese and a soft cucumber that will have to do. From the freezer, I fish out a bag of sausages. Beside the toaster is a bottle of Palestinian olive oil, one month short of expiry.

I fry up the cheese, then cook the meat in a different pan. Warmed by the familiar smells and sounds, I spoon out hummus into a bowl and drizzle olive oil over it, then toast the bread over a naked flame on the stove.

Lara enters just as I'm switching off the gas. 'Look at you, *hajjeh,*' she jokes, appraising my *dishdasha.* 'You haven't changed in the essentials.' Then she sees what I have prepared and looks like she might cry. 'Oh, I miss real food. I miss your cooking.'

I smile, immediately transported. Lara and Samira in my parents' kitchen, eating the endless supply of creations I would make – trials and experiments for my cake business: muffins, tarts, cakes and Arabic food better than my mother's dishes. In Amman, I missed my kitchen and the shape of the conversations that filled it. The invisible energy that floated between the women in my circle, keeping us together, making us feel whole, even when life threw us challenges. If I close my eyes, I am there again, bathed in the innocence and simplicity of another time; the fragrant smells of sauces and spices, the sound of cooking mixed with peals of laughter and stories.

Lara envelops me in a genuine embrace, her eyes shut tight. I remain still, uncertain, yet to let go, and allow her warmth to thaw me out. When she releases me, she goes in search of plates and condiments. Then she makes coffee. 'One thing I *can* do for you.'

As we sit down to eat, Lara places a cup of coffee in front of me, the foam topped with a dusting of cocoa in the shape of a heart. She bats her lashes. 'Aren't I talented?' Then she tilts her head to the side and studies me. 'You feeling well rested?'

I nod. 'I feel like I've been out for three days.'

'Closer to two.'

'What? That's not possible.'

'You arrived Tuesday night. It's Thursday.'

'God. Sorry.'

'You needed it. I just had to check that you were still breathing.'

Lara eats like a woman starved. 'Sorry about the lack of food,' she says between mouthfuls. 'I've been away, and I haven't done a proper shop. Food on tour is crap. Really bad for you.' She pinches her hips. 'She was always curvaceous and I can't decipher a great difference in her body. Perhaps she is slightly fuller, but as beautiful as ever.

'You don't look any different to me,' I tell her.

I take a sip of the coffee, immediately responsive to the bitter flavour. But the milk is a shock to my system. In Jordan, the milk was sweeter, usually condensed. I took to making a pot of aromatic Turkish coffee every morning, slavish to its comforting effects on me.

'I'm not sure how to behave around a rock star,' I say.

Lara snorts. 'Gawd. I'm not even close to being a star.' But I can sense the wish at the end of the sentence.

'You seem to be doing well.'

Lara nods, scraping up the remaining hummus on her plate with a piece of bread. 'I love it. It's like coming home. It's like ... do you know that feeling of relief when something just ... fits?'

'Uh-huh.' I ache at the memories of the things that 'fit'.

'So, I have an idea,' Lara says. 'I was thinking we could take a walk around the neighbourhood later. There are loads of bakeries and specialty cafes. This is hipster central. Maybe you'll be inspired.'

'Inspired to do what?'

'I figure you'll be wanting to restart your cake business. If you're staying a while, that is?'

'I'm back for good. But I'm not sure about the business.' My words hit me like a blunt knife.

'There's one particular place I want to take you to,' Lara continues. 'Sweets by Maggie. It's a dessert cafe with a little chocolate shop next door.'

The idea lands softly in my gut. 'That might be nice,' I say, my enthusiasm mild but growing.

'Maggie's kind of a big hit in the neighbourhood. All the social media geeks line up for her cakes every weekend. She's been around for a few years, but some influencer got hold of one of her cakes and Maggie took off.' Lara assesses me. 'Do you think you're up to it?'

'Of course.' I rise from my seat, already feeling overwhelmed, and start clearing the table to hide my expression. I'm in Sydney again. It should feel like home.

Then a sound splinters my thoughts and I look up to see Lara has dropped a key onto the kitchen table.

'It's a spare,' she says. 'Come and go as you please.'

'Lara, I don't know what to say.'

She rises from the table and downs the rest of her coffee. 'You don't have to say anything. You have no idea how happy I am to see you.'

I know she means it. I can see that, somehow, I'm a lighthouse to her, just as she is to me. With the familiar, we don't feel so alone.

***

Lara's suburb of Newtown is nestled in the inner west, an area of Sydney home to warehouses and wogs. Despite some upgrades, it's immediately apparent that its 1970s faded charm is part of its modern appeal. It has a worn-out quality, but it's clearly been revived by hipsters who recycle and favour retro settings. Beyond the apartments and houses lies the main street, filled with corner pubs, clothing stores, restaurants and cafes. The network of streets and outlets has a grimy quality. I see a tea shop and a store selling crystals and mystical wonder at eighty dollars an hour. We bypass shops with trendy clothing and leather handbags and only slow down for the food establishments.

I marvel at how comfortable and easy it feels to be here when this used to be the type of area our parents never allowed us to frequent as young women. Newtown was famous for its assortment of oddballs, misfits and people in various states of human confusion. I smile at the thought that Lara found her way here. Life gets it right sometimes.

Suddenly, a wave of reassurance moves through my body. I am meant to be here, walking these streets. There is something waiting for me, ready to burst into life.

I ogle a Japanese cafe with specialty matcha offerings. Beside it is a shop with tall cakes that show a clear signature style of marbled glazed surfaces and elaborate chocolate decorations. I file it away with a spark of interest as Lara forces me to keep moving. A few doors down, we come to a stop outside the cafe Lara mentioned, Sweets by Maggie. I peer through the window and see a jungle of bodies, some in a queue, others seated at a mess of tables and chairs. Beside the cafe is a chocolate shop, a hole-in-the-wall that is distinctive for its small window and gold lettering, which spells out the name: Small and Sweet by Maggie. It is strangely out of place but also exactly where it should be.

'Sweets first,' Lara says, steering me towards the cafe entrance. She pushes the door open and we are hit by the din of a space teeming with customers. We make our way through in search of a place to sit. It's a tiny shop, no bigger than an apartment, with small wooden tables packed together and a decent-sized display fridge. Lara flies over to a couple vacating a table in the far corner and we secure the spot. Then she dashes off to make some selections. I guard the table, trying to identify the contents of the fridge from a distance; I can see cakes, tarts, pastries and doughnuts.

A few minutes later, Lara places an assortment of desserts down before me.

'Coffee's coming,' she says as she takes her seat then crosses her arms in anticipation. She knows this is a language in which I'm fluent, and these desserts are impressive. There's a level of mastery to their design and structure. A chocolate dome looks robust, the chocolate thick and smooth, the surface shiny. Gold dusting and a sampling of raspberries adorn it. I suspect it will be bliss. Beside the dome is a vegan salted-caramel doughnut, glossy and enticing. There's a mille-feuille, plump with fresh layers of custard between flaky pastry, in some ways similar to the ones I used to make, but this one is topped with a luxuriously thick vanilla icing and gold leaf. Finally, an elegant panna cotta in a dome shape, infused with vanilla bean and topped with mint leaves and raspberry. Simple but suggestive of an experience.

'The chocolate dome is Maggie's signature dish. Chocolate is her thing, obviously,' explains Lara, indicating towards the shop next door.

As I start to sample the desserts, I wake up a little. The flavours offer mini explosions, brief teases of joy. As always, my mind starts to deconstruct the ingredients and steps that went into making each one. I compare my own approaches, but I also look for the faults. I'm like an actor who can never watch a movie without thinking about how it was made; a dentist who judges everyone's teeth.

Lara watches me. 'No?' she says, sounding a bit disappointed.

'Oh no, they're lovely.' Except the panna cotta, which is too heavy and thick. 'This whole place is nice.'

'I thought you might like it. Like I said, it's pretty popular.'

'Yes. Instagram famous. I can see why.'

A waiter arrives with our coffees, dropping them onto the table so quickly that the tops slosh onto the plates. Unperturbed, Lara takes a sip of her coffee and watches as I continue with the doughnut.

'So, is this the sort of place you might want to work?'

'Maybe.' I push away the plates, suddenly full.

'OK,' Lara says, placing her coffee cup carefully onto the saucer. 'Well, I know Maggie, because I know Leo. He's a mate, and Maggie's business partner. I think they're related, or they grew up together or something.'

'And they're hiring?'

'I don't know, but I can tell them about you.'

'I don't want a handout, Lara. I want to do this properly, if I'm going to do it at all.'

'Well, they're not going to give you a job if you can't bloody bake, are they?'

I think on this for a moment. 'I guess not.'

Lara sighs. 'Will you at least think about it? Just say the word and I'll give Leo a call.'

I nod and she breaks out into a grin and digs her spoon into the chocolate dome. She closes her eyes in rapture as she spoons some into her mouth, before widening them to a crazy size as she goes in for more. 'Oh my God. So good.'

Then her phone pings and she negotiates eating and texting, leaving me to drink my coffee while I study my surroundings. The coffee menu board reads like another language of roast origins and histories. Around me, people confidently go about their day. I watch as a woman takes a photo of her plate – an impressive, glossy lime-coloured dessert with shards of chocolate perched on top. I want to feel that ease and confidence, too. Like this is my city again, and I know my way around it. I don't know what this version of me will look like in this world, but part of me is anxious to find out, the part that wants not simply to survive but to live.

Phone abandoned, Lara speaks. 'You're so quiet. But so much is going on in that head of yours.'

I nod. 'You have no idea.'

'I want to, though.'

'I know. I just can't right now.' It all feels too large for this moment.

'Have you even checked your messages yet?' Lara says.

I shake my head. My phone sits heavily in my handbag.

'OK,' she continues, unflappable. 'I get that you don't want to share the full story yet, but enough with rules, Sahar. You look like you've loosened up a bit. Why don't you just have some fun?'

Her words are hollow to me. I have 'loosened up', it's true. But I feel lost, abandoned after a time of connection and purpose.

'Sahar, listen. I've calmed down a lot. I'm not anywhere near as wild as I used to be, and Lord knows, being with Hakeem means I'm disgustingly sensible in ways that I never imagined possible. I mean, I floss for God's sake. But I am your woman for regret: for dealing with it, and curing it. Just name your adventure.'

I don't want to hurt Lara's feelings. But I don't know how to explain that what fills my thoughts when it comes to my freedom is not the stuff people usually think a woman who has left her husband must want. I don't care about sex or a night on the town. I want solitude and space. I want to crawl into myself and out as I please while I process the path ahead.

I chuckle. 'I don't want to play *haram* catch-up, Lara. I'm fine.'

Lara studies me, disapproval etched into her features. 'Babe. It's not about giving in. It's about experiencing. Don't label it.'

'What do you think is going to help me right now?'

'I don't know. That's what I'm asking you to think about. You're in control here. You lead the way. Just tell me how I can help.'

I exhale noisily. 'OK. I need to work, to do something with my body. I'm antsy.' Full of all these emotions and nowhere to put them.

Lara is enlivened by my admission. She taps her phone against her face, looking up at the ceiling. 'OK. We know you can find work easily enough. The movement stuff ... why don't you do some dancing or yoga? I did pole dancing for a while. It was pretty cool.'

I sigh and shake my head. 'Never mind.'

'No, really!' Then she registers my expression, the conservative parts of me fanning out and constructing a boundary. 'OK,' she says, 'not pole dancing. How about you come to my gym as a visitor?'

A tiny thrill rushes through my body. Exercise sweeps away my anxiety better than intimacy, or even the stirrings of love.

I smile and Lara looks satisfied. 'Good,' she says with a decisive nod. 'Now, the day isn't over yet. Follow me.'

We navigate our way through the congregation of tables and emerge into the bright sunlight. I'm grateful for Lara's patience, but eventually, my history will surface. I cannot avoid it forever, and I don't want to. I want to share what happened, despite the fear that my friends will judge me for it. Sooner or later, I will have to explain how I fell in love in Jordan, but not with my husband.

***

Lara leads me to the chocolate shop next door. We enter, an old-school bell ringing out as we step inside. Several customers crowd the space that's deceptively larger than it appears from the outside. I head to a small counter where a variety of handmade chocolates are on display. Many of them are in bold colours – lapis blue, gold, silver, lemon yellow. Others are marbled, dusted, topped with an almond. There are pralines and shards in white, milk and dark chocolate. I crane my neck for a better look and see more elaborate offerings, as well as chocolates packaged in colourful boxes on a shelf, ready to go.

'Aren't they beautiful?' says Lara, coming to a stop beside me. 'And they taste amazing.'

'Stunning.' The craft involved, the care and delicacy.

'Sometimes I look through the window and imagine the flavours,' she says. Then her phone rings and she raises a finger in apology before escaping out the front door.

I direct my attention to the back of the store, where through a doorway, I can see the studio. A man in chef's whites is tempering chocolate on a metre-long marble counter, thick, wavy hair peeking out from under his chef's cap. His concentration is steady, his movements concise and clipped. He is not expressive, but what some might assess as boredom I recognise as ease; he is practised at what he does. Doesn't have to think too hard. He's in a creative zone, oblivious to the bustle of the shop.

Occasionally, he is eclipsed by browsing customers, but I stay in place, losing what must be minutes watching him work. He's good, and my body is responsive to the image. Very quickly, my hands itch to be doing the same. I catch myself almost imitating the dance of his limbs – one arm extending swiftly to scoop up the melted chocolate with a tempering spatula, his other hand swiftly removing it with a bench scraper. The sounds and scents flood my senses as if I'm the one standing behind the counter.

Muscle memory. I used to temper chocolate for cake decoration, but in much smaller amounts. I feel cheered by the feelings it has reawakened within me, my creative brain wearily emerging from its years-long slumber.

Chapter 3

Some things aren't lost, only misplaced.

Not far from Lara's apartment is an organic grocery store. On the way back from the chocolate shop, I drag Lara inside, insisting on gifting her some groceries because I'm an unexpected house guest. Besides, Lara's bare kitchen depresses me. She half-heartedly tries to stop me, but then her phone pings again and she leaves me to tour the shop alone.

The prices are steep but the produce is fresh. I move easily in these spaces, no matter how crowded they are, speaking an invisible language with nature. I choose generously from the bounty, undeterred by cost. Always frugal, never needing possessions, I have savings. Most of the money I made from my business went directly back into it.

I fill my basket with shiny red apples, stone fruits marbled orange and brown in appropriate amounts, a punnet of strawberries, a thin offering of blueberries in a small plastic packet. My entire body changes as I find my flow and build a menu in my mind. I will make dinner and dessert. I pile in some bananas, just shy of ripeness. Vegetables follow. I bypass the bagged lettuce and find a crown of cauliflower, to be fried until golden. Next, onions, then straight to the deli section. I opt for chicken instead of lamb, and I can already smell the *ma'loubeh* like it's in front of me. They have Lebanese bread, so I buy two bags. I take my time choosing the haloumi, worrying over saltiness levels. As a final indulgence, I buy a large tub of mixed olives. Then I remember the coffee this morning and circle back to find a Turkish blend.

As we walk home, shopping bags between us, Lara is quiet and I can sense something is awry.

'Are you OK? You seem distracted,' I ask.

Her response is delayed and hesitant. 'Nope. Just a gig thing. Don't ever become a musician.' She smiles brightly.

'Where can I listen to your music by the way?'

Lara's eyes light up, her look tentative. 'You want to hear something?'

'I have no idea about music, but if it's yours, I'm in.'

'We're doing a show next week. It's a classy place. Still a bar, though.'

'I'd like to come.'

Lara smiles wide and true. Then she looks grateful. It must be lonely being on her path, I realise. Minimal support, no anchor, even with a small place to call home. 'Hakeem might come too,' she says, but I can't tell from her tone if he generally attends her performances or avoids them.

I mentally chew on this, trying to form an image of me sitting in a bar with Hakeem that doesn't jar.

We continue on in silence, but I can't shake the sense that she is still hiding something from me. When we reach the gate to her complex, it becomes clear what it is.

I can see her at the entrance to the building: Samira, looking the same as she did the last time I saw her two years ago. She stands elegantly, dressed simply in black jeans and a blue knit top, her head-covering a turban, the kind I used to see Egyptian mums wear but which is becoming common among younger women negotiating their modesty.

My stomach drops. Samira is, in so many ways, a tattoo, a permanent imprint of my past and who I am. And here, I feel our connection erupt into life, even if our frequencies are out of sync, a little uneasy. Her expression differs from the last time we met: there's no joy in this reunion, no warmth to be found in her stern features. I detect something else. Confusion.

And there's more. She looks deeply disappointed.

***

In the kitchen, I drop my bags and start unpacking the ingredients for tonight's dinner. I'm reconsidering my initial idea of *ma'loubeh,* which takes time. It literally means 'upside down', because you cook the ingredients in a pot on the stove, then flip it upside down onto a large tray when it's ready to eat. There's an element of theatre – and suspense. The dish should retain its shape once it's been emptied from the pot. If it falls apart, something's failed in the cooking process.

Samira watches me from the side, leaning against the kitchen bench where Lara is perched beside her. She removes her head-covering and shakes out her hair.

'I'm sorry, Sahar!' Lara says. 'I broke. Samira called me and she could tell that I was hiding something from her. She can always tell!'

Samira rolls her eyes. 'Please. I didn't even have to take out a torture kit. Lara wanted me to know.'

I'm in trouble with the woman I've always considered my best friend, yet it strikes me that this scene is reminiscent of the many hours we lost together before adulthood took the wheel. The three of us in the kitchen of my parents' house, me commanding the space with ingredients as I cooked and baked, keeping my world neat and tidy and delicious. But this is some underworld version, more darkness than light.

'It's true,' Lara says. 'I suck at lying. Look, you don't have to tell your brother you're here, but you know Samira would kill us if we hid this from her. I just needed to rip off the bandaid.'

Samira comes up beside me. She takes a bag of fruit out of my hands and pulls me into alignment so that we're facing each other. My cheeks are burning red, as they like to when my emotions run high. My stomach turns as she stares at me. Her mouth is moving, but I'm mentally unpacking the steps for the dish: fry the cauliflower and onions; cook the chicken in the pot; add rice and cook for at least an hour. Maybe I should tell her that we can sort all this out after I've placed the ingredients in the pot.

'I'm so sorry, Sahar,' Lara says from across the kitchen. She looks contrite, but also burdened. 'I'm worried about you,' she continues, her voice lowered. 'Also, I ghosted Samira once and she didn't take it well. Samira is a bit scary now.'

Samira turns slowly to look at Lara, her mouth open in genuine offence.

'Strong! I mean strong.'

I forgot to buy yoghurt. *Ma'loubeh* is typically served with yoghurt and a salad. I have cucumbers and tomatoes at least.

Samira returns her gaze to me. 'Sahar. What is going on?' she says, her patience thinned out.

I wonder if she is simply hurt that she wasn't my first stop. 'I didn't want to intrude on you. It didn't seem right to just show up.' I expect she comprehends my meaning: the impropriety of my appearance at a house occupied by her husband, a man who is unrelated to me, and when she is a mother.

But Samira's downturned mouth and crossed arms, the slight inclination of her head as she investigates my expression, tell me she is not convinced. Even I know this excuse only has a certain amount of elasticity to it. I was avoiding Samira, and she knows it. But I couldn't bring myself to face her before I understood better how all of this looks.

'Please don't take it personally.'

'I've had it up to here with you two,' Samira says. 'How is it that I turned out to be the most normal one?'

Lara flinches, then leans forward from her place on the kitchen bench. 'Don't get cross at her,' she tells Samira. 'Getting divorced isn't as easy as you think.'

'Lara!' I say, my frustration spilling out.

'Oh fuck. I'm so sorry. I really suck at this.'

Samira's eyes brim with tears. 'Sahar. I'm not going to push you on why you didn't tell me you were coming. I just need to know if you're in any danger.'

I turn to find Lara looking at me expectantly, her face creased in worry. Samira is also staring, demanding the truth. I'm too exhausted to lie.

'I'm not divorced. Yet. But I have left Khaled, and I came here without telling him where I was going.'

Samira exhales. 'Did you tell him you were leaving the country?'

'In a manner of speaking. I left him a note.'

'Bloody hell,' says Lara.

A faint recollection takes shape in my mind. Lara's 'crazy ex' showing up on her doorstep, leaving unsolicited gifts of love, attacking her when she was closing up at work one evening. Then it clicks: I am being disruptive and selfish. I need to reassure her that I am not wreaking similar havoc upon her with my arrival.

'There's no danger. But I should get out of here sooner rather than later.'

'You don't have to,' says Lara, sliding down from the bench.

'Sahar, enough,' Samira says, her voice soft but firm. 'Stop being a hero.'

Lara is right. Samira is scarier now.

Samira pauses and when she speaks again, her tone is gentle. 'Are you here on your own?'

It takes me a moment to realise what she's asking, and I feel shame rising at my failure to stay connected with my friends.

'You mentioned a pregnancy or two,' Samira continues carefully. 'But you dropped off after the last announcement.'

'Four. I've had four miscarriages,' I tell her without emotion. Still, at any moment, the cracks will appear.

Lara's eyes well up, but to her credit she reserves the moment for me and does not get dramatic. Samira immediately softens and pulls me in for a hug. The emotion vibrates off her body in thick waves, but I feel nothing.

My body doesn't hold on to babies. I don't know why they came to me at all when they had no intention of staying. I fell pregnant in the first year, and miscarried a month in. More pregnancies – and losses – followed. I suffered the miscarriages quietly, refusing to be anything less than stoic.

I don't tell my friends that despite the pain of loss, there was a sense of relief the last time I miscarried. There was acceptance as a door slammed shut; a question truly answered. *You cannot have a baby. You are never going to be a mother. You cannot hide behind your duties. You will need to find something else to fill this gap. You don't have to be a wife anymore.*

In fact, a practical side of me lit up, reassuring me that it was biological –

and my fate. Now, it is accompanied by a sense of relief because Khaled and I do not belong together and a child does not deserve to have us as parents.

All I have left of the experience of being pregnant are moments of what it feels like to be a mother. Even when the foetuses were the size of a pea, I felt love vibrate through me, warming my insides and lightening my worry. I felt less alone, assured that no matter what lay ahead, I would be inextricably linked to another human being in the highest form of unconditional love.

It takes me a few moments to orientate myself again to my new reality, one in which my best friend has arrived on the scene and is holding up a blinding mirror to me. This is exactly what I didn't want.

Lara joins us in the hug. The embrace tightens and we linger in it, but I hold still, making room for their emotions until we finally separate.

Samira relaxes. 'So, what are you going to do now?'

'I asked Khaled for a divorce and he wouldn't give it to me.'

'The bastard,' says Lara, looking ready to fight the air in place of a man she doesn't know.

'We're kind of missing the first part of that story,' says Samira.

'Or all of it,' I say. 'It's a long story. Can I cook first and we can talk later?'

The tension has broken, but I feel chastised, my high mood from the outing dissolved.

I continue to unpack with Samira's help, while Lara picks at the fruit.

'I'm not scary,' Samira says, piercing the silence. 'I just don't take any shit from anyone.'

'She has kids,' says Lara.

'I have kids who test me every day.'

Lara nods and grins, popping a strawberry into her mouth. 'It's adorable.'

I smile appropriately, but my mind is elsewhere. Seeing Samira has advanced me further and faster than I wished to go. And now I feel like the rest must follow: I have to contact my brother. And I have to go to my parents' home and see what remains.

***

The next morning, I summon my courage and reach for my phone. I know before I've switched it on that Khaled has words for me and I will not like them. That he is disgusted with me. That he is disappointed and embarrassed. That despite his frequent refrain, I was never free.

I connect to the wi-fi and wait for the signal to solidify. Several minutes pass, but no notifications appear. A solid feeling lands in my stomach but I shake it away.

While my phone is on, I send Salim a brief message advising him that I'm in Sydney, knowing the more appropriate thing to do is to call him. But thinking of Salim makes me think of my parents. I don't know what talking to him will do, what thoughts and memories will erupt. Already the reminder that I'm an orphan now is turning my stomach.

My parents died too young, but even they would tell me if they could that this was simply their *naseeb,* their fate. No one gets out alive.

I hit 'send' then busy myself in the kitchen, cleaning the cupboards, arranging the rest of the new additions from the grocery store. I make a list of items I will need: different-sized mixing bowls, some baking trays, utensils. It's clear Lara never cooks.

An hour later, my phone rings. Salim's voice is drenched in cautious concern, like he's treading on thin ice that could crack below him at any moment. But there is an edge to his tone. My insides curl up and I feel a pang of anxiety.

'Are you going to stay at Mum and Dad's house?'

'I hadn't thought of that,' I tell him.

'Where are you now?'

'With a friend.'

'Samira?'

'Her cousin, Lara.'

Silence. Perhaps disapproval. Salim may have heard about Lara's new direction, her lack of piety. Laughable, I think, as I contemplate how much faith has held her together, even if she doesn't pray five times a day.

'Come over, see the family. We're here for you. You can stay here if you want.'

'I'll come by soon, *inshallah*. I promise.'

'Sis, call him. He's your husband. What am I going to tell him if he calls here?'

I hang up on a false promise to call Khaled. The truth is, I have no idea what to say to a man who never listens.

Chapter 4

Unravelling begins with a single thread.

Tonight is Lara's gig. It's at a modern 'upmarket' bar, she assured me, as if that should make a difference. I am wearing my obligatory singlet – the tight black one I wear under everything. The layers will slowly come on, blanketing me, hiding so many things.

Here, I threaten to completely undo it all.

I take the singlet off, so that I'm only in my underwear, and start to arrange my hair, rolling the long locks into a neat bun. My current way of wearing a headscarf is less voluminous. My neck is visible when I opt for the turban style. It suggests a fashionable quality I don't have.

How often have people told me I'm imprisoned in a headscarf? Yet I know the truth: I would be this person in any religion. Even without the heavy clothing and long headscarves, I've never felt free. Really, I am in recovery from myself.

Lara enters and I lose hold of the bun. My hair tumbles around my shoulders, and Lara immediately rakes the strands into her hands.

She looks stunning in black leather pants and a sleeveless, sequined black top. Her make-up is smoky, her hair beach-wave casual. I wonder if the boundaries of freedom have ceased to exist for her. She places her arms around me, smiling at the reflections staring back at us. 'You OK?' she says.

I lean into her embrace and nod slowly. 'I think I'm going to be very underdressed if that's what you're wearing.'

'Want to borrow something of mine?'

Lara steps back and takes hold of my hair again. She carefully rolls it into a bun and fixes it in place with an elastic band from the dresser.

In a second, her energy shifts. 'What's this?' she says, her tone grave.

In the mirror, I see what has caught her attention: the knotted scar that runs across my right shoulder blade. About halfway down my back, the skin starts to run clean towards my hip, where another, slightly smaller but still obvious scar maps the top of my right hip.

Every day I paint my skull with the memories.

There's so much she doesn't know. How long will I be able to pretend the past doesn't exist when the physical scars remain?

'It's a long story.'

'You keep saying that. We can make time for a long story,' she says, her frightened eyes meeting mine in the mirror. I smile, because thankfully, we don't have time tonight. She looks like she wants to say more, but she shakes it off and gives my shoulder a gentle squeeze. 'I'll grab you a top. Should be fine over jeans.'

'Is Hakeem coming?'

Lara shakes her head. 'Not tonight. He's in Melbourne with his son.'

When she leaves, I steady myself, placing my hands against the dresser. I take a few deep breaths, closing my eyes, a ritual that always rebalances me.

I finger the wedding band I still wear, before removing it and throwing it onto the dresser. It clatters against the wood then falls flat. I stare at it, marvelling at the weight of such a tiny thing.

I hook on my necklace: the thin gold chain I always wear with the pendant that says my name in Arabic calligraphy. I pat it against my chest, checking that it's secure.

Then I turn my focus to my headscarf, holding the thin bright purple fabric in my hands. It hits me with forceful clarity how ridiculous I'm being to wear a scarf that has lost much of its meaning for me. Perhaps that truth still exists somewhere, but not here, in this small room where nothing is familiar.

I am tired of the dishonesty of it all. I am burdened by pretence. I cannot enter into this new life the way I looked and felt in the one that preceded it.

I undo the bun and leave my hair out.

My mother used to talk about temptation like it was a delicious cake. 'Others will cut into it,' she told me, 'eat until they're sick and regret it later.

We don't do that.' Her eyes narrowed as she surveyed my response. 'We're not fooled by the exterior of things, the beauty that hides evil inside.'

I believed her because I knew: I would eat the cake if left alone. I would eat it until there was nothing but a crumb left.

***

The bar is an underground speak-easy called Musicale. 'Password-protected,' Lara tells me with a wink as she leads me towards the entrance. She knocks, provides the password to a man with a deep voice on the other side of the door, then grabs my hand like she thinks I might try to escape.

We follow a dimly lit hallway and emerge into a cavernous space that looks as if it belongs in another era. Crowding it are small tables for two covered in red-and-white tablecloths and tealights, each one topped with a tiny vase with a red rose in the centre.

'This is Leo's most popular venue.'

I don't know much about Leo, but he seems to have his fingers in everything. 'Is there anything he doesn't own?'

Lara chuckles. 'Are you sure you're going to be OK on your own? Leo's reserved a spot for you in the back corner. I figured you'd prefer that.'

'Perfect.'

I take a seat, grateful that Lara lent me a sparkly black top. I'm still underdressed, but it's too dark in here for anyone to notice me or care. My hair – long, tousled, slightly unkempt – falls down past my shoulders to the middle of my back. I feel exposed but not naked.

For a vague moment, I sense my mother's energy bearing down on me. Her words echo gently in my ears: 'It's the beginning of the end,' she would lament when she saw Muslim girls take off their headscarves. She took it personally. Would go out of her way to talk to them, like a concerned school principal. But it wasn't simply their decency she was protecting, it was their prospects of heaven in the afterlife. She also bemoaned human nature, the truth of who we are and why it was essential to fight it. 'Don't ever be complacent,

Sahar. Don't ever think a little thing is not a big one when it comes to your faith. God sees all. If it didn't mean anything, you wouldn't be changing it, would you?'

I take her point. It means little to me that I sit here so openly, my hair on display like an unusual statement of shame. This small thing is a big one. It can lead to more. Maybe this is the price of cutting away the old. Constant mental surveillance. But then, it was never my choice to wear a headscarf, not really.

I was once someone who embraced religion and its promises so completely. So how is it that I abandoned all of it when life challenged me? How is it that I, who never went a day without being a good Muslim woman, am now left without it?

Lara steps onto the stage. She sings soulfully. Exudes a knowing, the melody and the music inked onto her physical body. The moment embraces me, her words soft like invisible arms taking hold of me and filling me with warmth. She inhabits the stage with joy.

I close my eyes and think of him with a sense of shame. He wasn't mine to love, and it is here, in this cavernous, dark place, with the soulful voices and warm spirits, that this reality surfaces.

What we shared could not be defined as an affair, and yet, he was not my husband. So what was it?

***

When the band breaks midway, Lara arrives at my table, a bit sweaty and flustered, but her face is dewy and peaceful. Beside her is a man I assume is Leo. She had described him as Mickey Rourke, that 'hot actor but pre-plastic surgery before the really scary changes'. I had to look him up. But I don't see it. His hair isn't as long as Lara described, and it's dark with flecks of grey. He seems a bit younger, late forties perhaps. He's more an Anthony Bourdain. If he's related to Maggie, then he must also be Italian.

'Sahar, I want you to meet Leo,' Lara says.

I nod and extend a hand. Leo wraps it in both of his and gives me a warm smile. 'I've heard a lot about you.'

'Same.'

'I have to take care of something right now, but in case I don't see you later, I want you to email my business partner, Maggie. She might have something for you.'

Leo hands me two business cards then disappears towards the back.

I study the cards – one for Leo Mora, the other, Maggie Mora.

'He's the best,' Lara says, beaming at me. 'You need to email her. I'll have to get back soon, but don't feel like you have to stay. OK?'

I take her up on this. Twenty minutes later, Lara is onstage, and ten minutes in, I'm ready to leave. I walk towards the exit, grateful for the blast of cool air that hits me as soon as I step outside, the door swinging closed behind me and muting the music.

'Going already?'

I stop, startled. I turn to find Leo by the stairs, a cigar perched between his fingers on one hand, his phone in the other. He drops the phone into the pocket of his jacket and steps forward. Up close in the natural light of the evening sky, he looks a bit rough around the edges, skin like worn leather and dark brown eyes.

'I'm really tired. I think I'm still jet-lagged.'

Leo looks amused. 'I can always tell when someone is a Dorothy.'

'Excuse me?'

'Far from home.'

'Well, I grew up here. So, if anything, it's a return home.'

'Fair enough. Why don't you hang around for a bit? You hungry? I'll get you a plate.'

Half an hour later, I'm sitting outside in the back courtyard, sharing a bowl of potato wedges with Leo. The courtyard is not much to look at – an outdoor table with wrought-iron chairs, a small garden of neglected plants and flowers, untidy vines woven into an ageing lattice divider, all lit up by the light pouring out from the kitchen window. But the air is pleasantly chilly, the night sky bright and full of stars. The quiet hum of the music provides a soundtrack, the occasional soaring note from Lara piercing the night air.

As we share the plate, Leo tells me about his time with Lara. That's how he terms it: 'I did my time with her.' I don't need him to explain. Lara is like that. A hurricane that sweeps through. Like nature, she is just being herself, intending no harm, but no one is left the same.

'She worked with me for a few months, but I think she liked the idea of eating cakes more than helping me make them,' I tell Leo.

'Ah.'

'She used to challenge me a lot.'

'Oh?'

'I was pretty religious. She'd roll her eyes at me whenever I tried to lecture her. But then, she put up with it and never made me feel bad about it.'

Leo inspects me like he's seeing me for the first time. 'You *were* religious?'

'In a manner of speaking.'

'And now you're not.'

'No. I mean, I still believe, but ... I'm a lot of other things.'

Leo chuckles, but it's not mean-spirited. He leans in. 'You're a dark horse, aren't you?' Then he laughs warmly.

When we're done eating, Leo brings out a small box of cigars and a bottle of scotch. He pours the caramel-coloured liquid into two glasses then offers me one.

'No, thank you.'

'You don't drink?'

I shake my head.

'I've cut down.' Leo inspects the cigar, clipping off the end with the cutter. 'But Cohibas, I couldn't resist. With a scotch, I get a bit stupid with the happiness.' He lights up the cigar. 'Hope you don't mind the smell.'

'No, it's fine.'

'You ever had one?'

'No. But I've tried cigarettes. My ex-sister-in-law would get me to have shisha with her sometimes.'

'Hubbly bubbly?'

'Yes.'

Leo holds up his glass of scotch. 'Well, keep away from this so you can stay looking young and fresh, and avoid having skin like mine.'

'Like I said, I'm pretty vanilla.'

Leo puffs on the cigar a few times as though he's warming it up. 'Vanilla is a flavour. Don't know why people think it's not special.'

'We can't all be special.'

'Fair enough,' he says with a smile.

We make small talk for a while longer until it gets too cold to stay outside. Leo leads me to the footpath. 'You're welcome here anytime, by the way,' he says, then gives me a peck on the cheek. 'I'll order you an Uber.'

When I reach the apartment, my body feels lighter after an unexpected evening of connection. Then my phone signals a message. It's from Khaled. My stomach sinks.

Allah ye'samhik.

May God forgive you.

And he's not even religious.

***

Later, alone in my freshly furnished bed in Lara's apartment, thoughts of Khaled are replaced by *him.* He is ever present, a flimsy but eternal layer of my existence, even in dreams. That's where he visits me.

When he appears, I don't search for meaning or relevance. I know why he comes; we are linked by an invisible thread in some mysterious way, in a parallel place.

I didn't imagine our connection. The way he would look at me, like he was staring into my soul and finding a missing part in it. How easily I found myself reciprocating. Always with a look and a feeling. Always energetic, rarely physical.

It starts to hurt, the pain beginning as a small burn in the centre of my stomach, thinning out so that I can feel it from head to toe.

I slip into a fitful, dream-drenched night of sleep. A patchwork quilt of memories filters through, amplified and abstract. I am in a headscarf in my parents' home, but then wearing shorts and a bra on the street. I cover myself, but then I'm in the desert and it's not what I'm wearing that matters, but what I see. Him, watching me from a distance. Him, unconscious on the ground, bleeding out. Me, unable to scream or run.

Jordan

The second year

I'm growing accustomed to living in Jordan, but I still struggle with the loneliness – the distance from my friends and family; the unfamiliar. I often find myself alone in the villa; Khaled frequently travels, and his sisters are left to entertain me.

They don't seem to mind. Zainab sends me out shopping with Dina. 'We can be modest and modern,' she tells me over the phone. 'You are Khaled's wife now and we get to spoil you!'

I believe Khaled has put her up to this, but I like spending time with Dina, and her life is more interesting than mine. We go to Abdoun and sit in cafes smoking shisha while she regales me with stories of her social life. Sometimes, Dina, who is in the throes of her late twenties, is spying on a man she seems genuinely drawn to, who seems to reappear between crushes.

Dina sets me up at a local women's gym, while Zainab ensures I visit her house at least once a week for dinner. The semblance of a social life is being constructed for me, but the connections are still in development. The familiarity of childhood friends is missing and it often leaves me feeling sore.

It feels at times like I'm waiting for something, but I'm unsure what it is. Why am I here when it seems as if I have nothing to do?

Sometimes Khaled and I appear like two explorers lost in the wilderness, more weighed down by mutual disappointment than our individual baggage. We have little in common, and we have not bonded. He is my husband but he is a stranger. The big bed feels small even though we share intimacy in it. This is when he softens towards me. When, somehow, our differences melt away and we find each other through physical contact.

Khaled likes me on top. Likes my long hair to spill down my back and around my shoulders.

'Don't ever cut it,' he tells me one night, raking his fingers through my hair.

I start to enjoy physical intimacy, the rush I get when I see the desire in Khaled's eyes. Perhaps this is love, I tell myself.

***

Khaled returns from a business trip in the Gulf with some gifts – a bottle of perfume, some chocolates and a series of bright, small headscarves, shorter than the kind I usually wear.

'I don't know what you like with perfume,' he says as he shrugs out of his clothing.

I smile because I never wear perfume. 'It's very nice, thank you.'

He manages a stiff smile in return then excuses himself to take a shower.

I wait on the bed, wondering if he wants to be with me. But when he emerges, he is already dressed in casual clothing.

'I'm starving,' he says.

'I'll make you something.'

I feel disappointed but not surprised. The exchange flattens me a little, but later that night, he makes it clear that he wants to try for a pregnancy again. I never say no to Khaled.

Afterwards, I can't fall asleep. Khaled's one request is that we go to bed together. He does not love me – I'm not even sure he's attracted to me – but his pride kicks in at bedtime. 'A husband and wife should go to bed at the same time.'

But as I try to steady my breathing, he pulls me close.

'Repeat after me,' he says in Arabic, surprising me with his gentle tone, but also subduing my fears.

Allahuma gharit-in-nujoomu...

Oh Allah the stars have gone far away...

Wa hada'itil-'uyoonu...

And the eyes are rested...

For the first time, I feel that he could actually love me. The moment hints at some strain of belonging to each other.

I repeat the words after him, and eventually my voice crosses over into his. Khaled, the pick-and-mix Muslim, whose deep, melodious voice for so long seemed wasted to his religious wife.

Allahuma gharit-in-nujoomu wa hada'itil-'uyoonu...

Oh Allah the stars have gone far away and the eyes are rested...

Wa anta hayyun qayumon...

You are Alive and Infinite...

...laa ta'khuthuka sinaton wa la nawmon...

You do not slumber nor does sleep overtake You.

Ya hayyu ya qayoomu, 'ahdi' layli wa anim 'ayni...'

Oh Alive and the Everlasting One, grant me rest tonight and let my eyes close.

Chapter 5

I never do anything by half.

The next day I email Maggie, attaching a bare-bones CV that outlines my business history. I try to amplify my efforts in Jordan, but I'm not sure how to explain four years of odd jobs in refugee camps.

When Lara finally emerges at eleven thirty, I make us another Arab breakfast, but a proper one this time: scrambled eggs, fried haloumi, olive oil, zaatar, olives, cucumber and stove-heated Lebanese bread. I forgot to buy sausages. Next time.

I tell her about my conversation with Leo.

She shrugs. 'That's Leo. He's someone you'll always feel safe with. He's a bit protective.' She pauses. 'Did he call you "bella" or "kid"?'

'No.'

'Then he's not making a move on you.'

'I didn't think he was.'

Lara's eyes study me then she indicates my hair. 'Is it permanent or are you just trying it out?' she says carefully, ripping into the bread.

'My scarf?'

Lara nods. She stays busy scooping up eggs and cheese then fashioning the bread into an envelope.

'I think so. It just felt wrong to wear it to a bar.'

Lara nods slowly. 'And how did it feel not wearing it?'

I shrug. 'Honestly? Like nothing.' Naked but not exposed. 'It's been a long time coming, I guess.'

'You're not going to shave your head next, are you?'

I laugh, a bit startled at the thought. 'Why would I do that?'

'Because, I love you, but you tend to be a bit extreme.'

'I don't think cutting all my hair off is the kind of extreme I need right now.'

'But there's something more,' she says. 'If taking off your scarf felt like nothing, then there's more to come.'

My phone vibrates on the bench and I pick it up. Maggie has responded to my email.

Hi Sahar,

I've been expecting your email. Can you come in tomorrow?

M

At the bottom of the email is her full name, Maggie Mora, and a business logo for Small and Sweet by Maggie. It's pastel-coloured but not cute; it has an elegance to it.

The nerves rush in as I realise that this could lead to an opportunity, but also, that it means I would be working for someone else. I email Maggie back and arrange to meet her at the patisserie kitchen the next morning at 11am. She gives me instructions: enter through the green door between the chocolate shop (Small and Sweet by Maggie) and the cafe (Sweets by Maggie).

Then I move to the couch where I study Khaled's message, so lifeless and matter-of-fact.

Allah ye'samhik.

I trace the words on my screen, wishing they could reveal hidden information. I picture the tight expression his face would have held as he typed this. I feel his anger as if it vibrates in the space. For just a moment, I wonder if I acted impulsively.

Khaled's temper is short, but his elegance disguises it. And now that I think about it, even his message has a sophistication to it. He's not angry, he's making me feel guilty with his calm.

My hands tremble a little as I type a reply.

I'm sorry. I can't do it anymore.

When I hit 'send', I realise my whole body is shaking. Nerves, energy, I don't know. There's a much larger conversation to be had, meaning that has not been adequately transmitted in my response. Hurt that should never be unearthed or confronted.

My reply may be short, but at least I'm being honest.

Chapter 6

**_I don't know where to begin, or if
I have already begun._**

Maggie is folding pastry into croissants then brushing butter across them. She sprinkles thinly sliced almonds across the tops, then lays the croissants out neatly on a tray. There are only a handful of them, so I assume they are for her. She's not dressed in chef's whites like the three bakers working quietly behind us, but she wears an apron and is adorned in large resin jewellery pieces. Perhaps she is trying to tell me something with her demonstration. She is easy in her movements. The croissants are neat and evenly portioned. She is a pro, and this studio is her domain.

We're in the big kitchen at the studio where the baking is done. The chocolate studio is a smaller room, which sits adjacent to this one. It's like a hidden world, much larger in its offering than the outside would suggest. There are enough benches for five or six people. The walls have inspirational quotes against backdrops of the sky and the ocean, framed in rose gold. The one closest to Maggie has a quote by Joseph Campbell: 'Where you stumble, there lies your treasure.'

'So, Leo tells me I ought to give you a go?' Maggie says.

I smile at the thought. 'I'm not a complete beginner.'

She doesn't seem convinced. I go with the truth.

'I need to find a job. I've been away for a while.'

Maggie nods slowly. She takes the tray of croissants over to a large oven and with ease slides it in.

'I ran my own cake business for years,' I tell her.

Maggie closes the oven door, makes a note on a pad on the wall then turns back to me. 'I've had problems with people trying to steal my recipes.'

'I wouldn't need to steal them,' I say without thinking. I feel a burn set in my cheeks and I want to sink into the floor.

Her smile is one of amusement. 'Is that so?'

'I'm pretty good at copying things.'

'You mean like tracing a piece of art?'

I could just walk out now, but something holds me in place. 'I mean, I prefer to follow recipes or come up with my own ideas, but I'm good at this. I'm good with flavours.'

'So if I asked you to make one of my pastries now, you could do it.'

'I think so.' The thick custard of the mille-feuille was impressive, but not that hard to make. The flavour of the icing might not be note-perfect. And admittedly, I might struggle with the pastry – it was clearly made from scratch. I can do that, but it's been a while. 'Yes. I could.'

Maggie chuckles and starts to clean the bench. I look around and notice the man I saw tempering chocolate when I first visited the shop. He's working on a set of drizzle cakes at a counter behind her. I guess the cakes are lemon. He's staring at me, his lips curled in amusement. We make eye contact. I expect him to look away, but it's a while before he does. He smiles when he finally lowers his gaze, but it doesn't feel friendly.

'OK then. The tiramisu.'

I sigh. 'I didn't try that. It has alcohol in it and I don't drink alcohol.'

The man laughs to himself but continues with his work. Maggie's eyes widen. 'I'm not asking you to drink anything.'

'I think I should go.'

Maggie studies me then nods. 'I don't know if I trust you, but I feel in some way we were meant to meet. I have someone leaving next week, then my business partner dropped your name. I'll take that as a sign.'

My face flushes again. 'I wasn't being sneaky. I've only just met Leo.'

'What did you try?' says Maggie.

'The chocolate tart. The doughnut. The vanilla slice. And the panna cotta.'

'Never mind those. Take this bench. Make me a sponge cake with a cream filling and any kind of icing.'

'Can I make you something a bit more complicated?'

'Sponge cake. Cream filling. Some kind of icing. Go crazy.'

I look over and see two women standing at a counter behind the man. Below their flat chef's caps, I see that one of them has a half-shaved head, and the other has her hair knotted into an elegant bun that sits low, her make-up artfully done – elaborate black eyeliner, red lipstick that looks permanently painted on. They too are at work on desserts, and while I want to take a closer look at what they're doing, I have work to do.

I place my handbag to the side then wash my hands at the sink. I'm ready to set about making a sponge cake, with the filling and cream cheese icing, but I don't know where anything is. I don't even have an apron. I look to the man, but change my mind about seeking his help when I see how cold, or at the very least, disinterested, he seems.

I approach the women instead, and the one with the elegant bun leads me to a large fridge and the pantry. I thank her with a smile.

'No worries. I'm Inez, by the way.' She smiles back then wanders off.

In the pantry, the ingredients are clearly labelled and placed together alphabetically, and I feel a murmur of excitement. This sits well with me because I used to do the same in my own kitchen and the familiarity springs me into gear. I find a large silver mixing bowl, into which I place eggs, butter, caster sugar, self-raising flour, baking powder and cornflour. I add icing sugar to the pile and some thickened cream from the fridge to make the icing. It needs something more, but I'm not sure what. Cream cheese icing is hardly impressive. Then I spot it: a basket of produce, in which there's an abundance of passionfruit. It's perfect, available all year round, and I add three to my pile.

When I return to the bench, Maggie peers into my bowl of ingredients. Her eyes widen and she smiles before patting me on the shoulder. I have no idea if that means she approves or if I have already failed. It occurs to me how much is riding on this cake; I have never had to audition for work like this and perhaps it's sparking me into life because suddenly I am determined: I need this job, but now, I also really want it.

I have to impress Maggie. It will only take about thirty minutes for the sponge cake to bake, and it will need to cool for a few minutes before I ice it. I have enough time to make another dish.

I return to the fridge and find cream and milk, then I take a vanilla bean pod from the pantry. I never used gelatine in my strict days, but I'm not going to eat this, just make it, so I select a sheet of that, too. I will make panna cotta the way I like it, using a method I hope offers something new and impressive. It's not going to come out the same as Maggie's in thickness, but that's the point. It's more important that the flavours are on a par with hers. I recreate them in my mind, and try to recall the shape and look of it.

Maggie returns when I'm pouring the mixture into the moulds.

'This isn't a sponge cake.'

'I've done that and it's baking. I'm making a panna cotta as well.'

Maggie stares back in silence, her eyes wide in a new way. She purses her lips, nods once then moves off in the direction of the man who doesn't smile.

***

Maggie returns two hours later, just as I'm putting the finishing touches on the sponge cake. It looks as nice as a sponge cake can; it could probably be taller, more generous, but the icing is on point. A good sponge cake is never overdone. Maggie takes a knife to it, slices through to the centre easily, and says, 'Kept it simple – good.' I worry that she is making a judgement, but she does her little head-nod and seems to be reluctantly becoming convinced. She takes a second bite and closes her eyes.

I have already prepared the panna cotta. It would do better with another hour, but it has held its shape. I used some of the leftover passionfruit for a topping, not the strawberries that Maggie uses.

'You forgot the mint. And I use strawberries.'

She doesn't wait for a response, going on to check the wobble, which she seems to tick off with another sway of her head. She takes a spoonful and closes her eyes, stocktaking.

'What have you done differently?'

'The cream. I used seventy per cent cream, thirty per cent milk, instead of 100 per cent cream.'

Maggie considers this. She turns her attention to the man, who is watching, his amusement never-ending. It seems like Maggie is negotiating with the revelation. When she remains silent, I keep talking. 'It's lighter, less dense; more of a palate cleanser than a thick dessert.'

'Lighter,' Maggie repeats. 'What do you think, Luke? Does it work?' She procures a fresh spoon, dips it into the panna cotta then travels over to the man's bench. Luke accepts the spoon and tries it.

'Would make a great mousse.'

'Ooh, bit harsh,' says Maggie.

I don't know if I have impressed her or turned her off me completely, and I want to start again, to reintroduce myself. My cheeks flame afresh, but I refuse to allow Luke to deter me with a cheap dig.

'Look. It's nice,' Maggie says at last. 'But I asked you for one thing. A sponge cake. I didn't ask for a panna cotta, and I certainly don't want one that's meant to ... well, what? Teach me how to do it better?'

The panic sets in. 'Oh no, not at all. I just wanted to show you what I can do.'

Maggie studies me. 'The cake is good. I like it. Do you know chocolate?'

'I do, but not as well as you do. I used chocolate in my cake business sometimes.'

'Artistically?'

'For the figurines I used to put on top of the cakes.'

Well, I mainly used fondant, but I would use chocolate for eyes or props. Dancing elephants with the trunks up for luck atop a chocolate bucket. Lions with chocolate beach balls. White chocolate hearts for a happy couple.

'Used to?'

'I lived in the Middle East for several years, so I closed my business.'

'The Middle East.'

I nod. My olive skin, darker from the Jordanian sun, tells the story of where I come from better than anything else about me. I suppose my features hint at my heritage, too. Lara and Samira could pass for Anglo. I never could.

'And what did you do there?'

'A few things. I worked at refugee camps with an aid agency for a few years. I taught baking workshops for a bit. I mainly worked as a translator. That sort of thing.'

I keep my expression neutral as Maggie's gaze flickers down to my hands.

'But you grew up here.'

'I was born here, yes. I got married. That's why I went there.'

Maggie studies me for what feels like minutes. Her look is thoughtful, intense; she seems by turns frustrated and excited, like she is wrestling with herself.

'Will you be going back there anytime soon?'

I shake the idea away. 'No. I'm here to stay.'

Maggie smiles, her eyes curious. 'What is your story?'

'Which one?'

This makes her laugh. 'I like you. You've got spunk.'

'Thanks.'

'OK.'

'OK?'

'I think so. Yes. We'll give it a shot.'

'Thank you so much. Will there be a chance to learn more chocolate skills?'

'Well, we can work on that, but I want you in the kitchen supporting the senior staff to start with.'

My face must have fallen, because Maggie softens and moves towards me. 'The women you saw earlier? Inez, studied and worked in Europe. She's a *pâtissier* and is making us vegan-friendly. Kat, ten years in commercial kitchens. The best *décoratrice* I've ever had. And this one here – Luke. A qualified chocolatier. He's an OK baker.'

'All right, then,' he says with a more genuine smile, despite Maggie's dig about his baking ability.

They obviously get along well. I glance around and feel small. They all look like they're in their thirties, but younger than me. And so much further ahead.

'I ran a business for several years. I'm not a beginner.'

'In this space, you are. Now, that is what I have to offer. It's up to you. If you'd rather go it alone, not have to be the junior and do the hard yards to earn your spot, I understand.'

I am lost for words. A junior? Earn my spot? My head is screaming at me to retreat. Hole up in my parents' house and start baking. Take some professional classes and return to safety. But my insides are pulling me elsewhere. My body is speaking to me at the same time, and I know that my fear in this moment is not a warning but a demand. I am meant to be here.

'Would it be full-time?'

'Three days a week is all I can offer. Starting with a trial.'

I look down, fighting back emotion. My feelings are morphing too quickly for me to comprehend them. I glance up and find Luke watching me, even as he continues to drizzle the small cakes. They are uniformly done, lined up neatly, looking delicate and pretty, topped with a piece of curled lemon rind.

'Thanks. I'll take whatever you can give me.'

Then I exhale as I feel my first genuine burst of excitement in so long, mild as it is. I extend my hand. 'Just tell me when to be here.'

'Super.' Maggie takes my hand into both of hers and gives it a gentle but firm squeeze. 'Take the weekend. We're closed Mondays. Tuesday, 5am. But sometimes, it might be an earlier call.'

My eyes widen, but I recover quickly. 'I can't wait.'

'Check your email for a contract. What else? Wear black.'

I glance at Luke in the chef's whites. Not there yet. 'No problem.'

Maggie smiles dimly. 'I like your panna cotta. But my recipe stays. OK?'

'Of course,' I say, mortified. She thinks I was challenging her. I suppose I was trying to prove myself.

I start to clean up and Maggie places a hand on my arm. 'Leave that. Get some rest. This is going to be a big change for you. I feel it.' Maggie's eyes flash and she does a brief little dance with her shoulders, suddenly excited. 'Luke will be your primary contact. Go say hello and get to know him before you leave.'

Maggie departs, buzzing, like a puppeteer who has just received a delivery of new toys. And, briefly I wonder if she is and I have just signed on to be part of her next show.

'Hey,' Luke says. He abandons the last of the cakes. His blue eyes scan me as he wipes his hands on a tea towel.

'I'm Sahar,' I say, extending my hand.

He awkwardly holds up his hands – not yet clean – and I feel silly.

'Well, see you Tuesday,' he says. 'Congrats.'

'Do I need to bring anything?'

'A lucky apron.' Then he offers a faint smile and rolls his eyes. 'That was a joke.'

'Right. Is there anything else I need to know?'

'Don't be late. The early starts are hard if you're not used to them.'

immersion

Chapter 7

I hate being a beginner. I want to fast-forward to mastery.

'Sahar. Sahar. Sahar. Sahar. What. Are. You. Doing. Look at me. Look at me. Look at me.'

Luke.

At least once every shift.

Every. Single. Shift.

Another thing: 'Too many questions.'

At least he can say my name right.

It's September, and Sydney's weather is half-heartedly making an effort. I walk to work so early that I need a jacket to guard against the morning chill, but I leave the kitchen in the afternoon when it's much warmer, despite the temperamental skies.

As I journey there, I am always deep in thought – about something new I've learned, or something I could do better.

I understood I would be a junior, but I am more a janitor than an apprentice. When I ask Luke if I can make something – anything – he tells me I have to work towards it. I'm not sure selecting the fruit for a cheesecake will prove my worth in the kitchen, but Maggie's presence tempers Luke's control over how my day goes. Her main function is running the business end. She comes in and out, tending to admin and the cafe, and checking in with me regularly, but not in an overbearing way.

The benefit of being a crappy junior is that it's a masterclass in commercial kitchens: I help with orders, with equipment and the pantry. I quickly become well-versed in the ingredients we use the most and the least, in appliances I didn't know existed, and how to work smarter.

I study the month's selection of sweets and think about how they work as an ensemble. Maggie likes to throw in nods to her Italian heritage. Perhaps, if I ever get to create a dessert, I can work with the flavours and sweets I grew up with: the flavoured waters – rose and orange blossom; the mastic; the flaky, buttery *baklawa.*

Moments with the senior bakers, Inez and Kat, deliver more lessons. It was Inez, the woman who led me to the pantry on the day of my baking audition, who took me aside after my first week and offered some encouragement. 'Just go step by step,' she said in her measured tone. 'Don't worry about Luke. The simpler and quicker you work, the better ... for everyone. Also, never pitch Nutella as a hero ingredient. And when you get to whites, always wear a T-shirt underneath so that you don't see sweat stains around your armpits.' Then she asked me for my opinion on dating someone with a man bun.

Kat ('No one calls me Katerina') is a friendly 'butch' – as she calls herself – who oozes cool because she doesn't seem to care what anyone thinks of her. Her personality is louder than her voice. She casually uses words like 'wicked' and 'lit' and it sounds natural. She calls me *habib*. 'I grew up with Leb friends,' she says. 'I know all the good swear words. Also, I'm Greek, which is practically the same as being Arab.'

Kat regularly spars with Luke, especially about the music playlist. One morning, I watch in awe as they wrestle each other for power over the music system, like siblings fighting for the remote control. I hear Kat mumble an insult at him in Arabic under her breath. Outraged, Luke turns to me. 'What did she say?'

'I didn't hear her, sorry.'

Actually, Kat had called him a cunt.

I glance at Kat, who winks then stares down Luke. I smile and return to prepping ingredients.

Kat also throws insults in English. 'As always, you know how to take a shit then ask who farted,' she told Luke one day when he picked apart her work.

'What does that even mean?' Luke said.

'Who checks your work?'

Brimming with frustration, he walked off.

This time, when Inez tries to settle the conflict over the music, she drags me into it: 'Will you please pick something so they'll shut up?' She gives me a beseeching look, her bright red lips in a straight line.

I freeze, too timid to offer my opinion. 'I don't really know much about music.'

Luke sighs, seemingly annoyed that the conflict has been slowed down then punctured by an amateur. 'Groove Armada or The National?'

He is speaking a foreign language. 'I don't know either.'

'Did you grow up in a convent?' says Luke.

'No, I just don't love music.' I look at Kat, who deflates.

'Just let the little boy have his way. I'll go solo,' she says, then wanders off in search of her bag.

Inez continues working, not at all unsettled.

And that's how the antagonism between Kat and Luke differs to how Luke acts towards me. Luke isn't overly friendly with anyone, but when they bicker, the power dynamic between them is different; they are peers, both fluent in the language of Sweets by Maggie.

I am not like them: confident, uninhibited and outspoken. I don't know how easy their lives are, but in the kitchen, surrounded by Maggie's inspirational posters, life is a Pinterest board.

'*It is not the mountain we conquer, but ourselves.*' – Edmund Hillary

'*Stop acting so small. You are the universe in ecstatic motion.*' – Rumi

I have to remind myself that no matter my efforts, this is not my business. I am a junior-level employee.

So I just get on with it. I keep to myself. I am always professional. Even Luke notices my meticulous planning, the way I work according to lists. Even Luke can't deny that I work hard.

And I did try to make a friendly start. On my first day at work, I brought a tray of Arabic sweets – a kilo of sticky *baklawa* – as a gesture of my commitment to joining the team. We Arabs love to celebrate and give gifts. The way the team responded offered valuable insight into their personalities.

Maggie peered down at the cellophane-covered tray and lifted her head with a beatific smile. 'This is lovely!'

But she didn't try any, so I decided she was simply being polite. Luke's expression was neutral, while Kat and Inez rushed over and ripped open the cellophane, murmuring as they made their selections. Kat had one half-wedged in her mouth, and another in her left hand when she fist-bumped me with her right and gave me a solemn nod. 'You can stay. God bless Maggie's diversity garden.'

Inez lingered. 'Don't mind Kat. She doesn't mean anything by it.'

'Inez has a weird name and is a vegan nutjob,' Kat continued. 'Even if she looks like a goddess.'

Inez broke into a smile, clearly not offended. 'That's my thing. I'm the vegan pastry chef. Admittedly, I'm more vegetarian than vegan – I can't resist dairy once in a while.'

'I tried something of yours,' I say. 'A salted caramel doughnut?'

'That's me. You liked it?'

'It was amazing.'

'Anyway. Ignore Kat. Except when it comes to desserts. She knows sweets.'

Then Kat called out, 'Maggie likes to take in strays from different backgrounds. How do you think I got here? I'm a wog and queer, so she hit the jackpot.'

Inez rolled her eyes. 'We're all wogs. Even Maggie. Except for Luke. He's the token white guy.'

'I heard that,' he said.

'No, his diversity credential is old age,' said Kat.

'Fuck off.'

'Luke, come and get some of these before they're all gone,' Inez said, her eyes still on the tray.

Luke remained at his bench, not interested in me or the sweets. 'Will you be getting back to work anytime soon?' he responded.

'Suit yourself,' Inez said, peeling a lady's finger carefully away from its neighbours with one hand, while batting away stray hairs from her loosened bun with the other.

Everyone is a type or two at their core. I like Inez and her calm, no-nonsense demeanour. Something about her certainty reminds me of who I was before my marriage. But she's also quiet and that's how I feel connected to her. The discreet but diligent one. Kat is the fun and creative one. Luke is cold and a loner. Maggie is maternal and aspirational.

The same day they made fun of Maggie's diversity garden, I found myself in a corner of the kitchen I didn't often frequent. Then I saw it on the wall, something I had completely missed up until that point: a diversity charter. *No one will be discriminated against based on who they are and how they live.*

Am I a diversity hire, and not just Leo's recommendation? Is that why Luke doesn't like me?

***

One afternoon, about two months in, Maggie appears at my bench while I'm peeling apples and leans in like she's about to initiate a gossip session.

'How are you finding Luke?'

'He's kind of tough,' I say, then immediately regret it. 'I mean, I don't think he likes me.'

Maggie leans back a little, her mouth twisted in a near smile, as she assesses me. Mild amusement, I think. 'He likes you just fine. He says you work very hard.'

Sahar. Sahar. Sahar. Sahar. What. Are. You. Doing. Look at me. Look at me. Look at me.

'He gets frustrated when I ask questions.'

'Luke is a bit impatient. That's who he is in everyday life, so that's how he works. But he needs to learn some patience. I'll have a word with him.'

I feel like a child who's just dobbed him in. 'No, it's OK. He's not that bad.'

Maggie is about leave when she swings back. 'You know that you can use the kitchen after work if you want to flex your baking muscle? I just don't want you to bake anything that we do here,' she says, her piercing eyes alight. 'Experiment. Be creative. *Have fun.*'

I study the silver bowl of peeled apples. 'Thank you, Maggie.'

'I never intended for you to forget what you know or to stop practising, Sahar. But I work a certain way here and I needed you to reboot your baking brain. You can learn a lot from others just by being an observer. Some people teach themselves piano, but that doesn't mean they have learned how to place their fingers and read music.'

'I understand.'

'You should be baking all the time. This is a long-term relationship. You have to work hard at it. You have to love it.'

Everyone at Maggie's loves it. I can see it in the way they all fall into their own cadences. Even Luke gets in a zone. I admire his talent. He likes chocolate more than baking, but he is very good at both. Sometimes I catch myself just watching him at work, easy in his movements, more patient with ingredients than people. The rare moments I get to work in the chocolate studio, I concede Luke knows chocolate in a way I aspire to: the language of its moods and temperatures; the way it has to be worked; its extraordinary potential for beauty. And he softens in the space, like he is at home.

He also seems to notice my efforts, and there's no denying he will give me the more interesting tasks. But he doesn't seem to expect the same from the other juniors. They work to instruction but don't aim for perfection. And they get away with it. I don't.

One afternoon, as I put the final touches on a batch of caramel tarts, I look up to see him watching me, relaxing out of his usual expression of fierce concentration. A moment of eye contact, then a faint smile. 'Yes,' he says. 'Good.'

Chapter 8

Why is it that I can be forgotten but I cannot completely forget?

I work three days a week. On my days off, on Maggie's advice, I practise my skills. I've even purchased a marble board to temper chocolate. Every couple of weeks, I visit my parents' graves. I plant flowers and small stalks of sage, the kind that Mama and Baba loved to drink in their black tea, and say prayers over their plots of earth. I don't know what I was expecting to feel the first time I went, but the second time was a little easier and I sat for an hour among the ghosts of the graveyard, a loose headscarf wrapped around my head out of respect.

Each time I go, I ask them the same questions, wondering if one day I may be delivered an answer.

'What happens when you're gone?'

'Do you feel me like I feel you?'

'Does the separation hurt?'

It helps that I go to the gym, an industrial playground for adults. The equipment is sleek, gunmetal grey. Bright orange scaffolding lights up the floor, heavy enough that people can swing from it, or do pull-ups. I can't do pull-ups without a resistance band, but I like a challenge. I take up boxing and do strength classes at least twice a week. It helps to picture a source of angst in boxing and smash into it. I see Luke's face, with his trademark look of frustration, and punch in time with his clipped instructions.

Sahar. Sahar. Sahar. Sahar. What. Are. You. Doing. Look at me. Look at me. Look at me.

Jab. Hook. Cross. Upper cut.

I practise regularly, but my body has still not fully recovered from what it's been through: damage that is invisible, unlike my scars. Sometimes I feel it in a sudden movement, a sharp pain, and I lose my footing.

At work, Luke remains my primary manager, but now once a week I get assigned to one of the others – a day with Kat or Inez. They work differently. They are both friendly, but Inez respects silence in the kitchen, while Kat likes interaction. Kat's the first to ask questions of me and my life. She shows genuine interest in the modified version I give her, telling me that she has travelled to the 'homeland' (Greece) but really wants to see the rest of the world. 'Maybe one day I'll retire in Europe. Find a cottage on the Amalfi Coast and make limoncello.'

I like Kat, but I am cautious. One Saturday, she asks me to join them for drinks after work.

'I don't drink alcohol,' I tell her, but this doesn't seem to perturb her.

'That's what mocktails and energy drinks are for. Come on, it'll just be you, Inez, Luke and me. It'll be fun.'

Before I can stop myself, I grimace.

She shakes her head and winks, her mouth widening into a knowing grin. '*Habib,* ignore Luke. Honestly, he's not good-looking enough to get away with being such an arsehole. But, he's going through something. He wasn't so bad before he hooked up with Cruella.'

I have no idea what she's talking about.

'His on-again off-again girlfriend,' Inez explains. 'Her name's Bianca. He's changed a little since she's been on the scene.'

Kat grins again. 'But his obsessive Gordon Ramsay deal never changes. Don't let it put you off having a good time.'

'Maybe next time,' I say and Kat shrugs, mildly defeated or put out, I am not sure which.

***

Later, I share this exchange with Lara, who rolls her eyes to the heavens over a dinner of homemade pizza. She offers a surprising diagnosis on Luke's behaviour: 'Pigtail puller.'

'Definitely not.'

'Trust me.'

'Lara.'

'He wants to have sex with you,' she says, nonchalantly plucking off a piece of *sujuk* and placing it into her mouth. 'Which is not OK, by the way. How old is this guy?'

'Not everything is about sex.'

'He's imagining a lot of things.'

'I'm not sure how old he is. I think he's a couple of years younger than me.'

Lara shakes her head. 'I used to think boys being mean to girls they liked was cute, but now I think it's gross.'

I'm sure she's projecting her own experiences on to me. 'He's like that with everyone.'

'I know you're not used to getting attention, but you're not all covered up now. Not that that ever stops a guy. But the way you were before, no one would have come near you.'

'I still have the same face.'

Lara chuckles. 'You have so much to learn about sexual attraction, young Padawan. You think it's about a physical or a mental connection, and nothing else.' She sighs. 'You'll see. The more comfortable you get, the more natural it will start to feel dressing as you please and wearing your hair out.'

I don't want her to be right. I don't want my years of modesty to be justified if I'm now exposing myself to things that might harm me.

'It's fun,' Lara continues. 'It hurts sometimes. But that's the point. It's experience. And that's what you need. That's how you get better.'

'At what?'

'Everything. At life and not giving a shit. Imagine if my love-life ended at my teens. I'd be singing about a boy who didn't want to have lunch with me.'

***

Eventually, life starts to seem peaceful. I have had no further contact from Khaled, and at work, Luke softens his edges ever so slightly, but he still gets annoyed easily, and resorts to a smirk when I ask a silly question or get something wrong. I understand it. He's very good at what he does, and he's not built for teaching. He's made to do things, not watch others butcher a passion that runs through him like blood. Maybe I understand it because that's me, too.

Luke reveals little of his personality, and I only know a few things about him: he mentions vaguely that he comes from a big family, and he learned how to bake before he found a passion for chocolate.

One afternoon, he assigns me a task requiring more than admin: mini fruit tarts. I'm struggling with the fruit portions. The mandarin slices are uneven and it all looks sloppy. I can see this. I'm a perfectionist and I'm starting to panic. Before I can fix them, Luke arrives at my counter and lifts up the tarts for a quick inspection.

He shakes his head. 'You need to pay attention.'

I continue working, unsure how to respond, my face growing scorching hot. 'I'm sorry. The mandarins were a bit soft.'

Luke's mood has been even lower than usual. He's been in and out more frequently and his phone seems permanently attached to him. I want to make room for his personal troubles, but when his blue eyes stare into mine, I hold his gaze, my cheeks still burning. I could concede defeat, agree with his measurement of my abilities, but something harder in me arrives to stop me.

For a second, Luke's eyes widen as he returns my stare. Then he looks away. 'Start again.'

At this point, I wonder if I have imagined my business success. I want to look over the many photos I took of my creations and scrutinise them for faults and signs of beginners' luck.

'I can do it. I'll fix it,' I tell Luke.

Perhaps it's my tone, my sincerity, or what I suspect is a look of sheer desperation, but Luke nods. 'We'll go over the basics this afternoon. Again,' he adds.

As he walks away, I have to remind myself that I willingly signed up for this, that this is what I want. I have already fallen into patterns that feel familiar, even if they require an update. New flavour combinations fill my mind, and I find myself lost in techniques that are simple but new. Things I had never thought of before.

I am determined to get the tarts right, so I start again. I work faster now that I've done it once.

As I work, Maggie trails past in the direction of her office. Not far behind her is Leo in jeans and a light jacket.

Kat and Inez enter, cradling cups of coffee. 'He looks hotter when he's in the leather jacket,' says Inez.

'Huh?'

They share a look. 'Leo,' says Inez. 'Your friend?'

'He's not my friend. He knows Lara, my flatmate.'

They continue to silently assess me.

'What's wrong?' I say.

Inez shrugs. 'Nothing. Just saying, he's hot, and if he wasn't related to Maggie and an investor...'

Kat rolls her eyes. 'Not this again.' She pushes away from the counter and wanders off, leaving me with Inez. She has a look on her artfully made-up face that I'm unable to decipher.

'Are you OK?' I say, and Inez jumps a little.

'I mean ... technically I'm not his employee. Right?'

'I guess?'

'I think he has a girlfriend anyway.' Inez emits a murmur then gives me a mournful smile. 'Back to work.'

I watch her go and realise Luke is staring at me, but his expression is easy to understand. He's not impressed. I return to my task.

I produce a more acceptable batch of tarts and leave one on Luke's bench for him to scrutinise. Just as I do so, Leo emerges from Maggie's office. His gaze wanders around the kitchen, then he makes his way to the exit. He slows down near the doorway, his fingers running across the bench beside him.

I can understand Inez's attraction to him. There's something about Leo that I'm sure many women would find appealing – a certainty in how he walks, a quiet confidence. Maybe it's because he's mature.

He catches me looking and smiles, nodding once in my direction, then makes his way out the door.

I glance behind me to check on Inez, but she's at work, focused and diligent.

Chapter 9

Perhaps I need to start interacting more with the invisible instead of defining it.

I've been at Maggie's just over three months. I'm still on three days a week – Tuesday, Thursday and Saturday. Getting Sunday would be ideal because the pay is better, but instead, Luke asks me to prep on Saturday for the rest of the weekend.

It's a grey Sunday afternoon after a difficult week at work, and I pay a visit to my parents' graves. It's a train ride out west then a ten-minute walk to the graveyard. I don't have to work out the route to their site anymore. A headscarf wrapped around my head, I drop onto the grass, positioning myself at the end of the plots, between my parents.

My head is thick with emotion as I study the granite headstones. Our relationships were not close. I don't know that I miss our interactions, but there's no denying that their imprint remains; invisible fingerprints that tell me where I come from and who I am supposed to be.

In his last few years, my father seemed to soften and become smaller. One day, I saw him cry, something that terrified me because no one wants to see their parent cry. My father, an engineer who couldn't find employment, was forced to make money through a mixed business. For decades, he sat on bundled-up regret. For years, that was my inheritance.

The sage stalks from my last visit have withered and mostly blown away. I bring out a bag of fresh ones and throw them gently onto the graves like an offering.

'Mama, I miss you. Baba, I can still hear you clearing your throat.'

It's strange what remains vital.

'I don't know where you are, but I need you. I need your strength.'

I am sure that wherever they are, Mama especially does not approve of my rapid unfurling into someone who would never get into heaven. But my mother had her kindness, too. Her solutions always led to God, but I never remember her rejecting me outright.

How did I so callously forget all that my parents did for me simply because of what they withheld?

'You gave me a gift and I have wasted it. Can you please send me a sign? Please show me that everything will be OK.'

My father passed away two and a half years after my mother. I managed only to see my mother off, later watching two women wash Mama for burial then wrap her in a white cloth. 'She was in a rush,' one of them told me in a low voice.

I was numb, unsure about what to do with the information.

'How do you know?'

She smiled, her eyes on my mother's still body. 'They tell you.'

A thin line of connection seems to form between their joint memory and me as I sit under the grim sky. The clouds hang low and the air is heavy with the prospect of a storm. Eventually, a light patter of rain falls against the grass as I grieve. Around me, people trail through the rows of graves, some stopping to inspect the names, others knowing exactly where they are headed.

I sit there a while, eyes closed to a gentle breeze, which I imagine is Mama's spirit sweeping past me. Tears spill down my cheeks. I wipe them away and exhale.

I frequently wonder if the dead can see us, and if they can, do people change when they die? I wonder if my mother would have compassion for this version of me or if she would disapprove, the way she would have in the real world. Suddenly, I miss her. I would even face her disapproval if I could just be close to her again and feel the strength that came with her certainty.

In my religion classes, I was taught about judgement; about hellfire and coffins that become tighter the more you sin; about hell and heaven, even when both already exist here. I don't pretend to have experienced the worst human hell; I witnessed it at refugee camps, where people tried to carve out a new life when all hope seemed lost.

But somehow, when you lose someone, you know the shape of such belief changes. You can't see them encased in a box. They visit you in your dreams, looking radiant, healthy.

I made *wudu* before I came, my muscle memory kicking in to allow for a seamless purification. Water is helpful that way; a symbolic and practical way to remove the accumulated dirt.

I raise my hands, connecting them in supplication, and begin recitations, a prayer for my parents' wellbeing in the afterlife; a hope that it truly is better than this one.

***

When I get back to the apartment, Samira has just arrived.

'We're going out,' she announces. 'I feel like a proper night off and fresh air.'

Lara suggests Musicale, and Samira looks to me for a reaction. She is conflicted because of her headscarf.

'What?' Lara says, feigning innocence at Samira. 'They let in all types, even stuffy religious wom—'

Samira quickly but clumsily wrestles Lara to the carpet. Lara grunts, but they're fighting like siblings, so I'm not surprised when they tire quickly, mutually conceding defeat. They unlink then drop onto their backs, lying side by side.

'I'm not against going. But not tonight,' Samira pants. 'I'm in jeans for goodness' sake.'

I join them on the floor, inching myself close to Lara. 'Since when do you two wrestle? We used to be so civilised.'

'Since I had kids,' Samira surmises with a groan. 'I don't know how to be an adult sometimes. Everything is a battle.'

Restlessness. That's what we're all suffering from. The playfulness, a desire to connect, to smash into each other in a way that unloads the accumulated stress, but safely.

***

At dinner, we talk as we used to: about the everyday stuff that expands to seem like it takes up the whole world.

We're at a small Italian eatery in Newtown, walking distance from the apartment. It's not the most popular one, so the atmosphere is mellow and relaxed, the background noise a sea of low voices in conversation and the occasional guffaw, mixed in with a playlist of soft acoustic songs.

At one point, Lara starts to sing along, then she gives me a wink. 'I used to listen to this post-fuckwit ex. You always need a soundtrack.' When the song ends, she regales us with tales of being on tour. 'We all have second jobs that we hate.'

'At least you're doing something you love,' says Samira, who proceeds to roll her eyes as she describes the antics of her children and the foibles of her near-perfect husband.

'Honestly, Samira, it sounds like you're looking for faults to make us feel better about our crap love-lives,' says Lara, and we laugh because it's funny but possibly true.

'I haven't slept in years,' says Samira. 'Is there such a thing as surface sleep?' Then she frets over her maternal instincts. 'I am raising actual human beings. Every time they do something that shocks me, I blame myself. Why was I so hard on my folks? And I miss doing adult stuff, y'know?'

Samira is speaking to two women who are childless (or as Lara puts it, child-free), so technically we don't know. But I have a sense of her meaning. I know that my life and the changes I am making in it would be completely different if I had a child with Khaled. We would not just remain connected, we would be knotted together.

'Yes, but you married a Disney prince,' I say. 'Stop complaining. Hollywood was practically a food group for you growing up.'

'Burn,' says Lara. 'She has a point. You were definitely the most romantic one of us.'

Samira wears herself more loosely now. There's a maturity to her that feels earned. Out of all of us, she is the most womanly.

'You were also the most innocent,' Lara says to Samira, and it sounds like an accusation.

'Excuse me? I think Sahar gets that one,' says Samira, mock-offended.

'No. Sahar knew shit even I didn't know.'

'Is that so?' I say.

'You had a hidden stash of romance books, I'm sure of it.'

'We all had that!' Samira says.

We take a moment, then in unison: '*The Bronze Horseman!*'

We laugh, amused at how we passed Paullina Simons' historical romance around like it was a guide to romance and sex. Then we lower our heads in embarrassment as the people at the table next to us glance over.

'So many sex scenes,' Lara says in a low voice, fanning herself. 'Anyway, Sahar, you barely left the bloody kitchen, but you were always giving good advice about boys. You saw that Hakeem and I had a thing before I even knew.'

Samira leans forward in a challenge. 'Please, Lara, you were fooling around with guys while Sahar and I were just fantasising.'

'I had my limits.'

We give her a dubious look.

'What? Daniel was my technical first.'

'I hate that,' Samira says.

'We had fun. At least I can take that away from it.'

Then Lara gives me a curious look.

'What? I'm not a virgin, obviously.'

Lara rolls her eyes, then shuffles her seat closer so that she's right beside me. 'Obviously. But please tell me that your ex was at least a good partner...'

'Lara!' Samira is affronted on my behalf, but I don't mind the question. It doesn't surprise me coming from Lara, nor is it a shock that she might wonder about me, the uptight religious girl who couldn't talk to a boy without freaking out.

I shrug but my face warms up. 'The sex was good ... I think. It's not like I have anyone to compare him to.'

Even Samira looks curious now. But you left him. You obviously had big problems with him.

Lara shakes her head. 'That just makes it better sometimes.'

'Gosh,' says Samira. 'I mean, it took me a while to get used to it. I thought

I was in the wrong movie the first few times.'

We nod vigorously in agreement.

'So many people should be burning in hell for lying to women about having an orgasm the first time they have sex,' says Lara.

'Yeah. I needed an education,' I say. 'It was pretty uncomfortable for a while.'

Lara studies me. 'Oh my God. You watched porn, didn't you?'

My cheeks flare up without delay. 'Could you be a bit louder? I don't think the table in the far corner heard you. And it wasn't porn.'

'Oh. My. God,' says Lara.

Samira has her arms crossed and her eyes narrowed as she waits for my confirmation.

'It was a sex positions video on Khaled's laptop. I watched it a couple of times.'

Samira puts her face in her hands. 'Couldn't you just get an instructional book?' she says, sounding pained.

I hear a throat being cleared and look up to see a waiter standing beside us, his eyes wide. 'Did you want to take a look at the dessert menu?'

'Yes, thank you,' Samira says, and he escapes as quickly as he appeared.

Lara is about to cough up a lung. She can't stop laughing. 'I'm actually just kind of stunned right now,' she says eventually, but there's a note of pride creeping into her voice. 'It's always the innocent ones you have to look out for.'

By now we're all laughing, but the thought burns a little. Sex was not transformative. For too long, sex was painful.

'Porn is so fake,' says Lara. 'Not that I watch it.' She pauses, hands raised. 'But it's hard to miss.'

'It wasn't porn. Porn doesn't have narration.'

'Ah, it was one of those videos. Bet it was from like 1985. Am I right? I'm right.'

She is right. The hair was big, the women had bright pink blush and blue eye shadow. No one looked great. 'The music was pretty cheesy,' I say. 'But it helped.'

Samira is shading her eyes. She looks like she's trying to get through a period cramp, before she shakes her head, most likely repenting on our behalf, which was my daily bread years ago. 'You were the only person I knew who fast-forwarded the sex scenes even when your parents weren't around,' she tells me.

Then she and Lara lock eyes. '*Pretty Woman!*' they say and cackle.

I admit, the video was not an ideal entry point to understanding sex, but it did something, like flipping on a switch. I'd forgotten that natural, sensual desire you can have when you don't even have someone to think about.

'Faaark,' says Lara, wiping tears from her eyes. 'I'm checking your luggage for sex toys later, Sahar.'

'Lara!' says a pained Samira. 'Please.'

The dessert menu falls onto the table. I watch the waiter swiftly retreat to safety.

We shake with laughter. 'We should give him a generous tip,' Samira says.

'Look, I was desperate. I thought sex would be easy to get used to, but it was taking ages,' I say. 'It hurt.'

It would have hurt even if Khaled loved me.

Samira nods. 'Three months. And that's being generous.'

'Two,' Lara says, grabbing the dessert menu.

'Five,' I say. 'And I got a UTI every time.'

Lara and Samira wince. 'Yeah, where was that storyline in the romance books?' says Samira.

I suffered UTIs after sex for months. I suffered every time Khaled wanted me. His sister Zainab offered me a cranberry solution, but the UTIs continued. So I visited a GP – a man, who quietly prescribed antibiotics.

'Not just one time, OK?' he told me in broken English, his gaze on the prescription pad. He ripped off the sheet and placed it on the desk before me. 'One each time. *Yallah. Assalamu alaykum wa rahmatullahi wabarakatu.*'

It was the first time I realised how shame has no true anchor. It can show up at any place, from anywhere and fill you with remorse, even when you had no idea what you could have done to avoid it.

I withdraw from these thoughts to find Lara taunting Samira about her sex life and its regularity.

'No one has sex on a weeknight!' Samira whispers fiercely.

I shrug, because she has a point. But I'm sobered by the recollection of my husband.

'Khaled had a thing for Amal Clooney,' I tell them, taking hold of a menu.

'Fuck Amal Clooney,' Lara says. 'She's a unicorn. No one has Arab parents that easygoing.'

'Can you imagine if one of us tried to date a celebrity?' Samira laughs.

'Can you imagine if one of us tried to date someone openly, period? I'll have the sticky date,' Lara says, like it's a reward for a hard life. 'Anyway, my final thoughts on sex: thank God for foreplay.'

I'm caught in a laugh when my phone vibrates. Without thinking, I open it and find a message from Khaled. This time, it's in Arabic and English.

Inti talqa
I divorce you

A few seconds later, another follows:
Inti talqa
Then again:
Inti talqa
Inshallah the woman who is never happy can be happy now, Khaled concludes in English. In three texts, Khaled has ended our marriage. I feel the colour drain from my face as I stare at the screen. Melancholy and sorrow rise within me. It occurs to me that while my feelings have not changed, my perception – in just a few moments – has been turned upside down.

I must claim some fault here, too. He might have been the one who began unravelling something before it could be created, but I allowed so much to happen.

My friends want to know. They stop short of demanding that I tell them what happened to me, their entitlement as my friends.

I know in telling them, I risk making myself look bad, perhaps even immoral. And I know in telling them, I will have to disclose the most important thread of my story. I don't know if I'm ready, but at least some of it must be shared, and shed. I want to exorcise it from my body, in the hope that saying it out loud will set me free.

***

We're back at the apartment, a pot of Arabic coffee between us. Lara and Samira are watchful but patient, both facing me from their places beside each other at the dining table.

They already know it's a long story, so they are settled in. But when I struggle to get started, Samira opens the discussion.

'I should have been a better friend and told you the truth: it was madness to get engaged to a man you didn't know.'

Lara winces. 'To be fair, you can know someone for years and they can still be tossers.'

'No,' says Samira firmly. 'We spent hours dissecting my love-life. But this one comes back from Jordan with a ring and we think it's cute?'

I clear my throat. 'In case you've forgotten, I was shy but not stupid. I knew exactly what I was doing. Do you think I would've listened to you?'

Lara breaks into the tension with a wave of her arms. 'Guys, let's not go down a dark path right now. We can't change anything. And Sahar has a point. She wasn't confused like you, so there was nothing to discuss. It was her choice.'

Samira looks upset and I'm ready to call an end to the conversation.

'I don't need you to feel guilty right now,' I say. 'I have enough of that myself.'

Samira concedes this with a nod. 'You're right. I'm sorry.'

'I'm just going to be clear on this: Khaled was not a great husband, but I'm not innocent either. We were never a good match. I knew it when I went to your wedding, Samira.'

Samira had made sure to seat me near the exit, in case my nerves overwhelmed me. I almost danced in public that night, such was the excitement of the wedding. But what truly stood out was the joy stamped in her expression.

'I watched you with Menem, and your parents, and it was so natural and real. And I was going to Jordan thinking I would come back to Sydney, but knowing in my gut that it might not happen.'

'Why didn't you just back out?' says Lara.

'I don't know ... pride? I felt like I would have failed, and let people down. I thought I'd feel free being married, so I went from telling myself it didn't matter that I didn't love him to convincing myself it would come in time.'

'Eight years, Sahar,' Samira tells me.

My anxiety blooms. I'm quiet for so long that Lara lets out a groan. 'Oh my God, Sahar, you're killing us here. What the fuck happened?'

'I did fall in love.'

Lara's eyes immediately widen, but Samira's response is more tempered and cautious.

How do I explain that I had no choice? I fell in love with my husband's brother, and I really had no choice.

Jordan

The third year

Tonight is the first time I will meet Khaled's brother, Naeem, the revered eldest son. He is a permanent traveller, a doctor based in Dubai who spends many months each year providing his services in refugee camps and war zones. Everyone loves Naeem, even if they disapprove of his nomadic existence. 'What mother doesn't want to be close to her son?' *Amti* often laments.

He is in Amman for a few months to work at Zaatari refugee camp, and tonight is his first visit to his younger brother's marital home. With him is his fiancée, Magda, a cosmetically enhanced Arab woman with bright eyes and an infectious laugh. Khaled's sisters make fun of her lightly in my presence, joking about her maintenance costs. Naeem and Magda are to be married in a year. I have heard so much about them from my mother-in-law that I feel like I know them already, have conversed with them about life and served them tea. I can imagine how they speak and move.

Even Khaled's sister Dina, who is usually so unashamedly forthright in her opinions, speaks highly of Naeem. 'You will like him,' she tells me with a twist of her mouth, as though there is more she wants to add. I often sense, but can't confirm, Dina's belief that I don't belong here with Khaled. She often pokes fun at him and how uptight he is, but then she also mocks my conservativism. The first time she saw me in an *abaya* and headscarf, she scanned me then simply shook her head and said, 'No.'

The soft words of praise about Naeem feel like pinpricks of information, carrying an importance I cannot unpack.

I am feeling unwell on the evening of Naeem's visit, a little anxious and unsettled, like a storm is approaching but I'm not sure from which direction.

It's July and the nights are hot, the air full of the energy of anticipation. Khaled is in high spirits, pondering whether we should hold a party for Naeem after his first visit. He's excited in a way I've never witnessed before, not even on our wedding day, like a child who is finally receiving a long-coveted gift. He dresses up for the occasion in smart, tailored pants and a stylish button-down shirt. He looks handsome and even I find myself buoyed by his enthusiasm.

'Wear something bright and put on a smile,' he urges me. 'They are so excited to meet you. Let's impress them.'

Khaled often struggles with the way I dress, but tonight I don't mind and I choose a floral maxi Dina bought for me – black with vibrant red roses in bloom – with a cardigan and a light red headscarf, which I wear shorter than I used to, and looser. I don't want to be rude, especially as I know it will get back to *Amti*.

I have just finished applying eyeliner when I hear Khaled open the front door. I head straight to the kitchen to start preparing tea and sweets, serenaded by the sound of enthusiastic murmurs then the clap of a manly hug followed by deep voices. Magda's voice rings through louder, feminine and distinct in its high pitch, her words sounding like they could end on a laugh. I hear my name.

A few minutes later, I make my entrance. With Dina's help, I have become better at looking at people in the eye, but I am still a bit shy and uneasy around strangers. Khaled will get annoyed if I lower my gaze. His previous words echo in my mind: *It's rude. There's no harm in making eye contact.*

I enter the living room and immediately our guests shuffle out of their seats. Magda wears too much make-up, like an Arabic pop star, yet she is elegant and has a firm presence. Her hair is long and straight, a golden brown that is not her natural colour. Despite the plumped-up lips and fake eyelashes, she is beautiful, and I sense a maternal warmth. This is confirmed when she smiles and embraces me like an old friend. She takes a step back to assess me, placing my head between her hands. The praise in Arabic is poetic and overflows. 'What a moon! How she lights up a room! What a sweetheart!'

Inside I am cringing at the way she's infantilising me, but I smile and politely thank her for the praise. Then I look to Naeem, who undertakes a more sober assessment of me. He is taller than Khaled, and I have to tilt my head back to meet his stare. He has piercing light eyes and they widen a little as he extends a hand, his gaze unwavering, as though he is searching for truth in my eyes. It is startling, but there is an eagerness to his expression, a softness to his look that puts me at ease. He smells of *oud,* the musky fragrance that everyone wears in the Gulf, and being in his presence is like being wrapped in a warm blanket.

I find myself unable to look away as I take his hand. His grip is firm but not tight, his skin soft and warm. It sends a rush through my body. I am not used to it, and the feeling, rather than ordinary, is electric.

I don't know how many seconds elapse as we take each other in, Naeem's gaze unapologetic in its intimacy, but eventually I detach from his grasp and escape his look.

Naeem is attractive, like the rest of his family, but he is slightly more boyish than Khaled. Dressed in a grey suit without a tie, Naeem is thinner, rougher, distinguished in a very different way. His hair is short but curly.

I have never experienced anything like this: meeting a stranger but feeling as if something invisible connects us. When he first rose from his seat and appraised me, the look on his face moved from soft indifference to hard investigation. His gaze was not one of connection, but of reconnection, like he was trying to remember where he had seen me before. And I leaned into it without thinking because I felt the same sense of recognition.

As I take my seat, I snap out of this daze. If Magda and Khaled noticed the charge between us, they show no indication of it.

I have been married for three years, and even in my most intimate moments with Khaled, I have never seen a man look at me with such basic desire.

***

It would have been impolite for them to arrive empty-handed, so Naeem and Magda have brought us sweets from Dubai – dates stuffed with roasted nuts, candied orange peel and caramelised pecans. They also gift me a box filled with baking utensils. I open it, and with a tepid smile explore its contents. A packet of cake-decorating tools, some wooden spoons, a whisk and a mixing bowl.

'We asked them to show us what a proper baker would use,' Magda tells me, her hands crossed at her knees. 'I love the photos on your Facebook page from Australia,' she gushes. 'You have to keep going. I told Naeem that you would do very well here.'

I force some enthusiasm but tell her the truth. 'I don't think it would work here. It's very expensive to run a business like that.'

'You're in a nice area of Amman. Lots of people will pay for your cakes.'

'We'll see.' I add the term Arabs use to indicate that it's up to the fates: '*Inshallah.*'

I don't believe there is a market for my cakes here, but more importantly, I have lost my thirst to create them.

I thank Magda and Naeem for the gift and promise to make them something special for their next visit.

Magda giggles at my speech. She calls my Arabic *helou,* an interchangeable term that can mean sweet, pretty, or, as is her meaning, cute. It can be casual or condescending.

But Naeem gently scolds her in Arabic. 'What are you talking about? She practically speaks like a native.'

'She's improving my English and I'm improving her Arabic,' Khaled tells them, pleased. 'And you should try her cooking. It's like she's from the country. Next time you're coming for lunch.'

My eyes meet Khaled's, but he quickly looks away. I force a smile. Inside, I am burning. My husband is calling me a peasant.

'Amazing,' says Magda. 'If we had more time, I'd get you to teach me how to make something. Naeem always complains that I inherited lots of good things from the women before me, but not their cooking skills.'

She laughs, and I can't resist checking Naeem's reaction.

'Magda likes to exaggerate,' he says with a light smile, but he looks embarrassed – by her, or the accusation?

We sink into a stiff silence, with only the clatter of tea glasses to fill the quiet space. But I see Khaled's amusement play out in a tight but self-satisfied grin. He and Magda are more in tune with each other than I am with him. I know he isn't in love with her, but I wonder, for a fleeting moment, if there has been some wild cosmic mistake. Magda is the perfect match for Khaled, who loves beauty and ease in his connections. She is accomplished. I could have studied law or pharmacy; I had the grades to become a doctor like her. What I lacked was the temperament. I loved my cake business. But for the first time, I feel embarrassed by it.

Given her status, I am surprised that she is behaving like a *habla.* The kind of woman whose sweetness overtakes her energetic nature. The kind who doesn't think before she speaks and so will say too much, or the wrong thing, and the embarrassment will fall to the person she has implicated as well as her.

Without spending more than an evening with them, I can see that she doesn't match Naeem, who exudes a quiet knowing.

Khaled queries Naeem and Magda on their work. Naeem will be based in Jordan for a while, visiting the refugee camps to offer his services. Then he surprises us all when he addresses me. 'You should visit the camps with me one day. We could use your skills.'

Magda looks taken aback but quickly adjusts her stance, smiling as she shrugs her agreement, hands again resting at her knees. 'True. A lot of foreigners come through, but they can't speak Arabic.'

'We need translators,' Naeem continues. 'And you have artistic skills and they need to keep people busy. I'll put you in touch with the program director.'

I am surprised, but the idea electrifies me. Instinctively I look to Khaled, who shrugs, but does not make an effort to smile through his unease like Magda. He would say no, for sure, if he were the older brother. But Naeem has authority in this space.

'Do you think refugees want to learn how to bake? How is that useful?' Khaled says to Naeem, his tone neutral.

Naeem grins. 'Do you think people stop wanting nice things when they've lost the life they once had? Useful, *akhi?* It's never been more useful.'

I sense Khaled's insecurity against Naeem's authority. I turn to him. 'What do you think?'

Khaled shrugs. 'I don't know if it's useful, but if you want to try, Sahar, why not? *Inti horra.*'

***

My meeting with Naeem unsettles me. He is attractive, but I wonder if I am simply transferring my desires onto him. Khaled is an ideal tick-box husband in so many ways, but I cannot sustain a connection with him. In Jordan, my sense of self has become fractured, and I don't look to Khaled to fill the void. He struggles to look me in the eye everywhere except in the bedroom. Naeem has done nothing more than shake my hand and look into my eyes. But everything about him moves me. It awakens something in me, a fire, a need – genuine desire that physically hurts.

I try to shake off the feeling. But then, four days later, Naeem sends us the details of a direct contact at the aid agency. And a week later I'm on a minibus to Zaatari refugee camp. I am buoyed by new potential. I want to work, but the idea of seeing Naeem also thrills me a little.

Chapter 10

What once held me together has fallen apart. All around me, this wreckage.

I've said enough for one night. I pause here for my friends, who have been quietly listening. It will unravel, this strange history, but in parts, because tonight, I have nothing left. And while I know I'm only just getting started with the story, its essence lies exposed and a new energy fills the kitchen. Lara and Samira must now think I'm here purely because of Naeem. An extramarital love affair.

In the stillness, we find our bearings. Samira looks distant, head lowered, as she plays with the fabric of her top. Reliably, Lara punctures the silence, her eyes wide, staring into mine. 'Bloody hell. I thought you were going to tell me you're a lesbian. This is kind of worse, gotta say. Holy shit, Sahar.'

'I didn't sleep with him.'

But I imagined so many things. In my mind, I did everything with him. I gave him something I withheld from my husband. I reassured myself that Khaled didn't want it, but even if he had, I had already carved out an irretrievable space for Naeem.

When we're done for the evening, I walk Samira to the door. She collects her jacket and slowly shrugs her way into it. I get the door for her, but then she takes hold of my arm and leans her forehead into mine. My instinct is to detach, but she keeps me in place. I savour the familiarity of her scent; she always wears fruity perfumes.

When she looks at me, her eyes are wet. 'Love is everything,' she says, then rushes off.

I return to the kitchen, where Lara is trying to interpret the grains in her coffee cup. She exhales, abandoning it, then runs her hands through her hair.

'OK look. The scar. It wasn't your husband, was it? Did he do that to you?' She looks me square in the face and I shake my head.

'No. He was never violent with me. It was an accident.'

How it happened is an event I have managed to scramble in my mind so that it's not real. I have no intention of sharing it now.

Lara looks mildly relieved, but worry still creases her features. Although her eyes look misty, she's not crying. 'I've never known anyone as strong as you. But remember what I always used to say when we were younger and more innocent? Boys suck.'

'Yes. I remember.'

'Don't let it take over, you know?'

'There's nothing to get sucked into. Don't worry. We're done.'

Lara gives me a brief but fierce look then nods once, satisfied enough to end the interrogation. She starts to clean up, but my stomach aches.

So much emotion, and I haven't even told them the whole story.

***

A week after the divorce text, on an unseasonably grey and stormy Friday afternoon, I'm prepping caramel apple scrolls in Maggie's kitchen. Luke is in the chocolate studio, and Inez and Kat have disappeared. Two juniors, Justin and Olivia, float in and out, while I peel apples, core them then slice them. Nowadays, I usually have earphones in, playing ambient music or Lara's songs ('You always need a soundtrack'), but today the roof is being pounded by heavy rain and I feel comforted by it.

Being busy makes it easier to push away thoughts of Khaled divorcing me by text. I thought the divorce would feel more liberating, but instead it's been like a hard landing because my parachute didn't open. And oddly, some part of me is searching for a way to deal with the injustice of it, the searing insult of a bad ending to a movie I didn't even enjoy.

I am sure I am being gossiped about outside of his family, and the idea that Khaled's parents and siblings will be forced to indulge people's fantasies about who I am, and my worth as a failed wife, physically hurts. People will be diagnosing me as *majnooneh*; Khaled, the poor husband married to a woman who was not well. I push back waves of grief, anger and annoyance – at him then myself.

Maggie appears at my bench. 'You're my hardest worker, that's for sure,' she says, pulling over a stool then sitting down. We're in the same spot she first interviewed me.

'It doesn't feel like work.'

'Passion is not the same as obsession.'

'I don't understand.'

Maggie shrugs. 'I used to do that: stay so busy that I didn't have time to think. I covered up all my problems with things to do. Worked a treat. Until it didn't.'

'I'm not forcing this. It's easy for me.'

'No, I know. That's the problem. You love it, but it's still an escape. You need balance, Sahar. I've only known you for a little while. You're shy but no shrinking violet. You could run this place, but there's a reason I have loyal staff; they like what they do and they like working for me, too.'

'I'm not likeable?'

'Goodness, no, that's not it. But you're not flexible. You're compassionate. I can see that you feel very deeply, that you take things seriously and do them with care. But don't strive for perfection. The best stuff is the messy stuff.' Maggie rises from her stool. 'I want you to have fun, even when you're at work. Lighten up. The Gordon Ramsay intensity thing is a myth. Luke just didn't get the memo.'

'Maggie, did you hire me because Leo asked you to?'

Maggie looks mildly taken aback, but she recovers.

I look down at the apples, the discarded cores in one bowl, the skins in another. 'Sorry,' I tell her. 'I've just heard that he has a lot of influence.'

'Leo is my business partner. We also happen to be related. He doesn't interfere with what he doesn't know. And he doesn't know sweets.' Maggie softens, leans in a bit closer and places a hand on my shoulder. 'Don't look for meaning that isn't there, Sahar. Life is hard, but you seem to make it harder with that big mind of yours. You belong here. I would never risk my business with a handout.' She drops back onto the stool with a small sigh. 'I understand you better than you think, Sahar. I'm someone who finds it easy to see the light in the dark. But I was a wog when wogs had to laugh at the name. I know what it's like to make yourself smaller to fit into someone else's space.'

'It's not just being in a minority,' I say. 'Sometimes I feel like I don't have a centre and I'm constantly trying to find my balance.'

I'm surprised by my own admission, how my worries have now crystallised. I don't know who I am, constructed or authentically, and it's like having emotional vertigo.

'My father was an immigrant,' Maggie says, a bit wistful and reflective. 'Came from a tiny village in Italy, and it's like he carried it on his back every single day for the rest of his life. Worked himself to the bone – hard, back-breaking work; the kind no one respects. Even when I was a kid, I used to wonder why he struggled so much. It didn't make sense to me. He never got to enjoy life. Died of a heart attack at fifty-five. My mother never recovered.'

'I'm sorry.'

Maggie shakes her head. 'I used it. I wasn't going to be like them. And you are not what your parents told you to be either. Don't be a prisoner to anyone. I know how guilt works, and you can't let it take over you.' She squeezes my shoulder again. 'You are not what you've been through; just use it and power on. Be the rock in the stream. Things flow around you, not the other way around. Got it?'

I nod. 'Can I do more days?'

'Oh, the trial is over. I'd like you to come onboard full-time now.'

'Oh my God. Really?'

'Yes. We're getting busier. Do you want to do some time in the chocolate studio?'

'Of course. Yes.'

'We'll see how we go. Let's see if we can find your voice in there.'

I have no idea what this means, but Maggie has just shown that she has a genuine interest in my development. So often I feel like I'm trying to inflate a balloon with holes in it, but this affirmation tells me otherwise. I smile, a flutter of excitement rising in my chest.

'Let me know your size and I'll arrange the chef's whites,' Maggie says.

I haven't quite figured Maggie out yet, but she's hard not to like.

I'm about to return my focus to the fruit I'm preparing when Inez and Kat trail in. Maggie pretends to be unimpressed. 'Bludgers.'

Kat scrunches up her fingers and kisses them, throwing it towards Maggie.

But Maggie doesn't leave. She walks to the side bench and glances at the chunky, colourful watch on her wrist. A few seconds later, Luke enters, and the juniors also gather. Maggie takes a deep breath and claps her hands together. 'All right, then. Listen up, everyone! End of year approaches. Huzzah! December is always crazy for us. So to get ready, we're doing a team-building exercise on Monday.'

There's a collective groan, but Maggie waves it away and continues speaking over the rising din. 'This means your day off is not a day off if you're full-time. And if you're very good, I might even buy you lunch. OK? If this is going to be a problem, come see me before you leave today.'

Maggie commands respect, not fear, and I appreciate the difference. But team building? I've just been promoted and my first instinct is to contemplate escape.

As if she's reading my thoughts, Maggie stops at my bench on her way out and taps it with her index finger. 'As I said, you need to come out of your shell.' Then she winks and I feel like she's tricked me, even if it's not in a malicious way.

Predictably, my face responds while the words are stuck in my throat. I can feel my embarrassment colour my cheeks and my emotions rising.

Maggie's eyes glitter and she does her little head shake of delight. 'Fun,' she says, gently squeezing my arm. 'We're going to have fun.'

I offer a faint smile and Maggie begins a slow walk away, giving a couple of thunderous claps and yelling out for us to quicken our pace. 'Fun, fun!'

I watch her leave then catch Luke glancing at me. He looks pissed off, and this time I can appreciate his frustration. I manage a smile as I return my gaze to the ingredients. *Fun. Fun, fun, fun, fun.*

Chapter 11

I wish there were gentler, less embarrassing ways to truth.

Samira was once forced to abseil and scream her way down a flying fox for a team-building exercise. I baked her a cake in honour of the great feat, although it should be said that she was the one who booked it in the first place.

I am reminded of this as I stand in the Improv Parlour Theatrette with the bakery staff – Maggie, Luke, Kat, Inez, Justin and Olivia – and three cafe staff members I've never properly met: Jen, Harry and Dimitri.

The small warehouse we're in clearly has multiple uses. Against one wall are large wooden boxes, which I assume form a stage, and rows of conjoined seats line the opposite end. A small kitchen with a microwave, plastic toaster and matching kettle sit on top of a mini fridge.

We are about to do improvised theatre, and I am terrified. Right now, I would prefer to be scrambling down a cliff face attached to a harness than standing in this small performance space with my co-workers for the next two hours. Glancing around, I get the sense I'm not alone in this feeling. Only Maggie is alive to the experience, her eyes shining in anticipation, her mouth fixed in a closed grin.

To ease us in, our instructor, Zach, a dorky type in jeans, a hoodie and Converse sneakers, begins with 'icebreakers', including a zombie name game. He talks like it's the most exciting thing in the world, pausing, stretching out words and practically high-fiving himself.

We play games. Kat and Inez find a way into it. Eventually, Kat is no longer mumbling 'Fucken hell' under her breath whenever it's her turn to speak, and Inez actually appears excited, pumping her arms when she or someone else is clever in a game. I look for the light and find it when I see that Luke is struggling far more than I am. He has his arms crossed, and when he smiles, it's the conciliatory kind you give an enemy in a tournament. He hates it, and when we're forced to make eye contact during a game called Mirror – where one person leads the other with body movements – for once it's not a challenge. Somehow, both of us are able to do this without looking away, and for a moment, we seem to connect as the outsiders in this strange ritual. When we're done, he rolls his eyes and shrugs.

There's a notable difference in Luke beyond the almost-smile. He's dressed like a civilian – black pants and a short-sleeved shirt – and something in his demeanour is different because of it. The chef's whites give him a status he doesn't carry with him everywhere. But now he doesn't loom as large in my eyes. I see it so clearly that I am stunned.

'OK! Our next game is called Convergence!'

Oh for—

No. I don't swear.

***

I am barely over Convergence when Zach leads us into Musical Hotspot, where someone stands in the middle of a circle, belting out a song until someone steps in to save them. I make a beeline for the bathroom, but Maggie grabs my shirt, pulling me back towards her. She loops her arm through mine, then standing tall, taps me on the hand, I guess to reassure me before the slaughter. I get away with not singing by not stepping into the circle, but there's no escaping Word-at-a-time Story. I'm the worst at this because I pause for too long, disrupting the fast pace, not appeased when Zach says there's no good or bad. This is only partly true, because none of us are very good. Only Harry and Dimitri seem to speak the language, and this is because they're aspiring actors. The only person who gets as stuck as I do is Luke. Everyone else is starting to give in to the cheer and cringey hilarity, but while I'm plagued by excruciating stage fright, Luke is simply uncomfortable. I'm so mortified that during one game, when it's my turn to speak, I just stand there, frozen, and everyone laughs. It breaks the tension, and even I smile. Luke grins too, probably relieved that my mess-ups conceal his own embarrassment.

When Zach calls a break, I am filled with relief, but there's no chance for escape. Maggie makes sure of it. 'No one leave, it's only a five-minute break!'

When the break is over, Zach says he's going to slow things down. 'No more silly games, I swear!' He laughs, but we know it's a lie because we still have forty-five minutes left to endure.

'It's called ... Drum roll please...' he taps the air with his hands, 'I ... Love! Guys, *I love* this game. Each of you is going to get up here, and for one minute, talk about something you love.'

'Just one thing?' says Dimitri.

'A bunch of things is fine, so long as you can cram it into one minute. Don't try to be funny,' he continues, and Kat says, 'Ha! Nothing to worry about there,' and we all laugh.

Kat's monologue has us in stitches. She swears liberally then praises cussing. 'I fucken love what I do, but the best thing is showing people that you have more going for you than they think. My dad will always eat my desserts, and I fucken love that. And fuck using Cointreau in desserts. It doesn't work.'

When Inez speaks, she sways a little, hands knotted together at her lower back, as she explains her love of aerial performance. 'I love the way my body knows what to do without me needing to think about it. I love the feeling of movement, like I can float but I feel safe at the same time. And I *love* the sexy outfits!' she says, winking then giving us a cheeky hip swing, which is met with whoops and cheers.

Luke's runs for about ten seconds. 'I love the end product after a long trial period. Everything is experimentation, but sometimes you feel like you've reached the perfect ending and you have to move on.'

When it's my turn, I don't try to be funny.

'I love ... I love that I'm here. About ten years ago, I was a very different person. You wouldn't recognise me. I wore a headscarf. I practically lived in my home kitchen. I would never be in a place like this, or working with other people, or wearing my hair out like it's the most normal thing in the world. Then my whole world changed.

I went overseas and I felt like everything I knew was out of reach. I built a whole new world, but about a year ago, it all came to an end. I nearly died. For a little while, I thought it would have been better if I had. I feel ashamed saying that.'

I stop, momentarily panicked because I have said more than I intended, or would ever wish to share. But it came out, unbidden. I look over the faces watching me without judgement or even pity and I feel safe. Maggie has a maternal warmth to her expression, while Kat nods at me, encouraging. Inez gives me a mournful smile. Luke studies me, his expression intense but not telling me what he thinks. I look away. 'It does something to you, seeing real life up close. I'm glad I didn't give in to that feeling. I love that I'm here with you.'

***

Afterwards, we emerge into the fresh air and afternoon light like survivors of the Kokoda Trail, undeniably linked by the challenge but also filled with relief that we survived it. Kat pulls me in and ruffles my hair like a big sister, then releases me, allowing Inez to loop her arm through mine. I glance at Luke, who studies me, a curious look on his face.

We retreat to a nearby cafe for lunch, and the staff scurry around to move tables together to accommodate our group. Maggie takes a seat and orders a prosecco, to cheers from Kat.

'I've earned it!' Maggie says, looking delighted.

'We all have,' says Kat. 'But I want wine.'

Everyone is in high spirits, because in spite of our collective resistance to the team-building event, we had fun, and I think, even in that short space of time, shed some dead skin. I didn't expect it to unfold as it did. I knew we were meant to bond, but perhaps something about being forced to step outside of my shyness made me feel free, even if for a moment.

The drinks arrive and I take a sip of my lemon, lime and bitters, cherishing it like it's a long-desired reward. Maybe, just maybe, for the first time in my life, I'm starting to feel comfortable in a group, even if I'm not exactly at home in it yet.

Maggie makes a toast. 'To a successful afternoon of laughter and silliness. But please don't try for a job in comedy; you're much better at your current ones.'

There is gentle laughter, some half-hearted whooping from Kat, and we raise our bottles and glasses. It's a sound I never heard growing up except on television. Even with nonalcoholic drinks, my mother frowned upon toasts because of their association with non-Muslim celebrations.

As we wait for our meals to arrive, we start conversations between ourselves, chattering as we study the menu. Only Luke is quiet, sitting at one end of the table beside Inez. We make eye contact and his expression is new to me. He looks concerned, but I smile and he nods once before taking a sip of his beer.

After we've eaten, Kat tries to recruit Maggie for drinks, but she refuses. 'Early to bed tonight for me.' She rises from the table and says her goodbyes.

I wonder if she's going home to anyone. I've never thought about Maggie's personal life, and I realise it's because of her confidence. Sweets by Maggie and the chocolate shop *are* Maggie, and like she said once about Luke, how we are in life is how we are at work.

Kat turns her attention to me next. Neck craned, she extends an arm, reaching out to take hold of mine. 'You never come.'

'I have a gym class.'

Her hold on me tightens. 'Sahar.'

'I don't drink. I'm boring!'

By now, Kat has both arms locked around my waist and I feel embarrassed by the attention.

'Just come for one drink,' Inez says. 'I'll distract Kat so that you can escape early.'

I chuckle as Kat starts to shake me gently. 'OK, OK, I'll come.'

Kat leads the way to a bar down the street, talking Luke's ear off as he listens, head down, hands jammed in his pockets. Behind them are the juniors and cafe staff. Inez falls into step beside me, zipping up a light jacket, radiating calm as always.

'I'm not a big drinker, so you're not alone,' she tells me, raising her voice just enough to be heard over the traffic and Kat's guffaws.

'I don't understand why Kat insists on me coming. I'm happy to be the quiet, boring one.'

'She likes you,' Inez says.

'I know.'

'Do you?' says Inez.

'I'm grateful for you both. You know that, right?'

'Of course. And you're not boring,' Inez says with a sigh. 'Just intense.'

We continue in silence for a few moments before Inez speaks again. 'Sorry,' she says, bumping gently into my side. 'That came out sounding harsher than I meant it to. It's just nice to see you interacting with everyone. It's important. Especially with Maggie. We're not her staff, we're like her family. You won't have a future at Maggie's if you keep to yourself the whole time. And I know you want this.'

I'd almost forgotten the blunt scrape of shame, but my skin tingles in recognition and I immediately want to take back everything I did badly.

'Thanks. I guess I needed to hear that,' I say, my head down. 'I'm not a snob, I swear. I'm just not used to working like this, to being in a group.'

I'm not used to people wanting me in their group. Even in Jordan, I worked alone.

Inez gives me a long look. 'Today was good. It explained a lot. You're talented, Sahar. Keep going, OK? I know you're starting out a bit older, and it feels like it's going to take forever, but you came in with knowledge and experience, and so much passion. Do you see Maggie promoting the other juniors? Everything you did before you joined us counts.' Then she chuckles. 'God. I've been looking at Maggie's motivational posters for too long, haven't I?'

We slow down as we approach the door to the bar.

'You were really good today. Are you ever scared?' I say.

'Yes. All the time. I just don't want to lose myself trying to do better. I don't want to be a perfectionist. I get excited by experiences,' she says.

***

The bar is a dimly lit, wood-panelled, classy kind of place, where the music plays at a low hum and the bartenders wear aprons and have handlebar moustaches.

Inez, Kat, Luke and I find a booth and I manoeuvre myself into a seat. The other juniors and cafe staff have formed their own clique, but it was a natural separation. There was no tension, just an understanding of a natural divide. I'm surprised about which side I landed on, but choose not to overthink it.

Just as I'm wondering how anyone finds this noisy, dark place appealing, someone dumps two baskets of spiced popcorn on the table and I perk up.

'I want to know what kind of drunk you are,' Kat tells me with a luminous smile. She's already a little tipsy. 'My guess is, you're always thinking, so you'll be a sad sack.'

Inez shakes her head. 'She'll be on the tables dancing. I say happy drunk;

tells everyone how she feels deep down.'

Kat raises her hands, like she's about to reveal the answer to life's great mysteries. 'She'll be both. Happy then sad. I love it. I want to see drunk Sahar.'

They look to Luke to cast the final vote. He's less sullen now, but not cheerful. 'Militant.'

Inez gasps.

'Fuck off,' says Kat.

Luke straightens up and his whole body changes. 'I'm telling you. She's a perfectionist, so she'll be hard on everyone.'

I'm bewildered by this open and easy dissection of my character. Admittedly, I grow curious, too.

'Shall we find out?' says Kat. There's a glint in her eye as she crowds in on me and gives me a side hug. 'Kidding. We don't have time tonight. It needs to be done properly.'

Luke studies me throughout the entire exchange and slowly an almost-smile starts to form. 'Leave her alone. She's not a drinker.'

'OK, serious question,' says Kat, releasing me. She readjusts herself to face me. 'If you weren't hung up on what your parents taught you, would you want to have a drink?'

'Does it matter?' I say. 'Why is drinking so important?'

'OK, drinking, dating, anything you weren't allowed to judge as good or bad for yourself.'

'I let go of a lot of those things over the years. It's not that big of a deal.'

'Just play along.'

I'm feeling comfortable and emboldened enough by now to be more open with them. 'One of my best friends is already trying to get me to jump on the experience wagon. So get in line.'

Even Luke cracks a proper smile at that. 'You're going to write one of your lists?'

'I'm glad I'm amusing you all,' I say, surprised at how easy it is to be with them here. It occurs to me that I have never felt at ease with anyone besides my closest friends and family, and with Naeem. Not in school, university or even in my years of attending religious classes.

Inez raises her hands, a disapproving look on her face. 'Ease up on the girl. If she wants your help with her social life, she'll ask for it. But I reserve the right to interfere with work stuff. And clothing,' she says, mock-coughing into her fist.

Luke rolls his eyes. 'What is it with you women always needing to fix each other up? There's nothing wrong with how she dresses.'

I meet his eyes, but he quickly turns away and busies himself with his phone. I excuse myself and head to the bathroom.

The sound of the booming music mutes as the door behind me swings closed. My face is flushed, but in a good way. I wash my hands and face, top up my eyeliner and apply some lip gloss. I smile without thinking about it, a thin sprinkling of nervous excitement filling my chest. I am having fun.

I check my phone and see a message from Salim, a message from Samira with a photo of her kids' handiwork in the living room, and two voice messages from Khaled sent through WhatsApp.

Chapter 12

Some people are bad for you, and sometimes you are bad for others.

Khaled, a compartmentalised memory most days, is in contact again. I frantically play the first message. I place the phone to my right ear and stick a finger in the other one to drown out the noise.

'Sahar ... What were you thinking?' he says in Arabic. His deep voice, so familiar but so out of place here. 'You are your own worst enemy. I'm still trying to recover from you.'

My whole body is shaking from the shock of the old returned. I press play on the second message.

'Do you think I felt nothing? When I was with you, do you think it meant nothing? If only you had looked at me the way you looked at him.'

Khaled's tone is vulnerable. He sounds heartbroken, even though I know that what has ripped him apart is not me or my departure. He pauses a while, then sighs. 'Nothing would have made you happy. I know that now.'

He sounds like the victim, not the perpetrator. The words fall on me like bricks and I sink to the floor. That blunt scrape of shame.

When I was with you, do you think it meant nothing?

My body tenses at the memory of being with Khaled. It frightens me how easily I can conjure it all. The energy of him, the heavy scent of aftershave, the flare of annoyance in his eyes. The way he looked past me.

Don't ever cut your hair.

I don't know how long I'm there for, but I'm still in a daze, plaiting my long hair, lost in Khaled's words, when Kat comes into the bathroom.

'Oh my God, are you OK, *habib?*' Kat crouches down beside me and tilts my chin.

'I'm fine. I just needed a minute.'

Kat is not convinced, but then I exhale slowly and look her in the eyes, and she relaxes.

I take back what I told Lara about not wanting to experience things. I take it all back. Suddenly, I am overwhelmed by the desire to reduce my cage to ashes rather than make it so large that I forget it exists.

I want to try everything.

'Let's do it,' I say. 'Let's do that experience experiment.'

Kat looks shamefaced. 'We were just kidding around, Sahar. It's just, everyone had rules, and most of us broke them.'

I shake my head. 'No. You're right. I'm too afraid to admit that there are things I want to try.'

Kat slides down onto the floor with a heavy sigh. She speaks slowly, a little drunk, but her words are clear. 'Darling, I hate to break it to you, but you don't have ownership on being fucked up, or on your parents fucking you up.'

'My parents gave me religion. My ex-husband took it away. Then...'

Naeem. The in-betweener. The questioner who believed he didn't have the answers but also didn't think that the meaning of life was the most important question.

I need to figure out what lies between. A way out of this wilderness. Or find some tools to survive it.

I am quiet, ashamed at the thought that my parents' restrictions overshadow all the good they did for me. But it matters, how they taught us to exist in the world.

'Only girls with names like Becky and, I dunno, fucken Kayla or something had a normal childhood,' Kat says. 'And even then, they're pretty messed up, steaming their vaginas and shit.'

I start to laugh, properly, and Kat joins me. We are in hysterics by the time Inez comes in to check on us.

'Have you both lost your minds? We thought you fell in.'

Kat raises a hand and settles herself. She stands up then reaches down to pull me up. 'She's in.'

'What?'

'Sahar. She's going to try some things out. I'm calling it The Experiment. Capital "T", capital "E".'

Inez looks unconvinced. 'You know you can tell us to bugger off, Sahar.'

'I want to do this,' I say, and I mean it.

'Are you sure?' says Inez.

'It's going to help you figure a lot of shit out,' says Kat. 'Trust me. It'll tell you who you are. You think it's just an activity, but really, it's a test.'

And I have done enough of those to know how they work.

***

It was meant to be an early night, but Kat demanded we all stay back to devise the list. The crowd at the bar has thinned out, and only a drunk couple remains, swaying together on the dance floor to a screechy rock song.

'Leave me out of it,' says Luke.

'No. Fuck off,' says Kat. 'You're in. We all give Sahar at least one experience.'

I'm starting to regret my decision, but Kat's enthusiasm is hard to fault. I wonder what essential thread connects us, because she seems invested more deeply than the rest of the group. She carefully places a napkin down and digs out a pen from her satchel bag.

I drag the basket of fresh popcorn towards me.

'First, I'll take dancing,' says Kat.

'I know how to dance,' I say, and Kat raises an eyebrow. Admittedly, it was always with women, but we didn't hold back. 'In fact, I could probably teach you something.' I take another piece of popcorn.

Luke perks up. 'Them's fightin' words,' he says.

Leaning forward, Kat eyes me suspiciously. 'Have you done in-the-club dancing?'

'Not on my list.'

'Have you danced with a guy you like?'

Damn it. 'No.'

'Ooh, slow dance with a man. Yes! Write that,' says Inez, her mirth bubbling up.

'I've never even been on a date,' I say, stuffing my mouth with popcorn.

The table falls silent. The loud music continues to pound in my ears and I can hear my own chewing, but my embarrassment feels louder than both.

'You were married,' says Kat.

'I never dated him the way people date here.'

They're all staring at me, but their looks vary. Inez is sympathetic, Kat is horrified, and Luke is curious. At least I think he is, because he is scrutinising me intently, but not in the judgemental way he used to when I first started working at the bakery.

'You should totally go on a date. Go on lots of dates, even if half the guys you'll meet are fuckwits,' says Kat.

'You want to try Tinder or something?' says Inez, her beautifully made-up face etched with concern. 'I don't use it personally, but I can walk you through it.'

'No!'

'Not Tinder. Jesus,' says Luke.

'Is there a dating app for Muslims?' Kat queries.

'I don't want to swipe on an app for a date.'

'Just make sure he uses protection,' says Inez, lowering her voice, her eyes wide. I tied my tubes a while ago. I couldn't bear another pregnancy. But then Inez says, 'Safety from everything,' and she squeezes my arm.

'Dating a woman isn't much easier,' says Kat. 'Trust me, I know.'

'I'm not a lesbian.'

'The sex is better,' says Kat.

Luke groans and Inez chuckles.

'We know,' says Luke. 'You tell us all the time.'

'Fuck off,' comes Kat's tight response.

'I think my husband got turned on by that sort of thing,' I say, remembering Khaled's videos. One of them was for lesbian sex – at least, the way I think men imagine it.

'This is her without intoxication,' says Kat.

'And he's still your husband?' asks Inez.

'No, he divorced me by text. Not because of that, obviously.'

'It should be a little because of that,' says Inez.

'Adding dates to the list. No pressure,' says Kat, underlining the words.

'Do I get to tell you what I want?' I say.

'Totally,' says Kat. 'Inez, you take clothes shopping.'

'What's wrong with what I'm wearing?'

Kat winces as she scribbles down more notes, and Inez shrugs, arms raised in surrender because she is not the one steering this ship. 'There's nothing wrong, per se,' Inez begins awkwardly. 'But we need to put you in a sexy dress and take you out.'

'I've worn dresses like that before.'

Kat scoffs. 'In front of women only, I bet. Right?'

I'm silent and Kat nods, her smile growing wider. 'I know how it goes. I've been to those Lebanese girls' nights. The women go off. Don't get me wrong, it's impressive. But not what we want here. I'm adding sexy dress to the list.'

Inez takes my hand like she's offering me support during a difficult procedure. 'You don't have to do anything you don't want to.'

'We should all take drinking,' says Kat. 'That's a big one.'

The conversation is building around me. I should be offended, but I'm oddly touched by their investment in my wellbeing – even if it's their kitchen-sink version of it.

'I'll take mind, body and spirit,' says Inez and it starts to sound like a game show.

'Luke, you're up,' says Kat.

Luke is not impressed. 'I'll do drinks with you all,' he says, then drains his beer.

Kat shakes her head. 'Don't be salty. Have a think about it, and we'll come back to you.'

'What about something sporty?' says Inez.

'Rule: it has to be outside her comfort zone,' says Kat. She turns to me. 'It should scare you, Sahar. At least a little.'

'No, it should just be new in some way,' says Inez, ever the diplomat.

'I learned how to swim at school, but I wasn't allowed to go to the beach,' I tell them.

The two women study me, morose, and I hate it. 'It's OK. It's not like I was going to be an Olympic swimmer,' I say, looking to Luke, who shrugs. 'But maybe I could learn again?'

The pitying looks from the girls linger, breaking when Kat shakes her head and starts to scribble. 'I wanted to throw javelin and my dad freaked out. What would the church friends think? Instead, I broke their hearts by telling them I'm gay.'

'Are your parents OK with your sexuality now?' I ask.

'God no, but they still talk to me. We just pretend I never said it, or it was a breakdown. I've learned that if I want them in my life, I can't give them access to all of it. I pick and choose.'

I nod. I never had the courage to pick and choose. Now I don't need to, but it's lonely. My brother is distant, unable to align me with his way of existing in the world.

'You can't force your life onto people,' Kat continues, her voice lower. 'I don't want people trying to change me, so I don't mess with my sanity by trying to change them.'

'Maybe you should go back to javelin as a hobby,' says Inez with a teasing smile.

'Maybe I will,' says a sombre Kat. 'Maybe I fucken will.'

'Maybe we can all do something,' I suggest. 'Make it a group challenge.'

'Maybe let's focus on you for now,' says Kat. 'Who else is going to be the easygoing mum you never had?'

But Inez looks deep in thought. 'That's not a bad idea. Why don't we all do it?'

'Fuck off,' says Kat. 'I'm not the one hiding from life.'

Luke rolls his eyes. 'Likewise. Count me out.' He rises from his seat, momentarily leaning towards me. 'Tell you what. I'll teach you something cool with chocolate.'

I hesitate, unsure if he's joking. 'Really?'

'Sure. Last round's on me,' he says, then wanders off towards the bar.

Kat continues writing. '*That* she gets excited about. Not exactly what I meant by The Experiment, but OK.'

'There has to be something else,' Inez says. She steeples her hands together then rests her chin on them, inspecting me like I'm dessert.

'I wanted to join the circus when I was five,' I tell her, picking the most outrageous thing I can think of; I don't know how much more pity I can take.

But Inez's eyes look ready to pop out of their sockets. She's thrilled. 'Oh my God. You are coming to a Sexy Skygirls session with me!'

'Huh?' Kat and I say in unison.

'I do lyra!'

We both stare at her blankly, and she starts to flap her hands impatiently. 'Hoop! The aerial stuff I was talking about earlier, at my circus academy. But this class is all women and it's all sexy.'

'Do I look like I can do a circus act?' I may be a regular at the gym, but I still have the Arab curves and chest.

'All body types and levels welcome. You'll love it.'

'Added,' says Kat. 'And no, I'm not coming.'

Tipsy Inez does a faux sad smile but then scrunches up her face with glee. 'This is so exciting.'

Kat scans the list; I have no idea how she can read it in the dim light of the bar. 'This is looking good. Anything else?'

'I have one,' I tell her.

Kat waits. 'Shoot.'

'I want to cut my hair.'

'Really? But it's so nice and long,' says Inez.

'That's all I want. For now.'

'I can do it,' Kat says, and my eyes widen.

Inez smiles. 'Kat is brilliant with hair. She's done mine.'

'I had no idea.'

'There's a lot you don't know,' she says, head down as she adds my request to the list. 'My first job was sweeping up hair.'

'We can both do it,' says Inez, beaming. 'I'll do the treatment. Kat can do the cut.'

They wait for my response, but I'm still trying to process the rapid developments. 'Sure. Whatever you think.'

Inez's smile widens. 'And I mean it about joining in. I don't have a whole list to get through, but there's something I've been umming and ahhing about.'

Kat squints at Inez, a bit surprised. 'You don't keep secrets from me.'

'It's not a secret. Just something I've always wanted to do but didn't think I could. Or should.' Inez's face turns pink and she waves us away. 'One thing at a time. And, Kat, you're not getting out of this. And neither is Luke.'

'Whatever,' says Kat. She snaps a photo of the list on her phone, and a few second later, everyone's phones chime. 'Sent.'

Kat folds up the napkin and hands it to me. 'For framing.'

***

I come home feeling lighter than I should, given Khaled's message. I'm tired of feeling bad, of muting my emotions so I can forget. I need to find a way to be reminded of things and not internally fall to pieces.

Lara and Hakeem are on the couch watching a television show, Lara with her head in Hakeem's lap, his fingers caressing her forehead. It's dark but for the light of a tall floor lamp and the television glare, so I'm hoping I can sneak past and not interrupt their intimacy. But no such luck. Lara calls out to me to turn on the light. I switch it on, then approach them like I've been caught stealing. Lara sits up. 'And what time do you call this, young lady?'

'Definitely way past my bedtime.'

Hakeem smiles. 'Big night?'

'Bigger than I expected.'

'Sahar is making friends at work,' Lara says, straightening up. She pats the seat beside her but I shake my head.

'I just want to have a shower and go to sleep.'

Lara narrows her eyes at me. 'You look flushed. Were you drinking?'

'Nope. But everyone else was. Can you get drunk on fumes?'

Hakeem chuckles. 'Lara could.'

Lara punches him and he makes a guttural sound in response.

'Hakeem can't hold his liquor. We tried and failed.'

I look to Hakeem to see if he minds this revelation being so casually shared, but he shrugs. 'I wanted to try it. Turns out, I don't like whisky and I'm not missing out on much.'

'Actually,' I begin, 'it's funny you should say that. Lara, I know you were saying I should be experiencing more things ... My workmates have kind of convinced me it's not such a bad idea.' Lara is quietly watchful as I walk towards her, feeling a bit silly. 'We're calling it The Experiment.' Saying it out loud makes it sound stupid. I pull out the napkin with Kat's hastily scrawled but surprisingly legible list. She's even decorated it with flowers, hearts and faces projecting a variety of expressions. The haircut is an excited face; the dancing, a happy one. The one beside chocolate-making with Luke is a snooze emoji.

Lara takes the napkin with a curious expression. She looks to Hakeem then studies the list. 'Those little fuckers.'

Hakeem flinches.

'You're not their Barbie doll to accessorise.'

'Didn't Sahar just say this was your idea?' says Hakeem.

'And second, exactly. Fuck that, I put my hand up first.'

'I'm sorry, Lara. It just kind of happened. They were joking about it. Then Khaled left me some messages and—'

'Whoa, whoa! He contacted you?'

'Yes. I think the family is dealing with a lot because of me.'

'Shit. Are you OK?'

'I'm OK. I just don't want him to have power over me anymore.'

Lara softens. 'Well, I certainly don't think it'll hurt you to have a life outside of work and the gym.' She studies the list again. 'Can I at least add one item? Hakeem, you should do something. Samira will want to add something, too.'

Hakeem sees my pained look. He gently takes the napkin away from Lara and hands it back to me. 'Let Sahar decide for herself before you start inviting everyone into her experiment.'

'Lara, I promise we can do something,' I tell her. 'The list thing is a bit of a joke.'

'I'm going to think of something. And it'll be epic.'

'God help you,' says Hakeem, landing himself another sucker punch.

'You wouldn't need this if you were born twenty years ago, by the way,' says Lara with a sigh. 'It's our generation that's messed up. Now you go to the gym and Muslim girls are doing handstands in hijab and competing in the Olympics.'

Hakeem pulls Lara towards him. It's an easy movement, instinctive and certain. 'Why so worked up?' he says.

'I'm not worked up. I'm passionate,' she says with an intimate look.

My heart is full as I leave them, a little crushed by how the vision of them together revives a memory of love.

***

I am wired. I can't fall asleep. Despite the turnaround in the evening, Khaled's voice rings clear in my mind. He is gaslighting me, but he has ammunition. He knows more than he ever said; I suspect he simply didn't because to say something would have suggested an investment in our marriage he didn't have. I am sure he cheated on me during his overseas trips. There were things I found, in a suitcase, or a pocket. The scent on a piece of clothing, feminine and sweet, nothing like the heavy masculine scents he favours.

I reach over to my phone and unlock the screen. I open Khaled's messages and start typing.

Please send me the divorce papers. I'm in Sydney.

Without thinking, I give him my address.

Jordan

The fourth year

The hot sun beats down on us over the refugee camp at Zaatari. Naeem is giving me my first tour of a place so vast it's considered a city. He wears a long-sleeved shirt and tailored pants, insisting that, at least some of the time, he likes to dress as he would if he were in his surgery in Dubai out of respect for his patients. There is a lightness to him. He inhabits a space. It feels like something to be beside him and have his attention. With every beat of our conversation, he is leading me into new ways of thinking and existing in the world.

The religious girls I used to know in Sydney would warn that the brother-in-law is death whenever someone got married. Never be alone with your brother-in-law. He is not your *mahram.*

We're not really alone here, but our interactions feel private somehow. And meaningful.

It is Naeem who urges me to search for the beauty in my heritage and embrace it.

'No matter what people have told you to be, you are Palestinian,' he says. Some Arabs in the diaspora cling to their cultural identity. Most of the people I knew held on to their Muslimness. Nothing, not the brutality of public judgement post-September 11, nor the casual death threats lobbed at them as they went about their ordinary day, would sway them.

Salim, acting like a gentle guardian, suggested it would be OK to modify my hijab for safety reasons. Instead, I lengthened my headscarves and ignored the stares in the supermarket, and the intimidation at the traffic lights. I sought solace on the prayer mat. Occasionally, an invasive thought would sneak in, one that plucked at the emptiness I could feel following my prayers. How was it that I would recite so urgently my supplications but nothing would echo back to me?

***

The first time I worked at the refugee camp on the outskirts of Amman, Naeem and Magda stay in Jordan for only a month. It is seven months before they return.

Naeem pays us a visit the day he arrives back following travels to Syria and Palestine. The connection that had so startled me remains intact. He greets me with a look confirming that he too shares these confused feelings. I never knew so much could be said without words, but within minutes, my heart is unblocked, my stomach no longer tight, and the pain of separation has dissipated.

Khaled is tolerant of my work at the camp, but he lightly blames Naeem for taking me away from him. 'She prefers spending time with Syrians to being with her husband,' he tells his brother as we eat lunch.

'You travel a lot,' I say.

Khaled acknowledges my words with a shrug. 'What kind of husband would I be if I didn't prefer you to be safe at home?'

'What century are we living in?' Naeem says. There's an edge to his tone and it's noticeable.

The next day, Naeem surprises me by joining the agency team on the minibus. It is a thrill to be near him, and he angles his tall body into a seat too small for him in order to sit beside me, prompting a German volunteer opposite us to make a joke about it. He's so close I can smell the musky scent of his *oud* fragrance. His body occasionally bumps into mine. Every pothole, or sudden swerve by the driver, brings us together.

For months, I thought I had imagined Naeem into being, some kind of convenient rescuer. But whenever we're together, he proves to me our connection is real by finding a way to expand his knowledge of me and my world. He asks questions about my life in Sydney, and who I've left behind. He shares his thoughts on politics and the Arab world. He is an activist at heart.

It is strange but I never feel guilty. Perhaps it's because, technically, all that exists is emotional attachment and a hidden desire. It is also easy to hide behind Khaled's acceptance. Easier because it's not approval he displays, but indifference.

'Are you sure you don't mind me going to the camps?' I ask him a few times.

'I hate it when you ask me that, Sahar. I'm not your master.'

'OK. I'll go, then.'

'*Inti horra.*'

I get to know Naeem primarily on the bus trips into the refugee camps. At the camps, we are both hard at work. Occasionally we are brought together, but it's rare because he doesn't need me to translate.

One day, Naeem tells me he has arranged for me to upskill by learning first aid.

'Now you can save a life,' he tells me with a smile.

We work with the residents of the camp, from children to the elderly. We always speak in Arabic, but occasionally the younger ones will try to challenge themselves and share a sprinkling of English words they know. The older people I interact with pick apart my accent and joke about me being a daughter of Palestine as my language skills become stronger.

As I help them find creative outlets, some offer a skill in return. One woman, Farah, a quiet, thoughtful school teacher, helps me with my Arabic writing.

I make friends and expand my world each day that I'm at the camp. I come to understand how inflated my self-importance was in my youth, where I spent every moment worrying about how ordinary, simple acts could offend God. At the camp, I see how many small stories exist and interact. But rather than deflate me, they inspire me to be useful and give me purpose. I am not there for Naeem, but because of him.

***

One morning on the bus ride in, as usual, we fall easily into conversation. Naeem only speaks to me in Arabic. He asks me about my thoughts on life in a way Khaled doesn't, in a way I never even query myself. When he sees how I pepper my language with religious platitudes, he gently steers me towards neutrality.

His voice. His lively eyes. Naeem is handsome by anyone's standards – a beautiful face; masculine but not aggressive; tall but not perfectly built. I lose myself imagining how it would feel to be enfolded in his arms.

'Forget religion and read Mahmoud Darwish,' he says. Recently, he has decided to properly introduce me to Arab writers, most prominently the Palestinian poet Darwish and his displaced angst. 'You are like him, always lost and wandering, expecting the world to be fair,' he says with a smile.

'Are you sure you're not talking about yourself?' I say, and he laughs.

Naeem reaches into his bag and retrieves two books, which he then hands to me. 'I warn you: he will break your heart,' he says, his expression more serious.

I look down at the books in my lap. He wanted me to read Darwish's poetry in Arabic, but knowing that my reading comprehension is not as strong as my spoken Arabic, he has gifted me *Now,*

As You Awaken and *Exile's Poet* in English.

In that moment, I wonder if past lives are real; if he and I knew each other in another time, and if we suffered together in some way that links us in this life.

***

At home, after a long day, I fall in love again, with a poet who never found peace, his words weeping tragedy.

The exile tells himself: 'If I were a bird I would burn my wings.'

I find myself in Darwish. Tethered to an idea of place, but never at home. I discover that displacement can be expressed in many ways.

The next day, Naeem wants to know what I think. He cares. He values my mind and my perspective. And I tell him: how when reading poetry, I discover that immersion in lyrical pain can speak to you, list out the feelings you automatically stem. I had read the obligatory texts in school: Robert Burns, Henry Lawson, Banjo Patterson and his bush ballads, a war with nature. They were texts I studied but never connected to in any meaningful way.

'Of course you didn't,' Naeem says. 'Australia is a land built on blood. We Palestinians understand what it means to have your land stolen from you.'

Other poets steal my thoughts. Kahlil Gibran; no stranger but never appreciated until I read him under a hot sun at the Citadel in Amman, where I pretended to be a tourist.

And what is it but fragments of your own self you would discard that you may become free?

He shifts my understanding, shows me how my religion is missing a crucial component of genuine faith. Religion as a duty, rather than a feeling.

I cannot teach you how to pray in words.

I am used to working with my hands, but I learn to broaden my mind and sink into my heart. I returned to the mystics I first met with my Islamic teacher Hajjeh Noura. She would diligently work through a Saturday lesson in a high school classroom without air conditioning, still fully robed, even in the absence of men. She wasn't like the rest, who were pious in a quiet manner. She wore sneakers and played basketball with us after class. She made jokes about sex. She was nothing like the strict Muslims I knew, women so strict, they did aerobics to silence because music is *haram.* And she was secretly, I am sure, a Sufi, unable to share her longing for the Divine outside of the traditional scripture she was contracted to teach us.

I realise now that she felt no need to.

***

It terrifies me to discover how much I can feel for someone, what a look triggers within me. That time is not a requirement, only connection. Occasionally, I wonder if I am imagining this to be something it is not.

One morning, Naeem compliments me on my Arabic skills. '*Ya* Sahar. Do you know there are fifty words for love in Arabic? Shall I teach them to you?'

My breath catches in my throat. Is it a confession? I swallow my nerves, and his expression softens from playful to serious. My doubts are erased. I am not imagining it.

'I didn't know,' I tell him, and we lock eyes, neither of us willing to sever the cord between us.

In my marriage with Khaled, I always feel separate to myself, like I'm watching myself from a distance, seeing not feeling. In the bedroom, this only intensifies.

I don't think I will ever sleep with Naeem. We haven't even kissed. But our connection transcends the physical. It isn't pleasure he gives me, it is communion.

If anyone around us notices our connection, we are oblivious to it. Only Magda disrupts the union. Increasingly wary of my presence, she is no longer cheerful when she sees me.

'Do you think I'm stupid because I wear make-up and can't cook *mansaf?*' Magda tells me, and I have no response.

One stormy afternoon, as fierce wind and rain batter the tents at the refugee camp, a fellow aid worker gossips that Magda has broken off her engagement to Naeem. I listen for signs that the rumours involve me, but there's nothing to suggest this. I return to my admin tasks, rain pounding the metal roof as I try to clear my thoughts.

I seek confirmation with Naeem, but he seems regretful, not sad.

'You have to do what's right for you,' I say, because I understand the separation. I wish I could do the same with Khaled. I wish I had done it before my marriage. I am deeply in love with Naeem, and he pays me the attention a lover should; he would have destroyed Magda with his indifference the way Khaled almost did to me.

'I have to do what's right by her,' he says, 'and that means letting her go with her dignity.'

His tepid response leaves me feeling flat, but what else can I expect?

The end of the engagement prompts a response in Khaled. He eyes me with suspicion when I come home that evening. From his place on the balcony, which overlooks a sea of villas that glow a soft orange and yellow in the evening light, he asks me if I saw Naeem. He is smoking a cigarette, and resting beside him on the balcony is a cup of tea, still hot.

'I did.'

'He told you about Magda, then?'

'Yes.'

I expect Khaled to criticise her, loyal to Naeem as he is, but he looks disgusted. 'My brother is an idiot. He lost a diamond.'

I can feel my cheeks burning and I am seized by a feeling of panic. I search for the subtext in his words, the meaning of his disgusted look and if it relates to me. Khaled stares ahead, smoking, lost in his own thoughts.

'I don't want you going there so much,' he tells me.

'They need me.'

'I need you!' He turns abruptly towards me, his face etched in a minor version of fury, or perhaps it's hurt. 'I want to try again,' he says, indicating to my body.

'I've lost three.'

'Zainab told me about a doctor who helps women like you.'

The next morning, Naeem does not join me on the bus. In the afternoon, he finds me at the agency's HQ, answering emails at a computer in the far corner of the demountable. There are only a few of us inside, regulars who know Naeem and don't blink at his presence. It's a farewell.

'*Yallah,* I'll see you again soon,' he says, attempting a warm smile.

I can barely look at him. I stem the flow of tears threatening to erupt. The change in him shatters me. This mock farewell. A budget goodbye.

'*Assalamu alaykum,*' I say, returning his smile. I don't wait for Naeem's response. I turn back to my computer and continue to type.

experience

Chapter 13

How do you know who you are, deep down, if you don't challenge the structures others have constructed for you?

On a quiet Friday afternoon in January, a week after we devised the list, Inez and Kat appear at my bench while I'm mixing a bowl of pistachios and honey. They tell me The Experiment has begun. The first item to be ticked off is my haircut, and Inez books me in for 'something special' after work. Before I can enquire further, they wander off and my phone rings. It's Samira and my first instinct is to panic. She rarely calls.

I answer. 'Is everything OK?'

'I get to take your photo,' she says. I can hear traffic and there's an echo so I know she's on speakerphone in her car. Samira beeps the horn. 'Idiot! Pick a lane!'

'What are you talking about?'

'The Experiment thing. I'm taking your photo.'

'I've had my photo taken before,' I say.

'But you haven't been seen.'

She hangs up mid-curse at another driver. I stare down at the bowl of pistachios suspended in honey and centre myself. Bloody Lara.

An hour later, Salim calls me. I half expect him to declare that he too is taking one of the items on the list.

'Will you come over for lunch? We would all love to see you.'

The idea makes me nervous, but I can't say no. 'Um, of course. Let me check my calendar.'

We agree to an upcoming Sunday and I wonder what I should bake for them, because it will never do to show up empty-handed.

***

After work, Kat leads me to a nearby hair salon. 'Nez!' she calls out, familiar and loud, as she sweeps through the shop. Her grip on me tightens as she leads the way towards the back, where Inez waits, calm and poised as usual, her painted lips and nails standing out in the dim light of the room. She's out of her chef's whites and is dazzling, sporting a rockabilly look few can pull off. Vintage. She's in a sixties-style swing dress with cap sleeves; bright red cherries on black. Her shoes are red and shiny and make me think of Dorothy in *The Wizard of Oz.* Ruby slippers for courage to help her find her way home.

'You didn't flake,' says Inez in welcome, her hands resting on the back of a chair that's clearly meant for me.

The shop is empty, one side lined with chairs lit up in the half-dark.

'Where are we exactly?' I ask.

'My friend Tessa's salon. She's letting me use it after hours in exchange for cake and a free make-up job.'

'Generous friend,' I say, as Kat practically shoves me into the seat.

Inez steps in front of me, so close that I can smell the rose-scented perfume she wears as she runs her fingers through my long hair. 'A trim?'

I touch the top of my head. 'I was thinking something a bit more...'

'We're going to chop it all off,' says Kat.

Inez ignores her, still assessing my hair. 'Don't listen to Kat. If she had her way, everyone would be shaving their heads.'

I glance at Kat, who looks mock-offended. She runs a hand across her semi-shaved head and shrugs. 'And why not? I guess not everyone can rock this look.'

'Exactly,' says Inez, threading her fingers through my hair, reading me. She begins questioning me, searching for a history, asking for my story so that she can give me the right haircut. 'How did you get your hair so long? It's so thick and healthy, too.'

By now I'm seated and facing myself in the mirror. 'It's been under a headscarf for a few decades, remember?' As I consider my hair, I have to concede that it's healthy, but it's wog hair. Frizzy, wavy, ready to grow large at the first sign of humidity.

'I'm surprised that didn't affect it.'

'It did for a while.' My hair would fall out in clumps in my early days of wearing the headscarf. But somewhere along the way, balance was restored. I hadn't even noticed how thick it was until Lara's gig.

'So,' says Kat, dropping into the seat beside me. 'What do you want?'

'Short, but not too short.'

Kat studies me. 'OK, let's try again,' she says, softer. 'What do you want to feel?'

I pause, surprised by the emotion when I finally exhale, uncertain about what's rising up. It's just hair, a physical trait, non-defining. And yet it never has been. Never can be. Cutting it all off almost seems like a cliché. But I need to do something with it.

Kat waits patiently. I glance up at Inez, who gives me a sympathetic look. 'Everyone thinks chopping off their hair will feel good. It does for a couple of days, then they realise short hair isn't that exciting. Trust me. I know.'

Inez, with her beautiful glossy looks and hairstyles from another time.

Kat nods. 'This isn't a costume change you can take off after the show. It should reflect who you are now. Who you are becoming.' She demonstrates by folding my hair to show me how I would look with it short. Not particularly good, it turns out.

'That's a lot for a haircut to do,' I say.

'That's why we're here to help,' says Kat.

I try to find the words that will capture the essence of what the haircut means to me. 'I want to feel like it's the most normal thing in the world to have my hair out. I want it to look like I've never thought twice about it.'

I'm sure I make no sense, but Inez nods with approval. 'I like it.'

Kat reaches over to a stack of magazines on a side table. 'Want some inspiration? I mean, I'm not a pro, but I can do most things.'

I shake my head. 'No. I trust you.'

Kat's smile is modest as she gets up and ruffles my hair. 'Sometimes a new colour can make all the difference,' she says.

Inez leads me to the sink station, and for the first time, I can see her tattoos in full. There's an illustration on each of her upper arms, with titles: the one on her left arm reads 'The Fool', and features a man, chin up, a small pouch on a stick hanging over his shoulder. A little dog yaps at his feet and he's about to step off a cliff. The one on her right is called 'The World'; it's a striking image of a naked woman adorned in a wreath of leaves, arms outstretched, surrounded by symbols.

I take a seat in front of a sink, my back resting comfortably against the basin. 'What are those images on your arms? If you don't mind me asking.'

Inez looks for second like she's forgotten that her arms are painted. 'Oh, they're tarot cards. I love to read them.' She fiddles with her phone then the room fills with music. She powers up the water hose. 'Tell me if the temperature is OK.'

My scalp tingles at the force of the warm water and I nod.

Inez massages shampoo into my scalp, and I'm dizzy with the calming sensation it delivers. 'The Fool is the first Major Arcana card: setting out on a journey, not knowing where it will lead but working out the risks before you take the leap. The World is where you land eventually ... hopefully.'

'You get what you want?'

'It's liberation,' Inez says, switching on the hose again. 'It's everything.'

***

Two and half hours later, I consider Kat's work in the mirror with admiration. All she's done is cut my hair so that it sits at my shoulder blades, but there are layers, and subtle tints of golden brown. It has body and shape. It looks like hair you just have and don't have to think about.

'The layers will look even better if you straighten it.' Kat holds up a mirror behind me, moving it left and right so that I can get a proper look at the final result.

'I love it.'

Inez begins to sweep up the hair that's scattered around me.

'You should get Nez to read your cards some time,' Kat says.

Inez nods, all smiles. 'I'd love to. If you're up for it.'

'I don't usually buy into that stuff,' Kat says with a shrug. 'Bloody Greeks are like your lot – superstitious about everything. But Nez tells a nice story.'

'Sure, why not?' I say, rising from the seat, feeling oddly renewed.

Despite my curiosity about tarot cards, my *haram* senses are tingling. I've never doubted the power of intuition. I've always acknowledged, even as I've ignored, my gut instincts. But cards? My mother would stop speaking to me if she were around to disapprove.

'Do you see bad things?' I ask.

Inez leans against the broom, staring into the distance like a story's playing out in her mind's eye. 'I get a feeling about you, about what's happening. I don't think of it as good or bad ... just that there are emotions and things to deal with.'

'And it helps?'

'I think so. If you pay attention and do the work.'

Kat scoffs. 'She's a witch. She warned me about infidelity. A couple of weeks later, I found out my girlfriend cheated on me.'

I raise my eyebrows at Inez. 'I thought you don't tell people bad things.'

Inez gives a small smile. 'I showed her the way. That's not bad. The truth can be uncomfortable, but it will set you free.'

***

After Inez has locked up the salon, we commence walking down King Street, me wedged in between the 1960s queen Inez and Kat with her labourer look. We must be a sight. I realise that I'm still the plain one; always the one to blend into the background. My clothes aren't remarkable. I lack a style. The only thing that's distinctive is that I'm now rarely without a pair of earrings.

Kat slows down. 'OK, so, we're headed to a party. It's a queer dance party. Mainly wogs. What do you think? Don't worry, no one's going to crack on to you.' We start walking again, moving carefully to avoid running into people headed the other way.

'They might,' says Inez. 'She's *cute*. And well, now she has hair by Kat.'

'We could always go back and punk you up.'

'Bite your tongue,' says Inez. 'You're perfect, Sahar.' She takes my hand and gives it a squeeze.

'By the way, Luke's going to be there,' Kat says.

'Ugh.'

The sound is out of my mouth before I can stop it.

Kat laughs, her face etched in surprise. 'Wow, she emotes!'

I blush. 'Sorry. He just annoys me sometimes.'

'He annoys everyone. Don't take it personally. The dude is stuck somewhere in his teens and hasn't grown up, you know ... emotionally. Some people are addicted to suffering.'

I don't want to give shape to Luke's character. 'Is he gay?'

'No. But he lost a bet.'

'What kind of bet?'

Kat squirms a little and scrunches up her face. 'About how long you'd last. Don't be mad. We do it with everyone. Not many people can handle working with us, and especially with Luke.'

'Why does Maggie put up with him?'

'Eh. He's good. Knows pastry and chocolate. She can get a million juniors but Lukes are harder to find.'

'So, he wasn't being extra horrible to win the bet?' I say.

'God no,' says Inez. 'He's not cunning enough to do that.'

'He's just an arsehole,' says Kat. 'Which is why I'm very confident in placing bets. And right now, I'd wager you'll have a good time if you join us.'

'You don't have to do this for me,' I say.

'Do what?'

'Make me over like I'm a full-time job. Not that I don't appreciate everything you're doing.'

Kat pulls out a box of cigarettes and retrieves one. 'Would you look at this one?' she says to Inez. 'She thinks we're trying to save her.' But then she winks and I have to smile.

We reach the door to the venue and Kat and Inez swivel to face me like a pair of judges.

'Well? Are you coming in?' says Kat.

'I don't think I can dance like that. And I'm not gay.'

'Neither am I,' says Inez.

'They're not going to check your sexuality at the door,' Kat says.

'It's just an experience. You can dance or not. You can have some fun. Maybe have a tipple,' says Inez like a gentle counsellor.

I agree to go inside. Luke is the first person we encounter. He's standing at the bar, sipping on a drink when he sees us and waves us over. This is a proper dance festival, open to all kinds of personalities – even stuffy, uptight chocolatiers.

Luke, as always, studies me before saying hello. He gives me a smile, but I'm not sure if it's dry or sincere. 'Nice hair.'

I'm left wondering if he means it. It's possible he does, but then he said it in that annoying Luke way where the words can't be faulted but the tone grates.

'Thanks,' I say, embarrassed.

***

I am a wallflower for most of the night. Kat is dancing with Inez and another woman. They look over to me, try to get me onto the dance floor with waves and shoulder movements, but while it's invigorating being here, I'm tired and my bedroom is looking more attractive by the alcohol-soaked, trance-music minute. Just as I'm ready to make my exit, Luke comes to stand beside me.

'Usually at dance parties people dance.'

'I don't feel like dancing.'

'You don't drink. You don't dance. What did you come for?'

'The girls asked me and I didn't want to offend them.'

'I just mean, aren't you bored?' he says, gentler in tone.

I shake my head. 'Not at all. It's nice to see so much happiness in one place.'

Luke gives me an odd look.

'Anyway,' I say, glancing at him, 'I could ask you the same thing.'

'I don't dance either.'

'That's right. You lost a bet.'

Luke is momentarily taken aback by this revelation.

'It's OK,' I say. 'I'm not upset.'

'Lose the bet, you're designated driver.' He raises his glass, which I see contains water, downs the rest, then places the empty glass on the bar. 'Want to get some fresh air?'

'I think I'm going to leave, actually.'

'OK. Let me walk you out.'

'Will you tell Kat I had to go?'

'Kat is busy and doesn't give a shit.'

'Fair enough.'

The outside air is cool and refreshing, and I take a deep breath. We walk in silence up a set of brick stairs that lead onto the street.

'I can't figure you out sometimes,' says Luke.

'I'm not a crossword puzzle. We just have to work together.'

Luke flashes a smile. 'Fair enough.'

I start to walk away when he calls out to me. 'You're doing better.'

'Excuse me?'

'At Maggie's. You're doing good things.'

I'm surprised and touched, a bit emotional at my own response. For months I worried about proving myself because I began work at Maggie's feeling like I went from top of the class to a beginner – a fresh kind of hell for me, the eternal perfectionist. I realise now that I was good but not great.

'Thank you. That means a lot.'

'You were never terrible, by the way. But you know ... a commercial kitchen isn't a home one. And tempering some shards of chocolate for a cake topping doesn't make you a chocolatier.'

'Got it.'

I want to leave before he ruins the moment.

'Will you be right getting home?'

'It's a walk.'

'Let me walk with you. They'll be ages,' he says, indicating the subdued din below ground.

'You don't need to do that.'

Luke swears under his breath. 'Not trying to disempower you here, I'd just feel better knowing you got home safe.'

I consider my options: walk Newtown's backstreets late at night alone, or with someone who barely speaks to me? 'OK. Fine. Thanks.'

Luke closes the space between us. His expression softens and he seems to transform before me into a more relaxed, easier person. I wonder if this is him, who he has been all along, the edginess a mask I provoked him to wear.

Thankfully, he seems happy to walk in silence. Neither of us forces a conversation, but as we pass Small and Sweet, he finally speaks.

'I owe you a session in the studio for that list thing.'

'Yes.'

'How's it going anyway? What'd Kat call it – The Experiment?'

'Capital T, capital E,' I say, biting back a smile.

Luke chuckles. 'Bloody Kat. Always so pushy.'

I sense there's more to this observation – Kat calls Luke's ex Cruella, after all. Before I can talk myself out of it, I find I'm offering my own thoughts on the situation.

'Luke, I know it's none of my business, and you can tell me to bugger off, but whatever you're going through … I know what it feels like to want something that never feels quite right.'

I'm surprised by my own audacity, and Luke inhales.

I didn't time the moment well. We're stuck at a pedestrian crossing. But instead of getting offended, Luke turns to face me. He holds my gaze, his eyes bright, and I feel an unexpected warmth in my belly.

'Come in with some ideas next week,' he says.

'Ideas?'

'Chocolate ideas. We need some new lines. No rush, but start thinking. I'm getting stale.'

'I will think of plenty of ideas.'

I know he's not getting stale at all. He regularly invents new flavour combinations. His chocolates are immaculate, shiny the way tempered chocolate should be. I'm sure he gets some things wrong, but we never see it. He doesn't get dramatic about failure, just determined and intense. I suppose he's a perfectionist like me.

The pedestrian light turns green.

'I'm just a street away now. You don't need to come the rest of the way.'

Luke offers a bemused smile. 'Text me.'

I sigh, but then remember he's been nothing but a gentleman. 'OK. Goodnight.'

I cross the street, and when I reach the other side, I glance back to find Luke still standing there, watching me, his hands in his pockets.

As I trudge my way up the stairs to the apartment, my mind flits back to the look we exchanged. There was something about it that felt unnerving. The way he looked into my eyes. The fact that I let him.

The warmth in my belly returns, but I try to crowd out the realisation with the task of finding my keys and getting into the apartment.

Jordan

The sixth year

It's my third year with the aid agency and I've graduated to shuttling international journalists around the camp, trying to manage their expectations when taking them to a women's craft group doesn't meet their brief for an exclusive. The refugees are always hospitable, but I see how some of them laugh at the attention behind the journalists' backs. One day, I watch ruefully as two teenage boys walk home from school, role-playing an interview.

'And do you still eat normal food in this camp?' one boy queries, affecting the air of a seasoned journalist.

'Only earth worms, sir!'

The work has become significant. Other people's trauma is not a backdrop to my unfulfilled love story. I love my job, even when it becomes repetitive. I'm now a familiar face.

At one point, the agency asked me to travel to Lebanon and Palestine. Khaled drew the line. 'It's not safe,' he told me. Naeem had not been back for over a year, so I knew it had nothing to do with him. I shrugged my reluctant agreement. Zaatari feels safe.

As we feel the brunt of a fierce winter, I spend more time in the office demountable, catching up on paperwork, responding to emails, and working closely with the aid agency to create more programs. One afternoon, as rain batters the windows, I sense a figure approaching me in the dim light of the office. I'm typing when I hear my name. I look up to find Naeem standing before me in a heavy winter jacket, his hair more unruly than ever before, his eyes more piercing.

I try to register his presence. My throat feels blocked and I can't speak, a thin ache spreading rapidly through my belly. Eventually, I acknowledge him with a polite smile. 'Welcome back,' I say in Arabic, then return to my task.

But while I am playing it small, he is full of energy. 'I need your help today,' he says, his eyes searching my face. 'Your manager says he can do without you.'

'I'm really busy. Can you ask someone else?'

'It has to be you,' he says.

I smile politely and sign off my computer.

'Bring your jacket. It's bad out there,' Naeem tells me.

We walk in tense silence to the van that will ferry us to the hospital, the only sound our heavily booted feet crunching through a thin layer of snow.

It's Naeem who pierces the quiet. 'You're not going to speak to me, then?'

'What do you want me to say?' I reply, staring ahead, my arms crossed against my chest. It's bitingly cold, even with all the layers – thermals, cargo trousers, jumper, thick winter jacket lined with wool.

'Sahar.' Naeem takes my arm gently, slowing me down and turning me to look at him.

I struggle to, the humiliation of his sudden departure fresh, even after a year.

'I had to go. It was going to get messy.'

'It got messy after you left. Your brother, desperate for a child he knows

I can't give him, made me pregnant again.'

Naeem's eyes light up in fury. 'I'm sorry.'

'Can we please just go? Please? I can't do this, Naeem. I can't be your romantic escape from life.'

This only seems to infuriate him more. 'Is that how I've made you feel?'

'I don't know what you feel for me. All I know is that you gave me something then you took it away.' I detach from his hold and start walking to the van.

'Sahar.'

I ignore him, but he easily catches up to me.

In the van, I sit as far away from him as possible, my gaze fixed on the outside world through a frosted window as we trundle past empty demountables, the ones used as schools.

***

It's six months before Naeem is back again. We're in his clinic after his last patient for the day has left. He asked for me in the morning. I wanted to say no. Couldn't. Every time he returns, he brings with him a reminder of our connection, and an idea of belonging.

The tension between us has dissipated. We have been so busy that somewhere along the way, we found ourselves in a familiar rhythm. At one point during the day, Naeem checked in with me, his expression apologetic. He looked worried, but I managed a smile even as the pain of his presence seared through me.

The nurse leaves, and we're alone. It's strange, the things that tell you that you know someone. I know his silences. I know when he is encountering an uncomfortable or unfamiliar feeling. He comes to stand beside me as I unpack a box of donated supplies, not ready to leave, burdened by the fear that he will disappear again. He is so close that I can smell his trademark *oud,* and without seeing him, I can sense the patterns of his body, the way he moves. I can hear him breathing. From behind me, he brings his hands to my shoulders. They travel down my arms and land gently around my wrists. I feel his head drop on top of mine. He kisses it and tears spill from my eyes. So much pent-up emotion, and this odd sense of betrayal. He was never mine to have, so how can I be upset?

'I'm sorry,' he says. 'Please forgive me.'

I swivel around and move into his arms, my body shaking, and I softly let go for the first time in years.

Naeem allows it, but eventually he pulls back and uses a hand to lift my chin. His expression is one of agony as he takes me in.

'*Hayati.*'

I close my eyes, unsettled because it is an exquisite moment of tenderness and I want nothing and everything from him at the same time.

I try to step away, my entire body feeling like it's on fire. Three years in his presence, and nothing has changed. Perhaps it is simply the effect of unfulfilled longing, but it feels too heavy for me now.

Naeem uses his thumb to wipe away my tears and I laugh, feeling like a fool but also relieved because the connection between us remains. But then Naeem's eyes meet mine and he moves his hand to my face. He brushes away a few strands of hair that have escaped my headscarf.

'You don't need to wear that,' he says.

'Please don't,' I say. But then he shakes his head, his eyes intense, his look meaningful.

'I want to see your hair,' he says.

My breath catches in my throat. I linger in his gaze for a few seconds. Then my hands go to the back of my neck where I have knotted the two ends of my gypsy-style headscarf. The whole time his eyes are on me. I untie the knot and remove my headscarf, pulling out the elastic band keeping my hair neat. It falls down in a tumble, so long it ends at my waist.

I see the way it affects him. Naeem's eyes, always so full of energy, remain on me as he reaches out to touch my hair.

'Why do you hide?'

Before I can say anything, Naeem's hands are on my face and he is lowering his head. Without thinking, I reach up and meet his lips with mine.

He groans, moves his hands to my back, one taking hold of my hair. 'Sahar,' he says, but I'm too breathless to speak.

Naeem kisses me again, more intensely, faster, like he's trying to catch up. The energy in my body threatens to burn me out, but he doesn't pull back and I forget everything.

Chapter 14

Do you know I have a photo of you? Besides the necklace with my name in Arabic, that is all the physical evidence I have of you.

In my first few weeks back after New Year's, I am given more interesting work in the kitchen. I found it laborious when I first entered Maggie's kitchen; now I take pleasure in baking batches of sweets that people will enjoy the same day in the cafe, and I get a thrill seeing my work on display.

With Inez, I create a vanilla-iced rosewater doughnut, with dried petals as a garnish. With Kat, I work on a mini layered cake that has the appearance of the 'wog cakes' we grew up on – tall sponge cakes packed with layers of cream and topped with fresh fruit and jelly. 'But we'll make it more sophisticated, and with more complex flavours,' Kat says, bunching her fingers together and kissing them. '*Yallah!*'

This is the secret to Maggie's – riffing off classics, where the sophistication is in the flavours and craft, rather than inventing outlandish creations.

True to his word, Luke works with me in the chocolate studio beyond what is required. Maggie has assigned me to him one day a week, requesting I build up my tempering knowledge and ability, working with more than milk chocolate. But Luke brings me in twice a week sometimes. He says I ease his workload by producing the simple things: chocolate blocks and boxed hearts.

But I don't mind. Sometimes Luke leaves me to work alone, so I play music and lose myself in the movements. I am precise in filling the moulds. I learn to taste more as I go, making sure the flavours and texture are right. I come up with ideas but I keep them small and manageable, so Luke usually agrees to them. They are as simple as using chocolate buttons in white chocolate, or a fresh take on cookies and cream.

I start to see that Luke is different when working with chocolate. He moves easier in the space. And I discover new emotional strands to his personality.

One afternoon, he pulls me into the studio to help him with an urgent order of chocolates for a corporate event. We're tempering the chocolate but we lose track and mess it up.

'Damn it. I hate it when that happens,' Luke says.

'I didn't think that *could* happen with you.'

He gives me a wry grin, thankfully not offended by my observation. 'It does. I just know how to pretend it doesn't.'

I ask him about how he came into this work.

He shrugs. 'I was in the right place at the right time. I needed a job and I got one in a bakery, pretty low-rent work. I was doing what you were at the very start – all the shitty grunt stuff. But it was natural for me, using my hands that way. Got more interesting when I started making bread, then some pastries...' He ponders this. 'Never thought I would be a proper pastry chef. I prefer chocolate to baking, if I'm being honest.' He carefully brushes past me, and laments the size of the studio. 'It's too small in here,' he murmurs.

'You think Maggie should expand?'

'Small and Sweet isn't just the cafe and this shop. It's a philosophy. Maggie won't go bigger,' says Luke, still moving about. 'She won't even get a proper website.'

I sense longing in his words, which he confirms a few seconds later.

'I wish I could afford to buy this place, or one of my own.' He comes to a stop beside me. 'But I guess the fact that we even have this is something.'

We're both quiet, Luke watching me as I work, his body close to mine. There is an intimacy that feels oddly natural, but also unexpected.

Then Luke moves past me again, and, as though he's revealed too much, he shakes his head. For the remainder of the afternoon we work in silence. Occasionally, I look up to find him focused on his work. He's rolled up his sleeves to reveal his forearms, and a couple of tattoos peek out from his upper arms. He's in the zone, his hands moving easily and swiftly to create a series of bright red chocolates.

Outside, the light of day has dimmed, and Luke starts to tidy up while I continue to bag the chocolates. Eventually, I find the courage to offer up some more adventurous ideas. Luke is quiet but attentive as I tell him about Middle Eastern flavours – sage from the mountains of Palestine; the rose water my mother prescribed for an upset tummy but which fills Turkish delight; the figs that fall from the trees in my father's village; the penchant Arabs have for wafer biscuits.

'What's the idea?' he says.

'Heritage. Childhood?'

'OK ... But what's the idea?'

My face flames red because I'm clearly failing at the pitch. 'I think we could do some sweets that don't just look good but evoke an emotion. Something like: chocolate isn't just a flavour, it's a feeling.'

'Everything we make is meant to do that.' Luke indicates a set of trays covered in chocolate hearts. 'Who do you think buys those?'

'Well, yes, but love is so obvious.'

Luke finishes a bag of chocolates then carries his box to the stack near the entrance. 'You have to think about who's coming in and buying the chocolates. Sage means something to you, but most people think you burn it to get rid of bad spirits.'

'We can create stories with what we make. Don't you think people would feel excited about a box that has a little story on the cover?'

Luke is wrestling with the idea and I start to regret trusting him with it, knowing he's just going to torpedo whatever I suggest.

He gives me a long look and I return it, my heart beating faster. Finally, he shrugs. 'Try it, I guess,' he says, surprising me.

'Wait, really?'

He nods. 'Come in sometime and have a play. You know what you're doing in here. Enough not to burn the place down anyway.'

'Thank you.'

'Try to have some fun with it. We're not saving lives here, just trying to add some sweetness to them.' He analyses me for a few seconds. 'Sahar, if you'll take my advice, be careful. Don't limit yourself by thinking you owe anyone anything, or that you can only do what you know, that you can only work with flavours that are familiar to you. That's not what will make you good at this. And it's not what's going to make you special. You think something has to be hard if it's to be of any value.'

I look down. 'How do you know that about me?'

'Because you're like me.' Then Luke laughs, properly. It's not mean, it's strangely warm and knowing. 'And because I give you simple tasks to do and you complicate them.'

A smile tugs at my lips. 'I probably do.'

'Trust me, that's not how you prove yourself. You're allowed to fuck up. Even when I act like an arsehole, fucking up is how you learn.'

'I'm trying to be creative.'

'So think about what you don't know. Follow your curiosity. That's where the gold lies.'

I'm surprised by the eloquent advice, the easy flow of wisdom. Luke is more at home in the chocolate studio, which might explain why he seems so different here.

***

It turns out that Luke's odd mood wasn't an anomaly. The next week he brings me into the chocolate studio again, this time to assist with a new line.

He shows me the design of a new chocolate: different shades of blue, to be made in blocks and individual geometric shapes. The theme is 'water'.

'What do you think?' says Luke.

'It's beautiful,' I say. 'When it comes to chocolate, I think anything you could show me would get me excited.'

'You say that, but passions lose their charge over time.'

'Maybe, but if you really love something, you always come back to it.'

Luke hooks an eyebrow. 'What if you lost your ability to cook?'

'That wouldn't be great.' I laugh. 'But then, I did take a break for a while and I managed.'

I didn't bake much at all in Jordan. Now I can't imagine not being in a kitchen, the familiar scents and noises a comforting soundtrack, a confirmation that I am in the right place.

'I think you'd find another way to express yourself,' Luke says. 'I can't imagine you sitting still.'

'I guess.'

He moves over to the storage shelf and starts digging around for equipment. 'What do you love about what you do?'

'It's like the perfect outfit. It just fits.'

Luke nods, impressed. He hands me the tempering spatula and bench scraper, then dumps a bag of white chocolate onto the bench.

We retreat into silence for a while as we continue to work, the music filling the space, at odds with the sound of my tempering.

When I'm done, Luke moves the bowl over to the bench. 'You know, it's not a bad thing that you've changed. It means you've lived.'

I tempered the white chocolate perfectly, but soon it will be an aqua blue. 'I don't know who I am in the way I used to. Sometimes it's unsettling.'

'Whoever you were was just an idea. You're not meant to stay the same.' Luke is at the shelf, negotiating various shades of blue colouring. He gives me a sideways glance. 'We're all born into something. And we all have to climb out of it at some point. Better not to drive yourself crazy with things you can't control.'

'Is that how you feel?' I say.

He hands me a jar of food-colouring powder. 'I don't know. I guess. Sometimes it's like I'm holding on too tight.'

'I know what you mean,' I say, a little startled by his words.

I refocus my attention on the chocolate, but my mind is swimming. I want to probe further, but I worry about overstepping. I know so much about Kat and Inez, but Luke remains, in many ways, a mystery.

I clear my throat. 'I'm probably not the best person to be giving out life advice, but if you want to talk about something, I'm here.'

Luke looks up, our eyes meet, and there's a flash of understanding between us. I want to say more, but the idea is quickly extinguished by the rush of nerves through my belly.

'Thanks,' Luke says. 'Likewise.'

***

I arrive home to discover that Lara has invited Samira over, and she's bringing pizza so that I don't have to cook.

'I live with you and don't get to see you enough,' Lara says.

'Can we at least eat something healthier?' I say.

'No, Samira is already on her way.'

An hour later, Samira arrives with the pizza: two large margheritas with *sujuk* and extra olives. Lara looks ready to burst with excitement. 'Girls' night!'

We assemble in the kitchen and eat at the dinner table like proper adults. Despite Lara's enthusiasm, the atmosphere is a bit sluggish, and I'm not sure why.

Samira finally punctures the tension. 'Lara! What the hell is going on?'

I look from one to the other, confused. 'Have I missed something?' I say.

'Hello? Did you not see the ring on her finger?'

I refocus. Lara has shoved her hands in her armpits, but Samira is already trying to drag them out. She indicates for me to help and I scramble out of my seat to assist in revealing the evidence.

Lara looks guilty. 'I thought wearing it on the wrong hand would throw you off the scent.'

Samira rolls her eyes. 'You idiot, who do you think Hakeem called for help?'

Lara's face reddens. 'That little shit.'

'He proposed? Oh my God! Lara!' I feel mortified for having missed it.

Lara sinks into her seat. 'He's been talking about getting married for ages. But this time he bought a bloody ring and now I'm all confused.'

Samira and I look at each other, both of us wearing perplexed expressions.

Lara plays with the corner of a pizza box. 'He wants to do KK,' she says, 'and I just don't think I'm ready for that.'

KK – *Katib kitab* – is an Islamic marriage: the engagement we all wanted when we were naive about marriage because it meant barriers technically dissolved. It was the equivalent of dating the man you liked (or loved), but the stakes were higher because you were married in the eyes of God. You were moving towards a wedding and living together. A guy could still ditch you after KK and no one would blink, but it would be harder for a woman to leave. People would wonder just how far she took things with her husband.

'Where did you think it was going to go?' I ask.

'I just wanted to enjoy it not going anywhere for a bit.'

'Which you've done,' says Samira. 'Enough. Don't mess him around.'

I am hopeful for Lara and Hakeem. I want the mess of their separate experiences to fold into something beautiful and lasting. But I have to applaud her consideration. I wasted no time in agreeing to a hasty *katib kitab* with Khaled.

Lara's voice is quiet. 'I don't want to mess him around, but I don't think I could ever marry him.'

'Lara,' Samira says, 'you're obsessed with each other.'

Lara looks to me and I can guess what she is worried about. I shrug, because the past is so far in the distance, it's a speck. But the exchange annoys Samira.

'Oh, for goodness' sake, he was never mine,' she says. 'Not in any way. His proposal was ridiculous.'

'Hakeem proposed to you? When did that happen?' I say, blindsided that Samira kept this from me.

'Out of obligation,' Samira says, 'because he felt guilty for being so close to me.'

'It's not that,' says Lara. 'Honestly. It's me, my life. I'm finally doing what I want.'

Samira's eyes meet mine again and I can tell she is beseeching me to fix this.

I search for the right words. I know it's not Samira's innocent history with Hakeem that claims Lara's worry right now. She's worried that her fragile love affair will become a different kind of love story and that softer Hakeem will become fundy Hakeem again. I want to reassure her. Hakeem is different in the same way I am: a skin has been shed. Who knows, really, what is left to uncover? All I know is that I will not go back, and I don't think he will either.

Seeing Lara's look of quiet despair, my protectiveness kicks in. 'Lara, he was always yours.'

Lara looks put out. 'I feel like I'm treading water.'

I remember Lara's evangelism about Samira and Hakeem, and how on a difficult afternoon in my kitchen, I called her out on it. I told her what she struggled to see herself: she was in love with Hakeem. Therein lies the beauty of people underestimating you: they don't realise how much you see.

'I'm sorry I was mean about it all those years ago,' I say. 'I'm sorry about how I behaved, full stop.'

Lara rolls her eyes, but her body language is defensive. 'Don't be silly. You were a bit Neighbourhood Watch about everything, but I never took it personally. And you were right. I obviously liked the guy. I mean, after I ran into him when we were both single, things escalated pretty quickly.'

'People like Hakeem can only meet the truth in time,' I tell Lara. 'There was no way he could love you as he was. He wouldn't know what to do with you.'

I turn to Samira and study her, wondering where this moment is taking her.

'I believe what I'm seeing with you two,' I say, turning my focus back to Lara.

'I do love him,' says Lara. 'He shits me to tears sometimes. But then I think about how he is really there for me, how he doesn't try to change me.'

A few seconds later, Samira splinters the moment. 'Um, hello? Since when did you two become besties? I'm right here.'

It cracks open the sombre mood and our laughter quickly rises to fill the gap. Lara wrestles Samira in a hug. She motions towards me and I crowd into the embrace. There are many things I look back on with unease, but whatever happened in the past, I know it has to be made up of something good to have friends like these.

Chapter 15

Every opportunity is a new beginning.

On Tuesday, Luke steals me away from the bakery to help with a last-minute order.

'I thought we don't do those,' I say, following him in to the chocolate studio.

'We do when it's for the boss. Fancy event, and I'm already behind.'

The chocolates are made – milk chocolate ganache hearts, which we pack into little white boxes, topping them with a red bow. It's an easy task. Presentation has always been my forte.

When we're joined by Inez, she takes my instruction without fuss. Then Luke dashes off to complete another task, leaving us alone in the studio.

'So, remember how I told you I have an idea about what I want to do for my own experiment?' Inez says, a bit cautious.

'Yes. But I didn't want to harass you about it.'

'Promise me you won't freak out.'

'I won't freak out.'

'Well, you know how you're going to get your trapeze on with me.'

'Uh-huh.' I'm not ready for a sexy lyra class, so I agreed to trapeze.

'Well, I um ... I've been doing circus stuff with a twist.'

I stop mid-ribbon tie and look up. 'I'm listening.'

Inez makes a face, curling her hand below her chin. 'I'm doing burlesque.'

I laugh. 'Is that it?'

'What do you mean?'

'I don't know. I didn't know what to expect.'

Inez always seems so quietly confident, so I figured whatever she was doing it was going to be outside the box.

'Well, this is scary. It's showing a lot of skin. And it's performance. Very different to learning the hoop in a class full of women.'

'You're probably the most beautiful woman I know, inside and out. I'm sure no one will be able to take their eyes off you.'

Inez smiles, biting her lip. 'Will you come? To the performance? It's not for ages, but will you?'

'Of course.'

Inez abandons the boxes she's working on and pulls me in for a fierce hug. I laugh as she sways me from side to side, but then Luke sweeps in.

'Jesus, what are you doing? We're in a rush!'

Inez waits for Luke to leave again, then conspiratorially leans towards me. She describes the outfit she'll be wearing for the performance – a mermaid-like diamante-and-jewel-encrusted bodysuit. Slowly, the layers will be peeled away.

'But I don't think I'll go full nude,' Inez explains, like she's ordering a sandwich, and I marvel, astonished at the reminder of how differently women negotiate their bodies and what they show of them.

Then my mind wanders to Luke and Kat, who are yet to do their own experiments.

'What do you think we can do about them?' I say to Inez. 'Luke is unapproachable about it, and Kat says there's nothing she hasn't tried.'

Inez looks thoughtful. 'That's not exactly true. But it's a delicate situation.'

'Meaning?'

'We got approached by a food channel to do a segment once and I could see Kat wanted to do it, but they wanted to doll her up and she got upset.'

'Doll her up?'

Inez mentally calculates, still working on a box. 'Well, what I mean is, she felt judged. But I saw how excited she was to do it.'

'So, what happened?'

'She said no, and Luke and I didn't want to step in and take her place, so the opportunity died.'

'Kat would've been great.' I can picture it clearly. She is naturally confident, warm and charismatic, and so highly skilled. I'd watch her read a telephone book.

'Yep. So anyway, no one is free of desire. There'll be something Luke wants too.'

***

When we're done, Luke tasks me with making the delivery. 'Can you manage on your own? You can take an Uber.'

'I thought you said it was for Maggie.'

'It's for Leo. The silent boss,' he says, his expression grim.

It's only a ten-minute walk but there are 300 boxes, so I agree to the Uber. Luke takes hold of the bags and leads me out. 'You'll need to say a password. OK?'

'Yes, I know. I've been there before.'

Luke seems taken aback. 'To the speak-easy?'

'My friend sings there sometimes.'

'Right. There's your ride.'

***

Inside the venue, I'm met by a man who looks like he's in charge. He scurries towards me. 'I'm Dominic. You're the chocolates? Can you help me set them up?'

Dominic takes two bags off me then points towards the end of the room.

'Start there. Two boxes for each setting.'

'But they're the same chocolates.'

Dominic stares at me blankly. 'What?'

'People will be getting two boxes of the same chocolates.'

'Too many words,' Dominic says, then he sweeps off, crinkling bags in hand.

'What's the event?' I call after him, but he dismisses me with a swinging bag.

'It'll be fine,' he yells. 'Just do it.'

'O-K.'

I start at the corner table, methodically placing the red-ribboned boxes in concentric circles.

'It's an event to promote a new product. The theme is love,' comes a familiar voice. I look up to see Leo walking towards me. He's wearing tailored pants for a change, not jeans, and a nice blue dress shirt. I can't help admiring him, fully understanding Inez's attraction, even if I don't share it in the same way.

'I'm sorry I was late,' I say.

'You're not, it's OK,' he says. 'But you're going to hate me in a second.'

'Why? What's wrong?'

Leo winces. 'How many boxes did you make?'

'Three hundred.'

'I need another hundred.'

'OK.' I immediately do the calculations. 'We always make extra, so I'll rush back and see what I can put together.'

'How soon?'

'An hour?'

Leo studies his watch. Then he looks up and places his hands on my shoulders. 'Thanks, I owe you one.'

'Not at all.'

***

The next day, a flower delivery arrives for me. Inez is the first to come over and a moment later Kat joins us, tea towel in hand. Luke shakes his head. 'Guys. They're just flowers.'

It's a simple bunch with a bare-bones note.

Sahar,
Thank you for saving my butt last night.

Leo

I immediately look to Inez, and see a question in her expression.

Kat raises an eyebrow. 'Something you're not telling us, Sahar?' she says, taking hold of the card.

'He's saying thank you.' I hand the flowers to Inez and take back the card.

Inez breathes in the non-existent scent. 'Oh my.'

Luke is still working, but he indicates the flowers and addresses me. 'Why is Leo sending you flowers?'

'Because he stuffed up the order last night and I fixed it.'

Luke stops what he's doing. 'What do you mean?'

'I came back and made another hundred boxes.'

'Are you serious?'

'Don't get mad at me; it wasn't my mess. Someone ordered the wrong amount.'

'Why didn't you call me?'

'Because we had chocolates left over and I only needed to make a few more. What's the big deal?'

'Next time, call me.'

'Sorry,' I say, a bit stunned by his response. 'I didn't want to bother you.'

But he seems frustrated. 'I need to know these things.'

Which is fair enough. I should have let him know, so I murmur an apology and he returns to his task without making more of it.

Inez bites back a smile, still drinking in the flowers. 'He's hot and classy,' she says quietly.

I seek refuge in the pantry, where I pull out my phone and search for Leo's number. Then I type a simple text to say thanks. It's not a romantic gesture on his part, but I'm touched. I've never received a flower delivery before. I've never been the special one.

Chapter 16

If you have spent your life thinking about the next one, what does that say about your experience of this one?

On Saturday night, Inez comes over to Lara's apartment and we get ready together for a night out with Kat and Luke. In my bedroom, she mournfully assesses my clothing options. I have laid out two outfits, both involving jeans.

'What happened to the dresses you bought?'

On Thursday night, when the shops in the CBD were open until late, Inez and I caught a bus into town where she shepherded me through the major department stores and every clothing store in between. We discovered that I gravitate towards jeans in a variety of colours, and tops in bright shades. Inez nodded her approval but grew frustrated by the repetition. 'We need to get you something for a night out.'

This proved challenging. I rejected anything too short, too tight or too revealing. Eventually, we found some knee-length dresses that Inez was unconvinced by, but she had to concede because we were running out of time and still needed to buy shoes – casual, work and play.

Now she wants to see the dresses and the black shiny high heels I bought to go along with them.

'You can't wear jeans.'

'What are they going to do? Not let me in?'

'Basically, yes.'

I look at what Inez is wearing, and it's far more glamorous than a jeans-and-top combo, no matter how shiny or bright. 'You look really good,' I tell her, admiring her satin baby-doll dress. Inez is fit. She isn't curvy, and her breasts are tiny, but a push-up bra gives her chest some height, a bronze-coloured glitter eye shadow makes her eyes pop, and sexy high heels that buckle at the ankle complete the look. She falls back onto my bed and waits, feet tapping against the air.

I reluctantly pack away the jeans and bring out the dresses. Inez gets me to hold them up against my body. One is a bright red baby-doll type dress with a belt.

Inez shakes her head. 'Too Sunday picnic, though I could do a killer red lip.'

The other is a black shift dress with lace around the V-neck and a strip just under the breasts.

Inez makes a face and sighs. 'Hold on,' she says, getting to her feet. She leaves the room and returns half a minute later with a beaming Lara. But then Lara takes in the options laid out on the bed and her expression transforms to one of alarm.

'Babe, no. We can do better than this.'

Lara opens up her closet to me. 'To the left is the stuff I used to wear but shouldn't have. To the right is my current, sensible way of dressing.' She gives Inez a mournful look. 'I try to act my age.'

Inez does a stocktake of Lara's outfits, pulling out ones here and there to inspect them. If they pass the test, she places them on the bed. By the end of the inspection she presents me with three options: a tight, mid-thigh satin number with embroidered birds of paradise in metallic fuchsia; a blue, shimmery, floaty dress made of chiffon with large sleeves and a plunging neck; and a figure-hugging black dress with threads of glitter that will stop just above the knees.

Beside me, Lara, her arms crossed, her eyes wide, nods her approval. 'My pick is the black. Sexy but not too daunting for a newbie.'

Inez smiles. 'Agreed. Sahar?'

'I guess,' I say, but Inez is already shepherding me out of Lara's bedroom. She calls out to Lara. 'I need a chair to do make-up.' Then she turns back to me. 'And remember to take your flats, Sahar. You're going to hate those heels by the end of the night.'

I dress quickly, staring longingly at my boring purchase from last Thursday.

'You look great, don't second-guess it,' Inez says as she pushes me into a dining chair.

I struggle to sit still as she applies my make-up. I don't think I'm nervous.

And it feels strange to be showing my legs. But even before I put on the dress, I felt antsy, like I wanted to skip ahead to the end of the night, which is a worry given it hasn't even begun.

'Oh my God, what's up with you?' Inez says as she wipes mascara from above my eyelid for the third time.

'I don't know.'

Inez stops and leans back to inspect me. 'It's OK. We're going to have fun.'

'I know. I'm not worried.'

'You don't have to do anything you don't want to do,' Inez says, returning her focus to my eyes. The pressure of the pencil against my skin is pleasant and calming.

'Thanks for taking me out.'

'I'm not taking you out. You're coming out *with* us.'

Inez uses a little brush on my eyelids, then leans back to assess the result. She looks satisfied but continues to study me. 'You are a total hottie on a normal day, but now you have make-up by Inez. We are ready to go.'

***

Inez gives me a rundown on what to expect as we approach the queue. 'It's a club, so there's a bar and a dance floor, and it will be noisy. And guys will try to buy you drinks. Only let them if you're there to watch the bartender make the drink and hand it to you.'

From the outside, the club looks like any ordinary brick short-storey building, but for the fancy sign that reads the name: Ocean.

We take our place at the end of the queue and Inez cranes her neck to do a quick inspection. 'Shouldn't be too long.'

Looking around me, I'm glad Inez convinced me to wear a dress; no one here is wearing jeans. I'm regretting the heels already.

'Told you,' Inez says when she catches me inspecting my shoes.

As we approach the doorman, a bulky bouncer who looks a bit bored, Inez adjusts my hair, then tops up her lipstick. I can hear the music from out here, a thin layer of sound, and I wince at the thought of how loud it's going to be inside. When it's our turn, Inez smiles at the doorman, and without a word, he lifts the rope and indicates to the door.

The air inside is thick and smoky, the music loud, filling the entire space from floor to ceiling. It's also dark but for a flood of lights at the bar, which takes up a generous amount of space against a wall covered in shelves housing a variety of bottles. Beside the bar is a small stage where a man with multiple piercings and oversized headphones is DJing. I take a look around and see that the rest of the club is a dance floor surrounded by dozens of tables and chairs, some high, some low. The space is larger than I anticipated, and teeming with people who seem mainly to be in their late teens and twenties.

I struggled enough with getting used to big fat Arab weddings where the music was delivered by a very loud and live band – but at least the music was good and there was mezze.

Kat and Luke have secured a table and they wave us over. As we approach, I wonder at the low lighting and pumping, invasive music. How can anyone communicate in here, let alone enjoy a conversation? When I yell this to Inez, she shakes her head then yells back, 'No one's here for conversation. They're here to get smashed and hook up. You get used to the noise.'

We join Kat and Luke, but only Kat looks happy to be here.

'Did someone die?' Inez says, her eyes on Luke.

'Let's just get this over with,' he says.

Inez raises her eyebrows and mouths an *OK* as she takes a seat.

Then Luke exhales. 'Sorry. Sorry. Had a shit day.'

We make eye contact in the darkness, then my eyes flicker to his outfit – black tailored pants and a tight-fitting white dress shirt.

'You look nice,' he says, managing a smile.

'Thanks,' I say, unsure what to do with the compliment. For a moment we hold each other's gaze, then Kat's voice splinters through and he turns to face her.

'We'll start gentle,' Kat says and my nerves thicken.

'Start with beer,' suggests Luke.

'Yuck. Beer's an acquired taste,' says Kat.

'White wine? Or champagne?' says Inez.

'Yes!' says Kat. 'If you can stomach that, we can talk about stage two.'

My stomach rolls with anxiety. 'Guys, you're not planning to get me *drunk* drunk, are you?'

'Don't you want to get drunk drunk?' says Kat, scanning the drinks menu.

Luke is now watching me, as is Inez.

'Just drunk, maybe? Enough to see what the big deal is.'

Luke shakes his head, but his disapproval is not the same as Kat's. 'You don't need to do this at all,' he says. 'We're not in high school.'

'Fuck off,' says Kat. 'We're doing it. But Luke the school prefect here can keep an eye on you since he's the softest drinker.'

Luke shrugs. 'Fine.'

'Stage two will be mixers,' says Kat. 'Soft drink with vodka. Maybe rum and Coke?' She looks to Inez, who weighs it up.

'Ooh, vodka lime soda!' says Inez.

'What about spirits?' I say. 'Like whisky.'

Kat is amused. 'You have much to learn, little one.'

Luke chuckles and Inez winces.

'Give her some Pimm's,' says Luke.

At Kat's disgusted look, he holds up his hands in surrender. They continue offering up and knocking back suggestions, determining my fate, until, as decided by committee, Inez delivers me a glass of white wine. 'Take your time with it.'

I raise the glass to my lips, take a gulp and recoil.

'For fuck's sake,' Kat practically bellows. 'Go slow.'

'Be quiet and let the woman ease in,' Inez says, placing an arm around me and giving me a squeeze.

'I'm getting another beer,' Luke says, shimmying out of the booth. 'Anyone need a top-up?'

Kat holds up her glass, which has only a slosh of something dark red left in it. 'Another please. Shiraz.'

Inez gives me an expectant look. 'Are you OK? Tell me really.'

'I'm fine. It's just a very strong taste.'

I take a smaller sip and let it sink into my tongue. I don't recoil this time, but I'm not sure I can be bothered to acquire a taste for it.

I make it through the white wine but I don't feel tipsy. Instead, there's a thickness in my body, like jelly that has just set.

'Is it supposed to make me feel different?' I say.

'You've had one glass, calm down,' says Kat. 'Are you brave enough to try a mixer?'

'How about the rum and Coke?' says Inez, drumming the table with her elegant fingers, her perfectly painted nails dancing along the surface.

Luke returns and he takes a sip of his beer before plopping down on the seat at the end of the table. But he seems distracted and his eyes keep flicking back to the bar, searching out someone or something.

I watch as Kat and Inez turn to each other and have a silent conversation with their eyes. I have no idea what any of it means, only that it relates to Luke.

'Are you OK?' I say to him, and he looks a bit startled.

'I'm fine. How are you? Drunk yet?'

'Afraid not.'

I don't even care about trying more drinks, but I don't want to hurt their feelings. My primary hope is that I do not become obnoxious, loud and brazen. I assume these are my greatest threats because I am the opposite sober. But as I dip my toes into the alcoholic waters, I know that I'm in no danger of getting addicted to the feeling of intoxication.

Still a bit antsy, Luke jumps to his feet again. 'I'll get you that rum and Coke,' he says, and we watch him go.

'What's going on with Luke?' I ask.

'His girlfriend is here swanning about the place, probably,' Kat responds. She's now dancing in her seat, arms outstretched like a belly dancer's.

'I thought you said they broke up?'

'On again, off again. Have you met obsessive Luke? I mean, he's not a stalker or anything, but he's the kind who fully commits. I'll give him this: he's annoying but dedicated.'

Inez makes a face. 'They always are at the start. But his girlfriend isn't very nice,' she says in a near whisper, clearly ashamed for expressing a bad opinion about someone.

I watch as Luke casually approaches a woman standing in line at the bar. She's about his height, dressed in a tight red dress that doesn't hide a single blemish – and she has none. Her hair is long, straight and silky, and she's standing very straight with her arms crossed. In one hand, she's clasping a small sparkly black clutch, her hand flashing oversized costume jewellery rings, and a bangle covers a third of her forearm. Beside her, a woman dressed in a similar style stands close, like a bodyguard. No one looks happy.

'That's Luke's girlfriend?'

Almost as if they heard me, Luke and the woman swivel around and she evaluates us, her expression sour and unimpressed.

'Well, fuck me, la-di-da,' says Kat, brushing away non-existent long hair.

'Don't be mean,' says Inez. 'We've all liked the wrong people before.'

I find myself watching Luke, wondering about this woman's hold on him. He seems so different to the controlled, masterful Luke of Small and Sweet by Maggie, and it occurs to me that you can be a master in one domain and less successful in another.

A few minutes later, he returns to the table with more drinks. He hands one to me. 'Rum and Coke. Give it a whirl.'

I don't like this one much better. 'Do they all taste like medicine?'

Inez, who is now a bit tipsy, finds this hysterical. 'Yes. They taste terrible until they don't.'

After we finish our drinks, Kat and Inez push me onto the dance floor, and I kind of sway while they dance with more intensity and movement. Eventually, they steer me towards a man who's making it clear that he wants to dance with us.

'Talk to him,' Inez says under her breath.

I walk awkwardly towards this complete stranger, and wonder if it was actually Inez he was moving towards. He's a bit taller than me, and looks like he's come directly from an office job. He points at his body as he says loudly, 'Christopher!'

I yell back my name and he tries to repeat after me a few times before we spiral into an uncomfortable exchange of mispronunciation. Finally, I just give him a weak thumbs up and sway in my spot while he dances like he is bursting with emotion, eyes closed, punching his arms out.

I glance over at Inez and Kat, who are feverishly dancing but still have one eye on me. Inez winks and I shrug.

The rapid song, with its South American instrumentals and Spanish lyrics, picks up in pace. Christopher seems to go into a trance, his eyes rolling back as his body shudders like he's being electrocuted. I worry that he's having a seizure, but then he suddenly stops and starts to sway, using his arms like he's trying to clear a path ahead.

The song comes to an end and I immediately walk off the dance floor without a second thought about how it looks. But Christopher follows me and leads me to the bar.

'I bet I can guess what you drink.'

I give him a half-hearted smile. 'Impress me.'

'A Bellini,' he says slowly.

'Wow. I do like Bellinis.'

'OK, it's not a Bellini. You don't have to pretend,' he says, and I feel a bit sorry for him.

Christopher orders a drink, but I refuse his offer to buy me one, and he shrugs, non-committal, his eyes wandering across the dance floor.

We make small talk, which is harder than it would usually be given the pulsing music and people brushing past us to get to the bar. He asks me what I do and I tell him. As I finish a story about a tempering-chocolate fail, he glances around then nods, swigging down the rest of his drink.

'I'll be right back,' he says, then walks off.

Soon after, Kat and Inez rush over.

'Where did he go?' Inez says, out of breath.

'I don't know. He said he'd be right back.'

'What happened?' Kat says.

'We talked.'

'About what?'

'Chocolate.'

Kat and Inez look at me like I've just told them I have a terminal illness. Inez closes her eyes. 'Honey, no. Small talk not work talk.'

'Can I go back to the table now?'

Another drink soon follows. 'Mojito. See what you think,' says Kat.

I glance at Luke, but he is lost to his thoughts.

Then a song with a strong disco beat comes on, and Kat and Inez jerk their heads towards each other. 'Soul train!' they yell in unison.

'Oh God,' says Luke under his breath, and I'm starting to wonder if the only reason he came was to see his on-again off-again girlfriend.

'What's soul train?' I ask.

My words sound slow, and I suddenly notice how sluggish I feel, like I could take a nap. I definitely lack the energy and desire to throw myself onto the heaving dance floor.

'You'll see,' says Luke.

'You have to come,' says Inez, already shimmying her way out from the table.

'That's not going to happen.'

'Luke?' says Kat.

He gives her a look and she sighs. 'Of course, what was I thinking?' Then she considers me for a few seconds and clocks my expression. 'Just come and watch.'

I follow them to the dance floor, where the crowd has parted like the Red Sea. A voice starts booming through the sound system, geeing everyone up. Then it begins: a group of women dance, completely coordinated, while moving down the dance floor pathway. Everyone around me is cheering them on and I clap along, in awe of their confidence and bravery. Next are three men who do the same thing but with different moves. They seem to slide while the women use their hips and arms.

Then it's Kat and Inez with a few other women, rolling their arms like they're part of a school musical and I find myself cheering for them because they look amazing and effortlessly cool.

It goes on for ages, so eventually I return to our table, where Luke is sitting alone.

'You look really down,' I say, then feel like I shouldn't have said it, but my head is starting to throb and my eyes want to close.

'I'm fine. Are you OK? You look a bit pale.'

'I'm OK. Just a bit hot.'

'Come here,' he says, but he leans towards me. He places the back of his hand against my forehead and pats it gently a couple of times. 'You're OK.'

'I think I'll go get some fresh air.'

Luke nods. 'OK, just wait for me, all right? I'll be back in a second.'

He disappears into the crowd and I slide my handbag over my shoulder and make my way outside. The crisp night air is perfect. I close my eyes and breathe it in, spreading my arms out wide like an offering of gratitude. I walk to a bus stop shelter a few metres away. The street is quiet and I wonder what time it is and if the buses are still running. I pull out my phone and tiredly study it, forgetting why I pulled it out. Then I remember: I want to get home.

I don't know what bus to take. I search for Lara's number and wait while the phone rings.

But instead of Lara, it's a man on the other end.

'Hello you,' he says.

'Leo?'

In the background, I can hear music then a door closing.

'Sorry, I didn't mean to call you.'

'Sahar, are you OK?'

'I'm experimenting with alcohol. And I'm disappointed.'

Leo chuckles. 'Tell me where you are.'

'I'm at the bus stop. I'm just really sleepy all of a sudden. Is that normal?'

'It is if you're a tired drunk.'

I snort-laugh. 'Is that even a thing?'

'Yes, and apparently it's your thing. Can you tell me where you are again?'

I look around and locate the name of the bar or club or whatever it is, then begin rattling off my location like he's an Uber driver. I hang up and close my eyes.

Someone shakes me awake and I look up to find Luke towering above me, a bottle of water in his hand. He looks stricken, like a parent who's momentarily lost their child at the shopping centre.

'What are you doing out here?' He drops down beside me on the bench and seems to be assessing me for signs of harm.

'I needed fresh air. The music was too loud.'

'Jesus. You nearly gave me a heart attack. Have you met Kat? She would have murdered me if I lost you.'

'Why does anyone go to a place like that for fun?'

'To bump into each other and feel alive.'

My head falls onto Luke's shoulder, but he doesn't flinch. He unscrews the cap on the bottle of water and offers it to me. 'Drink. It'll help.'

I take the bottle and manage a few sips before returning it to Luke.

'You were supposed to wait for me,' he says quietly.

'Mmmm.'

'I think next time – if there is a next time – we stick to something light.'

'Yes.'

A solitary car speeds past, but otherwise it's as dark as a graveyard out here, save only for the streetlights and an impressive three-quarter moon.

'She's pretty,' I murmur.

'Who?'

'Cruella.'

'Who?'

'I didn't picture her to be your type.' We sit in silence.

'What's my type?' Luke says.

'I don't know.' I can't imagine her, but it unnerves me a little to think of someone captivating Luke more than chocolate. 'You don't like me much.'

'I like you just fine.'

I take a deep breath. My head is still on Luke's shoulder as I survey the dark sky and its sprinkling of stars.

'The moon is the same no matter where you are in the world, even if, technically, it looks different. Have you ever thought about that?'

I am incredibly impressed by my own lucidity. Clearly, I am a philosophical drunk.

Luke chuckles. 'Never thought about it, but I guess you're right.'

'I used to think about it sometimes, when I lived overseas – how the sky and moon and stars were the same as they were in Sydney, yet I felt like I was in a different universe.'

Luke is not immediately responsive. 'Sounds lonely.'

I shrug. 'It was sometimes. Which is weird given how much I like to be alone.'

'You're a hermit like me.'

'Why aren't you drunk?'

'I've only had a couple of drinks.'

'Why didn't you go dancing with Kat and Inez?'

'Bloody hell you ask a lot of questions.'

He doesn't sound mad, so without thinking I lean in closer, wrapping an arm across his chest.

He reaches an arm around me and pulls me towards him. 'Is this OK?' he says, gently tightening his hold on me.

'Yes.'

We drop into silence. More cars pass by. In the distance, I can hear the sound of a light rail bell.

'What's the worst thing you've ever done?' I ask.

Luke is quiet for a few seconds. 'The worst thing is usually the same for everyone. I've hurt people.'

'Same.'

The heaviness takes over. My eyes don't want to open.

'Don't fall asleep,' Luke says.

'I'm just closing my eyes for a bit. Then we can go back inside and I'll try some whisky.'

I can hear the sound of light traffic, and a man yelling profanities nearby. I let my eyelids drop, comfortable in Luke's arms, relieved because maybe he doesn't dislike me, after all.

Chapter 17

I swear I haven't forgotten you. But I'm letting the light in.

I wake up in my clothes and struggle to orientate myself. I have a moment of panic before I realise that I'm in my bed. My phone sits on the bedside table and the tiny notification light is flashing.

I pick it up, my eyes burning, and swipe it unlocked.

One message from Lara at 1am checking on me.

It's 9am now. Rousing myself, I head to the bathroom. My make-up is smudged and my hair is tangled and unkempt. I'm still in Lara's black dress, too. I wrangle myself out of it, then take a shower. I remove the make-up and apply some moisturiser. But the fatigue lingers.

Stepping into the kitchen, I find Lara sitting at the table, immersed in her phone while nursing a cup of coffee. She looks up.

'Hello, party girl. You had a big night.'

'How did I get home?'

'Luke.'

'What?'

'But apparently, you called Leo from a bus stop,' Lara says, looking like she's trying to complete some difficult arithmetic.

'Oh my God.' The memory quickly populates my mind as I recall the phone call, followed by sitting on the bus stop bench with Luke. 'Leo really showed up?'

'Uh-huh. But Luke brought you home in an Uber.'

'How embarrassing.'

'Which part?'

'Lara.'

'What? Why is it embarrassing? I think it's cute. And frankly, a relief. You don't get stupid when you get drunk, you get snoozy. And you called a friend. That's just sensible.'

'I am never doing that again.'

'Are you feeling hungover?'

'I don't think so? What does that feel like?'

'Well, I've only ever been hungover once, but I remember feeling like I wanted to vomit. And the person I was with told me to drink lots of water, which really helped.'

'I don't want to vomit, but I don't think I can eat. I just want coffee.' I drop my head onto the table.

'I'll make you one.' Lara jumps up. A few seconds later, the coffee machine groans into life.

'He's cute,' she says, over the machine.

'Who?'

Lara rolls her eyes. 'Luke. The guy who's pulling your pigtails.'

'He's not, Lara. I just challenge him.'

She shrugs. 'Same diff. He seems decent. Not that I have the best track record with figuring out the good ones. But I can generally pick out the tossers when they're focused on someone else.'

My head starts to throb, but I also want to exit the conversation. I have the vague sense I shared a tender moment with Luke, I just can't quite piece it together.

'Anyway,' I say, 'check alcohol off the list. I can say, hand on heart, it's highly overrated.'

'Most things are.'

My phone pings and I drag it to my eyeline. Messages from Kat and Inez.

Kat calls the night 'epic' then writes: **You're with Leo! Really?! Poor Nez.**

But she includes a laughing–crying emoji.

Inez laments my early exit and wants to check that I'm not feeling horrible.

How cute is Luke to get you home safe? He wouldn't let us leave. He didn't end up coming back tho. xx

'Did you have fun at least?' says Lara.

'I guess so. Maybe I've just missed the boat on this stuff. It feels a bit pathetic to try to catch up on some things,' I say.

'There's no age limit on trying new things, babe.'

'But shouldn't it feel ... more natural?'

'Maybe. I wouldn't overthink it.' She sighs. 'You're going through a big thing. You don't really know what you like, do you?'

'In relation to?'

'A lot of things. When I moved into my first apartment, like a proper adult after the fuckwit ex, I didn't even know what furniture I wanted, until I took a good look. That's what you're doing right now – taking a good look. Speaking of which: on Saturday, you're meeting me at my gig venue. I have a surprise for you.'

'It doesn't involve me singing, does it?'

'No. I promise. You will love it. This is my thing for you to experience and it's painless, with zero chance of humiliation.'

***

Back in my bedroom, I text Leo.

Please accept my apologies if I did or said anything inappropriate when I called you last night. For the first time in my life, I can blame intoxication.

I reply to Kat and assure her that I'm not 'with' Leo, then I message Inez and thank her for checking in. Then I ask her about a tarot card reading.

Her reply is swift.

OMG Yeeeeees. This week sometime.

BTW Leo?! He is so hot I could cry.

She includes a crying emoji.

I type a brief response.

Just ask him out already. ☺

Then she sends me a bunch of emojis that I interpret as excited confusion but there are still tears.

Next, a message from Luke arrives. It's to the point.

Hey ... Are you feeling OK?
Luke

I stare at his message, stuck on how to reply. But then Leo's response interrupts my thoughts.

Anytime. You are a terrible drunk and should not be left unsupervised.

This makes me smile. I quickly type out a reply to Luke.

I'm OK. Thank you, Luke. I'm sorry you missed out because I wandered off.

Luke replies within a minute.

I didn't miss out on anything. BTW you are the most analytical drunk I have ever met. ☺

I'm still smiling when my phone pings. It's Salim.

Is 1pm OK? Bring your appetite. The kids can't wait to see you. It's all they talk about.

It takes me a second to comprehend the message. Then I remember: I'm booked in to have lunch at his house today. I don't know that it's panic I feel. Instead, adrenaline kicks in. I have to do something about my appearance. I have to hide all evidence of last night.

Chapter 18

There is always a cost to freedom.
It's a matter of perspective.

Lara and Hakeem drop me off at Salim's house on their way to meet the sheikh who will carry out their marriage ceremony. Before we left, Lara had to ply me with more caffeine. She did her best with my face and talked me down from wearing a headscarf. As she pointed out, if I am truly going to evolve, I can't indulge in false starts so no one gets offended.

A quick stop at the bakery ensured I wouldn't arrive empty-handed, Inez tossing in a box full of treats.

Salim's wife, Naila, a pretty Lebanese woman from my old scripture group, is slightly taken aback when she answers the door, her daughter Aisha crowding her leg and staring up at me shyly. 'Oh my God, Sahar! You look ... so different.' She recovers herself quickly, offering a warm greeting and the obligatory three-cheek kiss (right, left, right). '_Mashallah,_' she says, smiling, but her eyes are darting around in a frantic inspection. But, I suppose, fair enough.

Salim approaches and hugs me, properly, then leans back and touches my hair. Behind him two more children wait, politely but with curiosity.

'*Mashallah,*' he also says, but it sounds more sincere and I am not sure what to make of it. 'Mohammed! Fatima! Aisha! Come say *salams* to your aunty.'

I am already aware of their sweet natures from brief visits to Sydney, and although I worry about looking as terrible as I feel, I receive their tender embraces easily, crouching down slightly to allow for a series of quick hugs.

When we're done, I make a wobbly rise to a standing position and smile brightly at Salim, who leads me to their living room – a white, airy space that looks straight out of a furniture store catalogue.

Salim is easy with his kids – two girls and a boy who are all primary school age – which is to say, he's nothing like our father, or mother. Naila is more intense, peppering her language with religious platitudes the way I used to. 'Subhanallah, I was just showing Salim old photos of us at the Sunday class.'

I mentally strap myself in, my mind flitting to the nightclub and the guy dancing like he was having a seizure, but I can't completely tune out Naila, who is playing with her long mane of hair and retelling Sunday school adventures like she's on a reality television show.

'They were good times,' I tell her, adjusting myself on the wide couch, my stomach becoming a little unsettled. Discomfort or alcohol intake? To be determined.

'We all looked so different,' she says, and I wonder if she thinks she's being subtle. I imagine saying the truth out loud: *Actually, the reason why I look so bad is because last night I got drunk at a nightclub. I'm also hanging out with men.*

But then I soften the mean edges of my thoughts. Naila's maternal energy is misplaced but not unusual. She reminds me of the Muslim women who used to talk about life post-marriage, keen to display their womanhood. They run households. They enjoy intimacy. They're proper adults, but nothing they do is *haram.* With sex, there is insider knowledge. All of them are sheltered, in a supposedly ideal life. And this is Naila now; not mean-spirited, but in a bubble she prizes.

Lunch is chicken from a local restaurant famous for its garlic sauce. Naila takes my plate and piles on bright pink parsnip, olives and pickles. She tosses on chicken-salted hot chips and practically half a chicken. I am struggling to swallow, but thankfully nothing comes up. I eat slowly and in a way that makes it look like I'm consuming more than I am. I discreetly sneak chips onto Aisha's plate and she looks thrilled, widening her eyes and trying to mute her smile.

I allow the conversation to be led by Naila, who trumpets the achievements of the children. 'I'm also thinking about starting a home business, like you used to have. I don't want to go back to accounting.' She looks at me expectantly, glancing at Salim, who nods supportively.

'That's wonderful. You want to make cakes?'

'Oh, goodness no. I was thinking events. There are so many sisters getting married, and I think I could make a living out of the people I know alone. Lolly bars and table decorating, that sort of thing.'

I smile and nod. Their home is elegant and beautifully furnished. 'I'm sure you'd be great at it,' I say.

The kids meanwhile are taking turns staring at me. I almost feel guilty when I see them watching me, in awe, with no clue that I could reasonably be considered the worst influence possible. This is only confirmed when Naila encourages them to show off their Qur'anic skills while Salim clears the table. I smile, transported by the familiar words. While my classmates took piano lessons and ballet, I went to scripture and memorised Qur'an.

Shortly after, the children proudly trail towards me in a line, faces beaming as they delicately handle certificates that they show off one by one – awards for athletics, swimming, spelling bees, monitor duties and so on.

They are gold-star students and I feel unexpectedly proud.

I try to offer encouraging words as I hand back the certificates, feeling more like a school principal than their aunt, but they each extend their skinny arms and wrap them around my neck in a tiny embrace.

I feel emotion well up, but I shake it off and give them each a kiss on the head.

'*Mashallah*. Keep it up.'

The girls want to show me their bedroom, so I follow them in and listen attentively as they break down the architecture of their toy collection. They call me 'aunty' and easily take my hand, their shyness fading. They become more playful, loud and brash with each other as they compete for my attention, correcting each other's long-winded stories and arguing over which toys and books to showcase.

'Do you have a Barbie doll?' I ask.

Fatima holds up a classic doll, with a thick mane of curly blonde hair, dressed in a white coat. 'She's a doctor,' she tells me. 'That's what I want to be.'

We play for a while and I tell them how I used to play Barbie with Samira when we were kids. I leave out that I used to put makeshift headscarves on my dolls. I was never very good at playing Barbie, unlike Samira, whose imagination was rampant with possibilities.

Afterwards, as Naila puts out the sweets, gushing over the impressive cakes, she seems more relaxed and I start to feel bad for my harsh thoughts about her. She is simply uncomfortable, unsure what to do and how to act around someone who was once more conservative than her.

The children start picking out their desserts and Naila urges them to be patient and take turns.

'They look like art,' Naila says, ready to cut into the sweets.

My heart stops as I realise that one of the desserts has gelatine in it, and the other liquor. I'm torn, but then I look at Naila, who is annoying but hospitable, and my brother who is only good. And then she's about to offer one of them to Fatima, who is insisting on the pretty bright pink one and I have to stop her.

'Um, you know what? The bakery gave me the wrong order. Two of those you can't eat.'

'Oh, really?'

'I'm so sorry.' I reach over and separate out the two cakes and smile apologetically at Fatima, who looks crushed. 'Gelatine,' I say, leaving out the liquor part.

'Tell you what,' I say to Fatima. 'I'll make you the same cake sometime and make sure it's halal. Deal?'

'Thank you, Aunty,' she says, shy but smiling so wide I worry her face will crack open. She looks at Naila in triumph and happily accepts a different dessert. There's plenty to go around and we fall into more natural conversation as we drink coffee and eat, the kids trailing off to their bedrooms with their plates. I tell Salim and Naila about my job.

'Just enjoy it,' Salim says. 'Don't make it harder than it needs to be. OK?'

'OK.'

'Find a middle place and sit there a while. We're here if you need anything,' he says.

I'm still trying to work out Salim's advice when he moves on to our parents' house and all of its belongings. I tell him that I plan to carry out a stocktake at some point. 'Is there anything you want?'

Salim shakes his head. 'I have already taken care of my stuff.'

Naila offers to help. 'When the kids are at school, I have plenty of time.'

I politely refuse and commence my exit. I arrange an Uber and rise from my seat.

'Thank you for having me,' I say. 'It was good to see you all.'

'Are you sure you don't want a lift?' Salim asks at the door.

'Uber's on the way. Ahmed. Four point nine stars.'

'Look, about the house...' Salim begins. 'I'm sorry there's so much stuff.' He crosses his arms, eyes on the ground.

'I haven't gone yet.'

Salim is surprised but he quickly gathers himself. 'Well, it's yours now, so you can decide what stays and what goes.'

'I still can't believe Mum and Dad left it for me.'

'And no mortgage, so consider it a gift. *Alhamdulillah.*'

'Why did they? I mean, they could have just left a small sum.'

Salim hesitates. 'I think they regretted how they did some things, Sahar. I think they wanted to make sure you weren't reliant on anyone.'

I digest this in silence. My parents saw my return before I did.

'Are you sure you don't want it?' I ask. 'It's big enough for you and the family—'

'I don't want to live there. I prefer it where we are.'

Naila arrives at the door and leans into Salim.

He places his arm around her and turns back to me. 'And they left me the business. Dad owned the property and the business, so we're good, *alhamdulillah.*'

There's money in the property, and a legacy in the business.

'Who's running the shop?'

Salim and Naila share a look before Salim clears his throat. 'I sold it a year ago. With the property.'

I digest this, too. Something has been cut from me, abrupt and sudden. It hits me with unexpected force that I will never see my father in his shop again. I will never walk in and smell the produce, feel the traces of our homeland in the walls and shelves heaving with imported spices and olive oil. I will never see my father again. For the first time, I try to understand properly how that makes me feel instead of relying on some vague sense of acceptance.

I farewell my brother and leave with muddled thoughts about our meeting; about Salim's life beyond our family, and his words of advice. He was always there for me, but perhaps I took his presence and patience for granted. I want to go back and ask him about the hurt that just rose to the surface, to pull out the words unspoken. Maybe he also felt like a guest in our parents' home, and now that they are missing from our lives, and we are building our own, the cords that link us, already strained, will finally snap. He has his life and people who need him in a way that I do not. I have my life, including problems only I can sort through and resolve.

I divert the Uber ride, deciding to visit my parents' graves since I'm in the area.

I don't quite know if it's guilt that wraps itself around me as I recall Salim's picture-perfect existence, or if it's my failed attempt at drinking catching up with me. Still, it's something. A sense of disquiet. Like I have let myself down, not my parents or even God. But perhaps this experience has just loosened my tightness around alcohol. The mystery has certainly come undone.

I'm glad I went to Salim's. His children remind me of how I once was – sweet and timid, a sense of politeness and respect in how they interact with the adults. That was me, before my parents' rules caused me to retreat within myself. Eventually I became fearful rather than reverential, socially inept rather than simply shy.

Who I have become has diluted the past and I don't know where the first significant change really began. Was it when my father first disciplined me? Was it the first time I was told I wasn't allowed to do something that seemed perfectly normal and innocent? The sidelined kid who was never allowed to go to school camp, who would gradually dismantle her natural desires because the effort to reach them was so exhausting? Or could it have been when my mother, days after I first got my period, approached me with a headscarf and urged me to begin wearing it. 'I am not going to go to hell for you,' she said, her tone matter-of-fact.

The day is warm and I spare a thought for Inez at the bakery.

I drop down onto the small patch of grass at the ends of their plots. I cross my legs, and slip on my sunglasses. It's hot and the sun seems extra bright. It's also quieter in the cemetery than I expected for a Sunday. I sit in reflection, wondering if there is some futility to these visits, speaking into the air, in search of spirits.

The heat sinks into my skin, warms my clothing. The air is dense with the sound of cicadas in full song, so loud it's like a cleansing of whatever layers remain stuck.

Words don't come as they usually do. I don't know what to say, or how to say it, because I am still yet to comprehend my own evolution.

With nothing to say, I cup my hands together and begin to recite prayers for my parents.

Chapter 19

Is choice an illusion when there is so much we can't control?

The academy Inez attends is for circus performers – which is to say, the people here are all insanely fit, toned and can achieve spectacular and unnatural feats with their bodies.

In one corner, bright, shiny sheets of fabric in vibrant hues of red, blue and pink drop from the ceiling. Opposite them are a set of hoops positioned at varying levels off the ground, several women contorting their bodies around them. Then there are the trapezes, again set up to accommodate every kind of user.

I'm ready to flee, but Inez stops me with a hand on my arm. 'Nuh-uh,' she says. 'You'll be fine. If you want me to read your cards, you have to stay.'

'Fine.'

Neither of us is rostered on at the bakery, so we're here for an early class on Saturday afternoon. Inez has agreed to read my cards afterwards, then I'll head off to see Lara at Musicale as promised.

We're all beginners in the class, but I am easily the most inept. The rest, it is clear, have athletic ability. I struggle to bring my knees to my chest and keep them there for the pike – the move that allows you to swing your legs over the trapeze bar.

I'm flooded by nerves and a deep sense of humiliation as I kick my legs up only to land on the floor again. But then the instructor, Amber, comes by and places a hand firmly beneath me. 'There are other ways to get up there, but let's try again.'

I reposition my hands on the bar then kick my legs up. In a choppy manner, I manage to lift my right leg and position it over the bar, followed by my left.

I feel tapped out and we've only just begun.

'You can let go,' Amber says.

I am filled with horror as I contemplate swinging freely and not being able to return my hands to the bar.

'It's OK, you're safe.'

I force aside my desire to get back on the ground, release my hands and let myself drop. The world around me is upside down. I can see Inez close by, easily positioning herself into a pose. Her hair is in an updo today, like she just stepped out of 1965.

'Thank you,' I tell Amber.

'I didn't do anything, that was all you,' she says. 'Now we need to get you up there.'

I know I'm not anywhere near as fluid or elegant as the rest, but my feet are off the ground and it's exhilarating to discover that I am not afraid of heights.

***

When the class is over, Inez and I go to an old-style diner not too far from the academy. Music from the 1950s plays, and the waiters are dressed like they've emerged from the same decade, in bright pink and black. We slide into a small booth, the red faux-leather couches squeaking with every movement. The Formica table is illuminated by an overhead light that is brighter than the sun. Beside me on the wall, Elvis Presley winks at us with his trademark smirk.

We place an order for fries and drinks then Inez takes a deep breath.

'Not the best place to do a reading, but we'll make it work.' She reaches her arms across the table in an invitation to join hands. I tentatively let her take hold of mine, my thoughts darkening with fear at what I am about to do.

Inez gives my hands a gentle squeeze. 'Have you ever had your cards read before?'

'No. But Lara has a deck, and I know people who read coffee cups.'

Inez plucks out a deck from her bag and starts to shuffle the cards. They're small enough to fit comfortably in her hands, the backs of the cards a light blue that contrasts heavily with her perfectly manicured fingernails. The sound of the rhythmic shuffling reassures me, like an energetic request is being made on my behalf.

'Now you shuffle,' she says, handing me the deck.

I am much slower, struggling to gain the same momentum as Inez. The cards get stuck at odd angles and some fall out.

'When you're done, split the deck into three, then put it back together in any order.'

I do as instructed, hesitating over the order in which I should reassemble them.

'Don't think about it.'

I place the sections on top of each other and hand the complete deck back to Inez.

'I'll read then you can ask questions. OK?' Her expression is soft as she lays down the cards face up in a cross formation. She stares down at them, intuiting a meaning I could not possibly extrapolate myself. 'Wow.' The word is larger than her voice. 'You really are going through some major changes. You must be feeling overwhelmed. This is nearly all Major Arcana.' Seeing my confusion, she adds, 'That's the big life stuff.'

Overwhelmed. Emotional. Tired – at least, I was for so long. So tired I existed in a place of no thought some days.

'See this?' Inez carefully selects a card and holds it up for me to see. It features three swords intersecting a bright red heart.

I lean in, suddenly curious.

'It represents your recent past. The Three of Swords is a card of heartbreak and separation. It might involve three people,' she says delicately, her eyes focused on the cards. She replaces the swords and moves on to the card at the bottom. 'This is Death. A new beginning. It's rebirth, burning away the old. This card is the question, the thing you need to understand. And here, in the centre: The Chariot. Also a major. This is about transformation, movement, a breakthrough. Crossing that is the Three of Cups. This is love and emotion. Joyful times help you to transform. It's friendship and celebration.'

'That sounds nice,' I say, a little nervous. Is this why people fall for psychics? It's so easy to tap into human despair. It can be a general truth and people deepen it to become theirs.

'You're thinking that you have to persevere and that, without a struggle, you haven't earned it. This is represented in your hopes and fears.' She points to a card called The Hanged Man, which depicts a clown hanging upside down, one foot in a sling, the other free. 'He thinks he's stuck, but he can come down at any time. In his mind, he's being delayed, things aren't moving fast enough. But he's still using this brief period of respite to see the world around him from a different perspective. Don't be afraid of this new view. It's bringing wonderful change.' Then, she triumphantly holds up a card called The Lovers. 'It can be a card of choice, or a love story unfolding.' Inez winks then stares down at the spread again. 'But I can't see who he is here. This is really about you. Oh, Sahar, I wish I could do justice to the feelings I get reading this spread.' She shakes her head, still staring down at the cards.

'You can feel it?'

'And see it. It's like a snapshot of your emotional world. This isn't about your future. This is about who you are and who you are becoming. You're reaching a place of genuine authenticity.

Connections are more meaningful, and your successes are longer lasting.'

'It sounds too good to be true.'

'It would be if the universe wasn't kicking your arse to get you there.'

'I think I've spent my whole life feeling like I'm going to be punished.'

'You're not being punished.'

'I'm being tested.'

Inez breaks into a wide grin. 'No. You're being shown what's possible.'

***

Afterwards, I walk to meet Lara alone, enjoying the crisp night air. I feel swollen with emotion from the reading, like I have just come out of a counselling session. It's not just what Inez said, but what she gave of herself in saying it, like she had access to my mind.

I arrive at Leo's underground bar, provide the password and a stranger lets me in. I follow the dim hallway to the bar. The cavernous room is set up differently to the spread of tables the other day. Tonight, it's intimate, with smaller tables designed for couples. Around me, groups of people murmur, and there's the occasional sound of instruments being tuned.

'You're here!' Lara hurtles towards me. She's dressed plainly in jeans and a buttoned blouse, but her make-up and hair are done. She looks beautiful and I smile.

'I told you I would come.'

'Now, I know you're spreading your wings and all that, so I wanted to give you something you can take with you anywhere.'

While Lara's talking, the band members gradually stop what they're doing and gather around her. They smile warmly, arms crossed, like a small army backing their commander.

'We're going to give you a soundtrack,' Lara says.

'I have your music already,' I say, but Lara shakes her head.

'Give me your phone.'

I dig around in my handbag, retrieve my phone and offer it to Lara.

She takes it then passes it to the tall man standing beside her. 'Solomon, you first.'

'Hey, *chica*,' he says to me, and it sounds normal coming out of his mouth.

There is such a thing as genuine cool. He starts playing with my phone.

'Each of us is going to contribute to a playlist,' explains Lara. 'Add or subtract as you want, but we're sharing songs that helped us. It's your soundtrack for this time in your life.'

I stem the emotion that travels up my throat and stings my nose.

'Good?' says Lara.

I smile. 'The best.'

Names are thrown my way. I don't know any of them. Frank Ocean. Florence and the Machine. Ray LaMontagne. Flora Cash. We Are All Astronauts. The Civil Wars. Dean Lewis. Tourist.

'We're putting some upbeat stuff in there for you to dance to as well,' Lara says, like she's dispensing a prescription.

'Who put Mogwai?' Solomon asks, inspecting the updated list.

A woman with wavy magenta hair and several ear piercings raises her hand.

'Bloody hell, Nikki. We're trying to help her recover, not sink her into a deeper hole.'

Nikki waves Solomon away and airily steps closer to me. 'It'll take you to the bottom of your soul and empty you out. You're welcome.'

'Oh, fucking fuck, no,' says Solomon, leaning in towards another woman beside him as she adds a song to the list. 'You are not putting in Taylor Swift.'

'I am putting in Taylor Swift,' she says, lifting the phone away to keep it out of his reach.

'Ginny.'

'She's the heartbreak queen.' Then Ginny looks at me and winks. 'You'll love it.'

After my playlist has been assembled, Lara leads me backstage. 'I have one more thing for you.' She stops at the door and her look grows more serious. 'I studied that list and I kept coming back to the sexy dress.'

I roll my eyes. 'Not my idea.'

'I've seen you in sexy dresses, when your curves were bigger and your cleavage was more impressive. Not that you've lost your boobs completely, thank the Lord.'

I think back to the segregated parties. Dancing with abandon. Dressed to look sexy and get judged by other women, but without the burden of men ogling us. In those moments, I would come out of my shell, elated at the freedom being among women gave me.

'I'm not going to let anyone cheapen you,' Lara continues, 'but you deserve to know what it feels like to wear the perfect dress out in the open, being the total babe that you are; to enjoy some attention, but more importantly, feel sexy as hell.'

Now that I think about it, I realise I have let people dress me my whole life. My mother enforced modesty. My cousins told me to embrace cosmetic beauty. My husband asked me to be presentable. No wonder Kat and Inez pick on my clothing. I never wear clothes that reveal anything about me.

Lara lifts a dress bag off a clothing rack and carefully unzips it. 'Something to try on tonight, and if you like it, to wear at my wedding.'

She pulls out a beautiful figure-hugging dress made of black satin. It has capped sleeves and a boatneck. It should go to the knees. My love for it is instant.

'It's a gift from Samira and me.' Lara holds it up against my body. 'I'm pretty sure it's the right size.'

My heart feels full as I take it from her and place it properly against my body. It will fit.

Lara looks at me, a request for confirmation.

'It's perfect.'

It's the sort of dress I would have once worn to a segregated event. It used to be enough to dress up at all-girls' parties, shock everyone with my made-up face, my curvy body in a tight dress. My hair, bouncing with curls, spilled below my shoulders. Hair is no small thing when you've spent most of your life hiding it.

'Will you wear it tonight?' Lara asks. 'It's sold out, but I've reserved a table for you.'

'You want me to stay?'

'Of course I do. Do you want to invite someone?'

I hug her. 'I'll be just fine on my own.'

***

About an hour into the evening, when I am comfortably situated towards the back of the room at a small table designed for two, a waiter arrives with a cocktail glass.

'Oh, I didn't order that,' I say, but he points to the bar.

'This is from Leo.'

I turn around and there he is, wearing tailored pants and a dress shirt. I smile at him and he nods, holding up his own glass.

'Leo says it's a special order. A mocktail.'

'Please tell him I said thanks.'

The waiter stares at me but doesn't move.

'Is there something else?' I say.

'Do I tell him to come over?'

'Oh, of course. If he wants to.'

He winks and wanders off towards Leo. I smile in Leo's direction, and a few moments later he arrives at my table. He indicates the empty seat beside me. 'May I?'

I nod, my grin widening.

'You're *wearing* that dress,' he says.

'Is it too much? It's new,' I say, a bit self-conscious.

'It suits you, don't worry. I just had to give the compliment.'

'Thank you. And thank you for the drink.'

'I thought we should keep you off the sauce.'

I feel the blush rising, so I fix my eyes on the red tablecloth, getting to know its intricate stitch. 'Sorry again about that. I don't know why I dialled you. Maybe because you're an "L" like Lara, or Luke.'

Leo is amused. 'I have no problem coming to your rescue, if you don't mind me saying that. I know it's very un-PC these days.'

'It's OK if it's true.'

Leo assesses me. 'Besides. I didn't end up doing much. Old-man Luke took you home. He seemed very protective of you.'

I look over at Lara, who's singing soulfully onstage, adrift in her own world. I take a sip of the mocktail and it has both sweetness and a bit of bite. 'He was just in charge of watching over me for The Experiment.'

'The what?'

'I'm doing this silly experiment where I'm trying new things,' I explain. 'Well, we're all supposed to be confronting fears ... the team at the bakery. Anyway, hence me being a failed drunk.'

'No one wins at being drunk, sweetheart. That's why I don't get drunk.'

'Isn't that the point of alcohol?'

Leo has a good chuckle at this. 'Depends who you're speaking to, I guess. But it's not for me. Tried it for a while, and life turned pear-shaped pretty quickly. You lose a lot when you switch off all your emotions like that.'

I realise how lucky I am to have never had alcohol as an option. I got the impression that Khaled indulged when he travelled for work.

Leo signals to the waiter to bring me another drink, then turns back to me. 'So, what exactly is involved in this experiment?'

I sigh. 'Well, there was the drinking because I don't drink – which obviously I am going to stick to going forward. Kat cut my hair for me, and we went dancing. I needed new clothes so Inez took me shopping, and she also read my tarot cards.'

Leo is deeply amused, hooking an eyebrow, his eyes wide. 'It's not the most daring list,' he says.

'Depends on who you're speaking to,' I say. 'I was pretty sheltered in my earlier years.'

'I get that,' Leo says. He looks lost in thought for a moment, but I can't tell what he's thinking. 'Is that it?'

'I'm still deciding. But sometimes I think I'd like to get a tattoo.'

Leo's eyes widen in surprise. 'What's stopping you?'

'Permanence,' I say and Leo guffaws. 'What do you choose that won't make you cringe later?'

'I got mine as reminders,' Leo says, glancing down at his arms as if to check his tattoos are still there. 'But some people get them to tell others who they are. They can be cultural ... a tribute. Some people just get them to show off. You'll know your reason.'

'What do yours say?'

Leo unbuttons his sleeves, rolling them up easily. 'This one begins here,' he says, tracing the elaborate lettering that runs down his right forearm, 'and ends here,' he continues, raising his left arm.

Up close, the italics become legible: *Every saint has a past, and every sinner has a future.*

'Oscar Wilde,' Leo says.

'I read him in high school.'

'And did you like him?'

'I disapproved of everything we read. I repented on behalf of all the authors writing sinful things, especially Oscar. But I was a top student. My parents pushed me pretty hard.'

Leo stares at me. 'I can't tell if you're joking.'

I laugh, but my embarrassment at my past innocence rushes through me, hot like fire. 'I found it very confusing. I was reading these books that moved me, but at the same time they seemed to go against everything I was taught to believe.'

'Belief is a dangerous thing,' says Leo.

'I don't think belief is the problem. It's what people do with it.'

Leo nods. 'Be an explorer instead.'

'But how do you find truth if you don't believe in anything?'

'You're here to experience life, not verify it.'

'You would not have gotten along with me when I was younger.'

Leo gets to his feet. 'Ditto. Anyway, enough of that. Let me know if you decide to get that tattoo. I can help you out.'

I'm touched by the offer. '*If* I do, then yes, I will.'

I watch him leave, and I'm swimming in the warmth of our easy exchange. I have never had male friends. They have always been family or lovers. Always protectors or oppressors.

Chapter 20

No matter how far I move forward, it doesn't take much to shatter the illusion of peace.

Luke has decided to return to 'go'. All day, he nitpicks at everything I do. He criticises the custard in my tarts, the tempered chocolate writing that graces the tops. But while he seems to find it easy to return to how things were, I don't.

I try to zone him out. But eventually, my resolve collapses and without meaning to, I snap at him. 'OK! I get it!'

Music fills the kitchen but everyone has slowed down to tune in to us.

'I heard you. I heard you the first fifty times you told me I was doing it wrong.'

I take a deep breath, and my fingers fumble with the knot of my apron strings, then I toss it onto the counter beside my imperfect custard tarts. Without another thought, without worrying how it looks, I leave, not caring if I never come back.

What I don't expect is for Luke to follow me into the office where I keep my handbag.

'Sahar.'

I turn to face him. 'What is your problem with me?'

'You have to listen.'

I shake my head. 'No. From the moment I walked in, you've made my life hell. What do you want? Blood?'

Luke surprises me when he says carefully, 'I just need you to work better.'

'Do you think I'm just some diversity hire or something? Is that it? Have I not bent over backwards to earn every crumb you've thrown at me? Done every crappy task to perfection just so you'll let me prepare a custard tart I could make in my sleep?'

Even in my fury, I'm surprised at how loud I am, at how the words spill out easily, how I don't say them with false courage, despite the tremble in my voice and the way my hands shake.

My breathing is heavy, loaded, as I gather my belongings. I don't remember ever feeling anger so intensely. This is drilled-down emotion, reserves of feeling I didn't know existed within me.

Luke hasn't moved. 'Look. I know you don't like being the least experienced, but you need to be able to take feedback. I don't ever think about your – whatever, diversity credentials?'

'My work is good. You don't have to be nice, Luke. I don't even care if you like me. But you should be fair.'

I shove my cardigan into my handbag and swing it over my shoulder. Hurt and confusion fill me as I make my exit, wondering if all my progress at Maggie's is going to end in nothing.

***

Halfway down the street, I hear my name being called and I turn to find Kat and Inez coming after me. Against my protests, they lead me into the hipster coffee bar we get morning orders from and sit me down by the window.

'Luke is emotionally stunted,' Kat begins. 'A lot has happened to him, and he doesn't know how to communicate.

He only knows how to be a soldier: he either gets orders or gives them.'

I stare at Kat blankly. 'What do you mean?'

'You know he was in the army.'

Inez sips her tea. 'He doesn't talk about it much.'

'Right. Well, I've experienced trauma, too. It doesn't mean I treat people like crap.'

Kat makes a face, like she is deliberating how much to say.

I stare at her. 'What? I am nothing like him.'

'You weren't the easiest person to get along with at the start either,' Kat says. 'You kind of just stuck to yourself.'

I feel a flush of shame travel down my cheeks and I shake my head. 'I was shy. I was new and junior. It's not the same.'

'Look, I'm not excusing Luke,' Kat continues, 'because he can be a fuckwit. But he's a fuckwit to everyone. Granted, it's different when you're working under him, but this is the first time he's had someone this talented to manage. It's doing things to him.'

Inez smiles. 'You are very talented. It was pretty obvious when you first started that you weren't a junior. You didn't really hide your frustration. But you weren't advanced either. Luke isn't easy, but he was toughening you up. I've seen worse.'

I stare down at my coffee, wishing that I could read my fortune in it the way so many Arab women do, the grounds weaving intricate pathways that reveal obstacles and ways forward. A well-read cup, I discovered in Jordan, is like a balm to a troubled soul. A good cup gives you hope.

I sigh. 'I'm sorry. You're right. I can be pretty obsessive and stubborn.'

'Like Luke is obsessive and stubborn?' Kat says with a wry grin.

Inez smiles into her cup. 'Two peas in a pod.'

'I would say get a room, but you work together, so I really don't think you should sleep with him,' Kat says.

'I'm not attracted to Luke,' I say, taken aback by Kat's casual tone. I glance at Inez.

'There's a thing there ... maybe,' she says with a shrug.

I am mortified. 'There's no thing.'

Kat rolls her eyes. 'Fine. Maybe you're a pea in a pod with Leo, then.'

'I'm not interested in Leo.' I turn to Inez. 'He's nice to me, that's all.'

Inez holds up her hands. 'I think he's hot, but he doesn't even know I'm alive. I have no claim on him.'

'If it's weird for you that I spend time with him, I won't.'

Inez gives me an odd look. 'Are you serious?'

'Of course.'

'Honey, don't be ridiculous.'

Kat chuckles. 'Would you look at this one? Doesn't know what to do with all the attention.'

I study my coffee, self-conscious all of a sudden.

Kat downs the rest of her coffee. 'Now, are you coming back to the kitchen? Trust me, you don't want to piss Maggie off with petty shit like this. I mean, we argue about music playlists, but nothing like this.'

'I know. I'll come back.' I drain my coffee. 'Thanks for coming after me.'

Kat raises a fist and I bump it. 'That's what we do.'

Inez puts a hand on my arm. 'You're not alone here. We really are like a family. And Luke drives everyone nuts. But talented people get away with stuff that ordinary people like us don't.'

When we return, I don't make eye contact with anyone inside the kitchen. Luke is at work at his bench. He glances up then indicates to my bench. 'Can you please finish those off?'

I nod. The words for an apology roll through my mind, but my gut steers me towards the counter. I place my handbag nearby and wash my hands, then get straight back to finishing the tarts. But my mind is full, trying to process my outburst – something I feel deeply embarrassed about.

And something else is being forced into view; I am trying to understand it. A glance at Luke and my remorse is compounded: how did I allow myself to take everything he does so personally?

I hate the lack of control that comes with working for someone else. Having my own business was a bigger luxury than I realised.

***

Luke and I are the last to leave. I consider making a quiet exit without saying goodbye, but I'm feeling calmer after a few hours spent working quietly at my task. Luke is still slavishly cleaning his counter with a sponge and something in me softens then breaks open. Are Kat and Inez right? Are Luke and I really so alike, and that's why we bump up against each other?

I clear my throat. 'I'm sorry for raising my voice at you earlier. But I really don't like how you speak to me. It's the way my dad used to talk to me, and it makes me feel small.'

Luke abandons the sponge and looks up at me. 'Apology accepted.'

It stings a little that he doesn't offer his own apology in return, but at least he has acknowledged mine. I'm near the doorway when I hear his voice call my name. 'Sahar.'

I turn and wait.

'You didn't deserve that. I need to be better. I was having a shitty day because of a personal—' He stops. 'It doesn't matter. It clouded my judgement. I'm sorry too.'

The relief I feel brings with it a burst of unexpected emotion. 'Thank you.'

There's a heavy pause but then he speaks. 'Can I buy you a drink sometime?'

'OK.'

I go to leave when Luke calls out to me again. 'How about now? It's been a shit day.'

'Sure.'

'I know a good place. Not as noisy as the rest.'

***

We walk in silence to the bar, a small hole-in-the-wall. Luke picks the corner table furthest from the front – the most sheltered spot. I'm relieved; it's the table I would have picked. He takes the stool, giving me the couch, the small table and a tiny bowl of spiced nuts between us. His mood is a bit stiff, our already odd vibe not fully restored following the dust-up. We start to debate who gets to buy the first drink, but I'm already up and headed to the bar.

The bartender has a carefully manicured beard. He is a genuine hipster. I order Luke a beer, reciting the name he gave me. 'Crown Lager, and I'll have a lemon, lime and bitters.'

'You don't drink?'

'Nope.'

'Want something a bit more interesting?'

'Depends on what you define as interesting,' I say, a little uncertain.

He leans forward, a smile forming, his eyes dancing. 'How about I surprise you?'

'OK,' I say, and can't help the smile tugging at my lips. I pull out my wallet and hand him two tens.

'Just the beer,' he says, taking one ten-dollar note. 'Yours is on me.' He places my change on the counter, then begins selecting ingredients and shaking canisters, looking chuffed. I glance over at Luke, who is scrolling through his phone.

A minute later, the bartender places down a bottle of beer and a very pretty-looking drink in a tall glass. It's a swirl of yellow and green, topped with fruit and mint.

He smiles. 'Tell me what you think when you're done.'

'Thanks so much,' I say, grinning like an idiot. I feel embarrassed but also flattered.

'I'm Aiden.'

'Sahar.' I extend my hand and he takes it.

I carry the drinks over to Luke and his eyes widen as my glass lands on a coaster.

'Do you drink that or eat it?' Luke says and I smile.

'The bartender insisted on surprising me.'

We look over to the bar where Aiden is focused on another customer. He glances over briefly, long enough to wink at me, and I reach for my drink to hide the rapid burn in my cheeks. I'm nearly forty. Why is this so hard for me?

But I know, of course. I am living out my twenties now, if not my teen years. I am not innocent. I have experienced significant milestones, but they are selective, like I missed important in-between moments. Mine has not been a normal graduation to adulthood, and while it feels like I'm cheating to try to rectify that now, to stay as I was is not an option.

'Did he ask for your number?' says Luke.

'No.'

Luke tips his bottle in my direction and we clink our glasses without saying a word.

We talk about work for a while, and by the time Luke has finished his beer, the awkwardness has started to dissipate.

I ask him, tentatively, about his time in the army, a fact that irks me even without knowing the full story. I don't know if I want to unpack what lay beneath his decision to enlist. I don't want to know what his experiences in a foreign country did to his mind and how he sees the world in case it's as bad as his mood most days.

Luke stiffens but just as quickly he loosens up. 'I was there for four years. I was twenty-one and needed a place to go.'

'Did you go overseas?'

'I was deployed, yes.'

I sip my drink, a bit uncomfortable.

'Afghanistan. And I hated it. Do you want another drink?' Luke rises from his seat and waits.

'Still going, thanks.'

Luke has one more beer, but Aiden's specially crafted drink is more than enough for me. Then Luke asks me about my time in Jordan. 'The camps. You said you worked with refugees?'

'Yes. For a few years, actually.' My mind is ready to travel there again. It still floors me sometimes how quickly I can not simply remember but be transported there. Especially to that last day.

'Sorry,' Luke says. 'You don't have to talk about it.'

'No, it's OK. I went there to do some programs with the women, but I speak Arabic well so eventually I began doing more. I was a translator for the foreign volunteer doctors ... and at one point, I was a media liaison. Lots of journalists came through.'

Luke studies me. 'I find it hard to imagine you doing that.' Before I can make sense of the comment, he waves my unspoken words away. 'I just mean, you're a loner and a bit timid sometimes. It doesn't seem like your bag.'

'I guess it wasn't really. But we can always surprise ourselves.' I look down at my drink. 'It saved me, I think.'

Luke nods. 'Tragedy can do that sometimes.'

'It sounds horrible, but it wasn't their tragedy; it was having a purpose. Being there ... it felt like I was doing something useful.'

We fall into silence, but it's not uncomfortable. The bar is slowly filling up, and the counter is two-deep. I don't even realise I'm watching Aiden at work until he turns to look at me. His gaze is soft and meaningful, and I quickly look away.

A moment later, Luke suggests we leave. Aiden watches us thread our way through the crowd, and I feel a pang of remorse for not saying goodbye to him. But then he calls out, 'See you again soon?' and I nod.

As soon as we step outside, I inhale deeply. The fresh air is like a blast of cold water, waking me up.

'Well, thanks for a nice night,' I say to Luke.

'Are you in a rush?'

I glance at my phone. It's only eight o'clock and Luke is buzzing with a low hum of energy.

'No,' I say, because I can't lie.

We walk on for a while, passing crowded restaurants, the occasional clamour of a kitchen competing with street traffic and passers-by.

'Do you live far from here?' I ask.

'Inner west. But a bit further in than you.'

'I don't know how much longer I'll be here.'

Luke slows down. 'You're leaving?'

'No, I mean I don't how much longer I'll be living nearby. My flatmate is getting married.'

'Cool. Look ... that chocolate lesson I owe you ... how about now?'

I laugh. 'It's late.'

'Fuck it. Let's go.'

I feel an odd sense of anticipation as we circle back to the chocolate studio, where Luke starts setting up. 'Let's try something different.' He's not drunk, or even tipsy, despite two beers, and I assume it has something to do with his size. He links his phone to the speakers and the space fills with music. He adjusts the volume so that it's soft rather than invasive.

Next, he pulls out some half-sphere moulds, a bag of couverture milk chocolate buds and some stencils. He rustles around on another shelf and retrieves a small airbrush gun. I watch him work. He looks more at ease than he has all night. He rolls up his sleeves and ties on an apron. He doesn't bother with a chef's cap, so his wavy hair falls in his eyes as he leans down to locate the chocolate, and he uses the back of his hand to brush it away.

'You never panic with chocolate. You work quickly but never panic. It goes everywhere,' he says, ripping open the bag and spilling half its contents onto the marble counter we use for tempering.

Luke goes to the sink and washes his hands thoroughly. I follow suit then wait for instructions.

'Start melting,' he says. I am used to this part. Melting the chocolate in the microwave at thirty-second intervals. At first I was surprised to learn they didn't use the bain-marie, but Maggie says the volume of chocolate and lack of space makes it impossible.

Luke stands watch, his mood softer now. He studies my form, occasionally offering encouragement, checking in about temperature.

'That's it. Faster.' He stands close, arms crossed. He sways a little, nods to his own beat, conducting a symphony. 'Faster.'

I find that I am enjoying myself, heartened by the certainty I feel that this chocolate will turn out well. Done incorrectly, chocolate can seize or bloom and end up chalky. Good tempered chocolate is not simply about the shine and the famous crack when it's split open; it should be silky and smooth in texture, and, of course, taste delicious.

'It's moody, remember,' says Luke, brushing past me.

When I'm done, I scrape the mixture into a large bowl at the end of the counter.

Luke drops a sphere mould onto the bench. 'Fill four of these up. You know what to do?'

'Yes.' I pour the tempered chocolate into the mould, filling four circles.

'Don't forget the tap.'

I tap the mould against the counter to remove any air bubbles and ensure an unblemished surface.

'This is a polycarbonate mould,' Luke continues, pottering around a shelf nearby. 'You can use silicon, but it's not going to be as shiny.'

I am about to scrape away the excess chocolate when Luke takes the mould out of my hands. 'Give it thirty seconds.'

I do as he says, then tip out the excess from the mould into the batch of tempered chocolate.

'Now scrape it,' says Luke. He positions a sheet of parchment paper on the counter. 'Five to ten minutes on that.' Then he gestures to the next bench. 'Let's do some stencils.'

He shows me how he makes patterns using plastic sheets – some designs simple, others more intricate and elegant. My focus is on his hands, working easily and fast. But the difficulty is low; it just requires patience and a methodical approach. Fill, scrape, lift.

'Nice. You're precise,' Luke says, and I am focused but manage a smile in response.

Five minutes later, I lift the circle moulds off and there is no liquid chocolate left.

Luke takes the mould and gives it one last scrape before placing it in the large industrial fridge. 'Ten minutes.'

My heart is in my throat when it comes time to pull the chocolate away from the mould, but the half-spheres easily come out and Luke nods approvingly. 'Well done.'

'Are we gluing them together?'

'Yep. You can use them as dessert cups, but let's make a dome.'

There are different ways to melt the edges, but Luke keeps it simple. 'Hot ramekin. Place it top down so we can use the bottom as a hot surface.' Luke moves closer and places two ramekins in front of me. We're side by side, my arm grazing his, when he takes a half-sphere and gently circles it against the surface of the ramekin. 'Carefully. You don't want to melt too much of it. Now you try.'

I am a bit slow but eventually grow more courageous. I realise how intently I have been working, not at all worried about impressing Luke. His easy approach makes it possible.

I hand Luke the half-spheres and he carefully but expertly glues them together. He wipes away the excess drip then carefully places the complete sphere onto a tray lined with parchment paper. 'You do the other one.'

As I massage the half-spheres into the ramekin, Luke clangs about in search of other ingredients.

'How about some gold dust?' he says, emerging with a medium-sized jar of edible lustre dust. Then he grabs a small bowl and a bottle of clear liquid. 'Can I use grain alcohol?'

I nod.

'You can use any type of extract, but this is my preferred one. And I don't have any lemon extract.'

'It's OK.'

Luke drops a teaspoon of the lustre powder into the bowl then adds a couple of drops of the alcohol. He stirs it until it is smooth and silky with a metallic shine. 'We're going to airbrush the domes. Hand-painting gets a bit messy. See how I've got that watery consistency? That's what you want.'

I lean in, feeling completely at ease with Luke, who has never been more patient or informative. He may have been the least enthusiastic about The Experiment, but he has delivered the best experience so far.

'Have you used one of these before?' he asks, holding up the spray gun.

'Years ago, on my cakes.'

Luke hands it to me, and I adjust the needle, loosening it then moving it out to prevent it getting stuck. He brings over the tray and places it in front of me.

I glance up at him. 'Should I just cover it all?'

Luke shrugs. 'Yeah, why not.'

A few minutes later we have two golden domes.

Luke nods his approval. 'Now you're going to melt the bottom off – enough to cover a surprise inside.'

I reheat the ramekins while Luke warms up caramel in the microwave. He asks me to fetch two large bowls and ice cream from the freezer.

He pours the hot caramel sauce into a small jug. 'We don't have fresh fruit, so ice cream by itself will have to do. Now it's my turn,' he says and I stand back to observe.

Luke scoops ice cream into the bowls then carefully places the carved domes over the top. He breaks off the chocolate we stencilled earlier and places the shards against the dome.

'Now, the fun part.' Luke pours caramel sauce over the top of the dome and I watch as it melts the chocolate, which collapses gloriously into the ice cream. My tastebuds awaken and my stomach groans in anticipation. I haven't eaten dinner, but this is a more appealing option.

Luke hands me the sauce. 'You do the other one.'

I bite my top lip, feeling a bit silly about how excited melted chocolate makes me feel.

'A bit of theatre,' Luke says. 'And super easy. One day, when you're on *MasterChef,* you're going to laugh at how I tried to impress you with this.'

'That's never going to happen,' I say, smiling at the image of me as a guest chef, lifting a cloche to reveal a complex dessert. 'I couldn't even get through half the games at improv and that was with people I know.'

We take our bowls to the step in the hallway that links to the shop, and in near darkness, we eat the dessert.

A strip of light comes in through the hallway, illuminating Luke's face as he speaks. 'It gets more complicated when you make your ice cream from scratch, or if you're making a complex shape with layers inside. But I wanted to take away some of the mystery.'

I smile into my dessert. 'An uncomplicated complex dessert. I like it.'

We're both quiet a moment, the music from the studio a distant hum.

Luke turns to face me. 'You're going to surpass me soon enough, I think.'

My stomach lurches and I exhale. I look at him and find his eyes locked onto mine. His expression is sombre, but I think sincere.

'We make a good team,' I say, and I mean it.

All of a sudden, he reaches out to wipe something off my face. 'You have chocolate and caramel ... Can't take you anywhere.'

The tenderness of the action eclipses my embarrassment. But then I go to check it's all gone and he immediately withdraws his hand.

The moment is severed and Luke rises from the step and grabs the bowls. 'I'll clean up.'

And it's the strangest thing, but I don't want him to go.

***

Sitting on the step in the hallway, I can hear Luke cleaning up inside, and I know I should go in and help him, but all of a sudden I'm feeling self-conscious. And there's something else ... something I don't understand. Perhaps it's simply what I have known all along: watching Luke work moves me. There's something about him that's familiar, and I feel oddly connected to him even when we disagree.

I stand up and take a deep breath, ignoring the thick roll of nervous energy that is dampening what felt so light only a few moments earlier.

I enter and see Luke at the sink, cleaning the moulds and the bowls. He has switched into another mode and I don't want to disrupt it. I begin tidying up the remaining bits and pieces, and wait until he's finished. When he turns around, Luke looks almost surprised to see me.

'You can go,' he says, not unkindly. 'I've got this.'

I feel a wave of disappointment. I'm not sure what has happened, but something has shifted from the gentle movement between us to stiff discomfort.

'OK then. See you at work tomorrow?'

Luke nods slowly a couple of times. 'And I want more ideas. Not just the feelings. Give me a creation.'

'Got it.'

I grab my handbag and walk through the store to get to the front door. I'm halfway across the room when I feel a hand on my shoulder. I turn and Luke is there, pulling me towards him. He cups my face in his hands, uses his thumb to rub my cheek, and his touch causes me to shiver.

Our foreheads bump against each other before his lips meet mine in a soft kiss. He tastes like alcohol and chocolate. The kiss deepens, and it feels like *something.* Luke kisses me again, and I find myself saying, 'Oh my God.'

'Fuck,' he says suddenly, pulling away. 'I shouldn't have done that.'

Luke steps back, holds a fist to his mouth and centres himself. But my insides are knotted. I want to kiss him again.

'No, it's OK,' I say shakily.

'Sahar, I'm sorry. That was very unprofessional of me.'

My stomach sinks and I nod. 'I understand. I'll go.'

I leave quickly. But my whole body is alive to what just transpired. Something in me has shifted to a place of desire. I feel it from my crown to my toes, in the restlessness of my limbs, the way the burn doesn't end at my stomach. I can feel it in my hands.

On my walk home, I am flooded by waves of different emotions. At one point, my mind wants to guilt me. I almost mistake the deep burn in my gut for shame. It's not. It's excitement.

I wanted to give in to Luke; to honestly and wholeheartedly let go without any thought of what came next, the default punishment setting extinguished. I wanted to experience the moment – so unexpected, so unimagined – in a pure state of acceptance. Maybe it's impossible; perhaps my ability to do that was lost years ago. And yet, when he kissed me, I gave in without thought. If he hadn't ended it, I would still be in his arms.

My stomach is burning by the time I reach the apartment block. My phone pings and my heart rises to my throat. But it's not Luke, it's Lara checking up on me. It slows me down, flipping me back to the real world. I look up at the apartment building, and while my insides are raging, through it all I feel gratitude that at least, in all of this confusion, I have a place to land.

But as I unlock the door to the apartment, I feel heavy. Perhaps it's guilt because the last person I kissed was Naeem. So it's no surprise that his image starts to push through. I remember my final day at the refugee camp, the desert chaos at complete odds with where I stand now, in a small, slightly outdated apartment in Sydney's inner west.

I walk down the small hallway.

I feel my feet traipsing across the hard earth of the camp.

I place my handbag on the side table then poke my head into the living room.

I am face to face with Naeem in his temporary office.

I enter the bathroom and wash my face.

We are both upset. A reckoning.

The memory pulls me open then apart.

***

There's a light on in Lara's bedroom. I know she will be alone, but I knock anyway and wait for her response.

'Sahar?'

I open the door slightly and poke my head through. 'Can I come in?'

Lara is reading a bridal magazine, but she immediately puts it to the side and sits up. 'Of course. Are you OK?'

'Why do things have to be so hard when they should be so natural?'

Lara sighs in the way that a teacher does when a student demands the answer to a tricky question. 'It's hard,' she says, 'trying to be normal when the normal we grew up with was so ... out there. Are you feeling guilty about something?'

I shake my head. 'I feel angry.'

'You seem pretty calm to me.'

I want to tell her about Luke, but I have no idea where it begins and ends. I rest my head against her shoulder.

Lara swivels onto her side and places an arm across my stomach. 'You know, I think the trick is to be able to find peace even when things are crap. If you can stay balanced in a storm, you can manage anything.'

I think about this for a few moments. The unevenness of life and what gives and takes.

'You're sensible,' Lara continues. 'You could have come back and gone wild just to make a point. But you didn't. I mean, you probably have hot guys at your gym losing their minds over you and you haven't even noticed.'

I scoff. 'I somehow doubt that.'

'Trust me. When you're leaning down to get a kettle bell, someone is checking out your arse.'

'Not helping, Lara.'

'Are you seriously telling me that no guy has ever tried flirting with you at the gym?'

Clearly, it has happened to Lara, and I have only ever seen her at the gym once.

'My circuit instructor told me I have a cool name. Is that flirting?'

'Was he cute?'

'I think so? I mean, he's a trainer and he has a good body...?'

'How did you respond?'

'I said "thanks" then continued my deadlifts.'

'Oh Lordy. Oh Sahar.'

'I don't care if the gym instructor thinks I'm cute.' I know I sound a bit whiney, but I don't want Lara to taint the one simple thing in my life – my workout.

'It'd be OK if you did care, though. You know that, right? If you wanted to just have some fun? Men can bloody well do anything they want and no one blinks. Who the hell are they doing all that stuff with?'

'Honestly, I'm just trying to keep my head above water half the time.'

Lara sits up and gazes down at me. 'Hand on heart, I love Hakeem and have come to terms with the fact that I've ended up with a Muslim despite being a terrible one. But I can't see that for you right now.'

'Wouldn't that be hilarious?'

'Fundy Sahar with an Aussie and crazy Lara with a Muslim.'

'Stranger things could happen, I guess.'

'I'm not surprised,' she says quietly.

'I don't think I'm going to end up with anyone,' I say.

Lara doesn't immediately respond. 'It's not like you have to.'

'It's weird. I think that's why I'm finding this so hard. It's not guilt; it's knowing that I have no desire to ever get married again. I just want to be free. But I also still want to connect.'

'You want to have sex.'

'Intimacy,' I say.

'That too,' Lara says and we cackle.

'I'm so proud of you,' says Lara, pulling me close. 'Think about how far you've come since you first got back.'

We lie like that for a while, easy together. Lara has been like a lighthouse these last seven or eight months.

An idea gains momentum. 'We should do something before your wedding,' I say. 'You, Samira and me. Maybe you can invite your favourite cousin, Zahra.'

Lara groans. 'Oh God. She's a total social media mummy now. She matches her outfits with her kids. I shit you not.'

For a few moments, I ruminate on what motherhood would have looked like for me. How would I have extended love to my children? What would I have taught them when it's clear that I am an eternal student? Would they have loved me without condition?

'Do you want to have kids?' I ask Lara.

'I don't know. Hakeem has one, and I like where I am. The music is fun; I feel alive every time I'm onstage. But I don't know how much longer I can do the little gigs and tours as back-up for the back-up. You know I was pregnant once? With fuckwit ex.'

'Lara!'

She waves me away. 'I miscarried, but I would've been a single mum. I don't know, if it had worked out, I probably would have loved it. Shit, I would've been that loser who buys her daughter sunglasses when she's one.'

I can see how the memory inflates then deflates her. We're quiet again. A moment of silence for what never was.

'It's not too late,' I say. 'And with the right person, your body will take care of you.'

Lara stares into my eyes, hunting for truth. 'Is that what you really feel? Because you are crazy psychic and I trust you.'

'Well, I wouldn't place bets based on what I think. But yes, that's how I feel.' In my bones. I can see the possibilities play out like an apparition in my mind's eye, an energy coming into form. 'I think you'd like it. You'd make it fun.'

Lara hugs me. 'Thank you.'

I return her hug, properly, allowing the connection to sink into my skin and warm me.

'I would like to call her Aurora,' Lara says, still clutching onto me. 'If I have a little girl.'

'Yeah. Don't call her Aurora.'

We share a laugh then separate, gently pulling away from each other.

Eventually, our conversation becomes lighter, more drawn out.

Lara closes her eyes before I do. I'm thinking of Naeem as I lay my head down on the pillow. When I close my eyes, his face appears so suddenly I almost think he is in the room with me. It's not long before I'm asleep and seeing abstract visions of a wintry desert landscape, a sea of ripped tents and empty schools, an ether of shattered dreams.

Chapter 21

I have no idea how many different outcomes have played out in my mind. Some lead me to you. Some have us never knowing each other at all.

The next day at work, Luke is friendly. Which is to say, he is acting weird. Kat notices it too and I hear her prompting Inez to ask me about it.

'We had a drink and talked about his army days,' I tell them. 'That's all.'

But I worry that I should have done more to prevent Luke's fall from grace last night. Not that I minded it. I am surprising myself with just how little I minded it.

The truth is, I miss being with someone, but I don't think I could fool around with a stranger just to sate my physical hunger, no matter how much Kat wishes for it. It's on her list, which seems to be ballooning by the week. I'm not even sure when she added it, but she left me a print-out: *Hot sex with a stranger.* I crossed it out.

I have plenty to do, but I'm distracted. At one point, Inez corrects me when she walks past and sees that I have used the wrong fruit in a custard tart. Luke glances up then returns to work.

I am not going to do this, I decide. I am not messing this up over a guy.

***

Samira comes by on Friday night, looking flustered, almost breathless with a frazzled energy. She's dressed in her usual jeans-and-top combination, and a gypsy-style scarf.

Lara is singing at Leo's place tonight, so it's just the two of us.

Samira's cheeks are pink and shiny. 'I swear, a military strike takes less effort than me leaving the house. Menem distracted the kids, otherwise I never would have been able to leave.'

'You're not in Guantanamo.' But I understand her energy now: she's made a mad dash for a brief period of respite.

'I miss my freedom,' Samira fake-whimpers. 'I miss wasting time on useless stuff and watching movies without interruption.' Then she makes a case for the usual pizza order.

I laugh. 'Are you deprived of pizza at home?'

'Shut up,' Samira says. 'Pizza is a food group. And I don't let my kids eat it.'

I shake my head. 'Tonight, I'm cooking.'

I throw a loaf of garlic bread into the oven while we do a round-up of news. Lara has found a dress – not a wedding dress, something formal in off-white. Samira approves. And I need to find a place to live because Lara will be moving out.

I begin work on the pasta. Nerves inhabit my entire body, like a show is about to start, but I have no idea if it's a drama or a comedy.

Samira half-heartedly offers to assist with dinner, but she's scanning my phone, engrossed in the playlist Lara and her band compiled for me. 'God I feel old,' she says. 'I don't know any of these singers.'

The linguine is drained, and I drizzle it with olive oil and toss through two different kinds of cheese, all the while keeping an ear open to Samira. 'I don't know them either.'

'Like that makes a difference. I used to listen to music every day.'

I sprinkle on cracked pepper next, mildly annoyed at myself that in my distracted state, the pasta is not quite silky.

Samira abandons the phone with a sigh. 'So, this is Lara's thing. When am I taking your photo? Stop trying to get out of it.' This was Samira's one request: she gets to take my photo because I am yet to 'be seen'.

'I'm not trying to get out of it, I swear. And thank you for the dress, by the way.'

Samira beams. 'Isn't it the best?'

'I wore it straight away.'

'But that's not my thing on your list. Have you at least given the photo some thought?' Samira goes to the fridge and rummages around, emerging a few seconds later with a bottle of soft drink.

'All I do is work and go to gym classes. I haven't exactly had time.'

We sit at the table in the kitchen, and I spoon pasta onto Samira's plate.

She watches me with interest. 'What classes do you do?'

'Boxing. Weights. I've just started trapeze, but I'm not very good at it.'

'Are you joining the circus?'

'I'm already in the circus, didn't you know?'

We share a laugh and Samira breaks into the garlic bread. 'Can I come?'

'To trapeze?'

'Yes.'

'You want to do trapeze.'

'Of course not. I want to take a photo of you doing trapeze.'

The idea makes me want to laugh as the vision of me struggling to get onto the hoop populates my mind. Another set of nerves rushes through me as I contemplate how embarrassing it could be.

'I don't know, Samira. I can only do one thing – and barely.'

'There's more to you than cake, Sahar,' Samira says in a faux-solemn tone. 'You need to know that.' She stares at me like she's Oprah interviewing me about a serious topic and we break out into laughter again.

'OK, fine. But I'll have to ask for permission from the academy.'

'Ooh the academy. Fancy. Don't worry about getting permission, I can organise that. I do that stuff all the time. Just give me the details.' Samira rips apart her garlic bread and runs it through her pasta. 'I won't have to set up much, just one light probably.'

'And the photo's just for you, right?'

Samira shakes her head. 'I told you. It's for you.'

***

The following week, I fall back into a routine, but this time it's different. Luke doesn't badger me. He has retreated into himself. I go to the gym, but I also make a lot of chocolate. Hours spent in the studio feel like only a fraction of the time. Thankfully, Luke increases my work doing chocolate while he spends more time in the bakery.

All the while, I feel Kat's watchful gaze on me. One afternoon, she calls me over to her bench to assist with a dessert.

'Want to pick the music?' she says, which immediately alarms me. But then

I take a deep breath, and maintain a neutral expression as I queue up a playlist of old love songs.

'Niiiice,' Kat says with a smile.

We get to work, filling biscuit shells with caramel and thick chocolate, and sprinkling sea salt across the top. A couple of times I sense Kat is inspecting me, but I keep my head down. Eventually though, she breaks the silence.

'You OK?' she says, steady, serious.

'I'm fine.'

'He's not a bad guy. But you work together, and if it goes south, you're fucked.'

'I don't know what you're talking about, Kat.'

'Rightio then,' she says, but from her expression, it's clear she doesn't believe me.

I am not attracted to Luke. I just miss connection.

connection

Chapter 22

Find a way out of the wilderness, and experiences to survive it.

It's been more than three weeks since Luke kissed me, and he has only grown more distant. I am mourning the loss of normality. At least before there was an energy between us. Even at his crabbiest, Luke was engaged and attentive. I could learn from him.

At one point, I catch myself getting irritated by his lack of interest, so I retreat to the pantry and busy myself with a mundane task.

I have other things to distract me. Lara's wedding cake, for starters. My mind is heavily at work on the cake design. Fondant icing or butter cream? Flowers or props? Kat and Inez offer their feedback, steering me towards simplicity.

When I tire myself out, adrift again, I reach a state that can only be corrected in the chocolate studio.

One evening when I'm feeling particularly restless, I decide to make use of the keys Luke gave me, disappointing Inez, who's been trying to summon me for an impromptu drink after trapeze.

The store is dark, and I fumble with the keys, but eventually the lock clicks open and I enter. The scent of chocolate hits my nose before I've taken two steps.

Inside the studio, I slip on an apron and start the playlist Lara and her band compiled for me – enough music to last me a few hours.

I rip open a bag of milk chocolate buds and spill a portion out onto the marble counter. I forget time as I descend into the ritual – melting then tempering, losing myself in the motions. Despite the sweeping movements, there is a stillness to tempering. It demands obedience to its rules. It is about heat and movement. I have no choice but to pay attention and to work fast. I follow the same routine for small amounts of white, dark and ruby chocolate. My thoughts dissolve through the thickness of my mood. They move from reality to imagination. I have an idea, and it's only here, now, in a studio empty of other people and away from the bustling street and all its stories, that it starts to make sense. I want to play with flavours to create chocolates aligned with tarot cards.

In my mind, I can picture the Major Arcana tarot cards Inez taught me about. A journey that starts with The Fool setting out on a risk-filled adventure, not laden with baggage but still needing a lightness and trust in order to go through the challenges of being human to reach liberation. The Fool – something fruity in white chocolate. The Devil – a hint of chilli in dark chocolate. The Hanged Man – marbled milk and white chocolate sprinkled with rose-gold dust. Milk, white, dark and ruby chocolate combine in a prototype of what would be The Magician. This is the trickiest card to flavour-define because it is the card of mastery. A magician has many talents and abilities, and all the elements at their disposal, hence my decision to incorporate all four types of chocolate.

What seemed like a swirling mess somehow comes together. It could be a box set with a striking cover. I draft a rough sketch on paper of how it might look, regretting my lack of artistic ability.

I'm so caught up in the task that I don't hear the door or the footsteps.

'Sahar?'

I jump and let out a scream. 'Oh my God!'

It's been so long since I've been overcome by such a deep state of creativity that I have to catch my breath, my hand against my rapidly beating heart.

It's Luke and he looks surprised to see me. 'It's after ten. What are you doing here?'

'I lost track of time. I'll clean up and get out of here. Sorry.'

He approaches me slowly. 'You don't have to leave. It's OK, I just wasn't expecting to find you here.'

'I needed to do something with my hands.'

'I was feeling the same.'

We're both quiet as I start to tidy up.

'What are you making?' Luke says.

'It's an idea I have. I wanted to surprise you. But I guess I can tell you now.'

'No. Surprise me,' he says.

The silence following his words feels full, weighted. I've never been good at hiding how I feel, at keeping things below the surface. But I realise I have got much better at pretending. And right now, I need to pretend, because I can no longer deny that Luke is having an effect on me.

Eventually, I stop cleaning and look up to see what Luke is doing. He's standing there, examining the mess on the counter, picking up the print-outs of tarot cards and chocolates. We are so close and I can hear my breath, smell his aftershave.

'Luke, I don't care that you kissed me,' I say. 'Maybe it was a mistake. But I'm not upset.'

Luke finally looks up and we make eye contact, and I search for meaning in his expression. 'I liked it, too, Sahar. But we work together.'

I nod, conceding his point. 'You can have the studio,' I say, my hands flying to my apron.

Luke shakes his head then steps away. 'Do you know what you're saying?'

'I have no idea what I'm doing most of the time. How do you think I ended up being such a mess at this age?'

'You're not a mess,' Luke says.

'I'm filled with pain and sorrow, and everything I do is just an attempt to survive it.'

Luke's eyes are still on me, but he maintains some distance. 'You have to change the shape of it somehow.'

We stare at each other and my insides stretch out in a thin burn. I am the first to look away, then Luke turns and exits the studio. I watch him leave.

When the door has swung closed, ringing the old-school bell, I return my focus to The Magician. I need to finish the prototype so that tonight is not completely wasted.

***

At midnight, my fatigue arrives like an unexpected storm. I have no energy to continue. I think of Maggie and her warnings about staying so busy you can't think. But Luke's appearance has scattered my thoughts.

I feel emotion rise up but I shake it off. I clean up quickly, the music playlist still running. Even in all this confusion, I'm glad to be here; to be feeling so deeply, with such raw emotion. I feel alive, even if I'm also scared and uncertain.

Something else occurs to me. I am using my body and mind in ways I never thought possible. I am finding elements of womanhood I never allowed myself access to. I wonder how long I have hated being a woman, sunk by the anchors of shame and guilt.

I give the studio one final look. We're closed tomorrow, and I don't want to leave it in disarray. When I look up, I see Luke coming tentatively towards the doorway of the studio.

I am both surprised and not at all taken aback. Whatever connection is threading itself between us is taut, intact.

'It's late and I didn't want you to walk home alone,' he says.

'I don't need you to take me home, Luke.' I challenge him with my eyes.

'I find it very hard to be around you,' he says, quiet, hesitant.

'I'm sorry.'

He shakes his head then moves in close. 'Sahar.' Now he's in front of me, his hands cradling my face, his eyes boring into mine.

Luke kisses me softly, tentatively. I reach up and thread my arms around his neck, raising myself to meet his lips as he deepens the kiss. Soon his hands are roaming my body, and that familiar heat runs through me, so intense I can feel a sharp, electric sensation travelling through my fingers.

Luke releases me, but I'm still in his arms. He brushes my hair away from my face, his expression serious, uncertainty marking his features.

'Fuck,' he says. 'Not here.'

***

We go to Luke's apartment. My mind is full as I refuse his offer of tea. I know that if I stop to think, the spell will be broken.

I only take a few minutes in the bathroom to freshen up, splashing water on my face and centring myself.

In Luke's bedroom, I kick off my shoes then drop onto the bed. I lie down, and Luke positions himself beside me, resting on his right arm so that he's raised above me.

He plays with my hair, studying me. 'Are you sure?'

I nod.

'We can go slowly.'

I pull him towards me and Luke kisses me again. He starts at my cheeks, then moves to my forehead before returning to my lips. He continues to kiss me softly before eventually angling himself so that his upper body is above me, his hands finding their way to my face. He is still kissing me as he knots his fingers in my hair.

'Sahar,' he breathes, his forehead against mine, and this moment of intimacy stills me.

He starts to pull away, but my body aches with need. 'No, come back,' I say.

I raise my arms above my head and Luke meets my gaze. I nod and he lifts my top off. His response is instant, a low groan escaping him as he lowers his mouth to my breasts.

He lifts his head to meet my eyes once more and I can see he is no longer uncertain; he wants me. I sit up and our movements become more fervent, my arms wrapped around his neck, the heat in my body rising as he reaches around to unclasp my bra. We don't know each other's bodies yet. This newness, so intoxicating.

Slowly, I think faintly, as we kiss, breathless, excited. *We will go slowly.*

Chapter 23

I can't unbelieve things, but more than one thing can be true at the same time.

I wake up alone in Luke's bed. I grab my phone and see, panicked, that it's morning. Then I remember that I don't have anyone to answer to. Even Lara is out of town.

I slip on my clothing then wash up before heading out to the living room, where Luke is playing with his phone. In the morning light, I see the apartment more clearly – minimalist but with character. The furniture matches, and the kitchen looks well stocked. The room fills with music, and soon a man's voice rings out in the small space, singing of loss. I recognise the song, I just have no idea who it's by. The warm feeling is instant.

Luke comes towards me, a smile on his face. 'Can I have the slow dance from your list?'

A flutter of nerves cascades through my body as I reach out to take Luke's hand. I'm relieved; for a moment I wondered if I would be met by a regretful Luke.

'Are you good at this?' I say.

'No one is good at this. It's slow dancing. We just sway together.'

I move in close and he places my arms around his neck.

'This is the good bit,' he says. 'The leaning in, the bodies touching, the kissing.' His fingers lightly graze my body, then he kisses my neck and I laugh.

'People don't usually laugh,' he says. But I can't stop laughing, and even Luke starts to smile.

'I'm sorry,' I say. 'This is not going well.'

But Luke just closes the gap between us again, placing his hands around my face. He leans in and I feel like I can't breathe. It's surreal, being in his space, seeing him in his ordinary state. His tiny flat – and knowing how little he needs to be content – makes me respect him more.

I place my head against Luke's chest and close my eyes, tuning into the lyrics of the song. They're about separation. The man is expressing sorrow about his actions. It's a song about punishment.

'Who's this?' I ask.

'The National.'

'My friend, Lara, put together a soundtrack for me with her band. This is on it.'

'A soundtrack for what?'

'Recovery.'

Luke nods, and I know he understands. The profound effect of being connected to him right now fills me completely. In this moment, I feel no separation. His hands are around the back of my head, running down my arms, his eyes on me. It's intense and soon he is kissing me again.

Eventually, I detach. He steps back a little and caresses my cheek.

'You OK?'

I nod. 'Are you?'

'I am. But I'm not sure how we do this. At work.'

'We don't have to tell anyone, if that's what you're worried about.'

'I think we just need to take things slowly. I don't want us to get fired. So you might have to lie about who ticked off slow dance with you.'

I laugh. 'Sure. I'll say that bartender taught me.'

'That hurts,' Luke says with an exaggerated sad face.

When the song is over, Luke makes us a breakfast of granola, yoghurt and fruit, and stovetop coffee using a silver moka pot. I tell him that I'm getting used to the capsule coffee that Lara adores, and he shudders.

'You can't be perfect, I guess.'

Luke's espresso reminds me of my Arabic coffee, its bitter flavour and strong fragrance bringing up memories.

'I'll make you an Arab breakfast sometime,' I tell him.

Luke tries to minimise his smile, but he seems excited by the prospect. 'That would be nice.' Then he asks me to stay. 'We have the whole day.'

We fast-forward to the ordinary as we settle on the couch and try to watch a movie. But we're both nervy and wound up, and Luke can't keep his hands off me. Soon, we're entangled on the couch.

We return to the bedroom.

Afterwards, I have no trouble lying beside Luke. I don't mind when he slowly draws me close so that he's spooning me, as if we are not still new to each other and learning each other's secret pathways.

'How many tattoos do you have?' I ask, always fascinated by the choices people make with tattoos.

Luke kisses my neck before moving his mouth to my shoulder. It's comforting to have him so close, to be so unapologetically held and touched. 'One on each of my upper arms. The snake on my right, a quote on my left.'

I swivel around so that we're facing each other. Then I raise myself up to inspect the quote, simply written in italics. '*Ancora imparo.*'

'It means "I am still learning".'

I raise my eyebrows. 'What's the story there?'

'It's a long one. But the short version is: there's no end to what the world can tell you about yourself. And, um, learn from the deep shit you get yourself into.' His body shakes with laughter and I smile, absorbing the words.

'I like it. Did it hurt getting it done?'

'Not really. The more meat, the less it hurts.'

I wonder if I should confess how I lack the courage to get a tattoo myself.

'I have to admit, the reminder helps,' Luke says. He pauses, then scans my face. 'My ex ... got in my head in a way I didn't expect. Not her fault, we just weren't a good match,' he says quietly. 'A relationship can't be your whole world.'

I nod, meeting his gaze. 'Is that why you've been a bit off?'

Luke is silent for a few moments. 'Remember that time you told me you know what it's like to want something that isn't quite right? What you said, and the way you said it ... It was the exact thing I needed to hear at that moment.'

The night at the queer dance party, when Luke walked me home. 'I remember.'

'Sometimes all the things I want to achieve seem bigger than where I'm standing. Does that make sense?'

'You're capable of more. I get it. I worked in a home kitchen for years and it felt huge. Now it would feel tiny.'

Luke's arm still rests on my body, his energy easy, familiar. I touch his cheek, study his lived-in features and blue eyes. 'You are so surprising to me.' He presses his lips gently to my forehead. 'I'm going to sound like a twat, but I think you're beautiful. And special.'

Then he is tracing the scar on my shoulder, the tips of his fingers gently tapping my skin. His hand trails down my side and lands at the second, smaller scar at my hip. I have studied them so many times, awkwardly swivelling around in front of the mirror to examine the contours of both, properly. I know them by heart. As he uses his fingers to softly caress their edges, they feel larger than they are in my mind.

He kisses the scar on my hip then the one on my shoulder at the top and bottom. 'That must have hurt.'

'It looks worse than it is.'

'Do I get to know what caused these?'

I want to tell him. To reveal the past and set it free, because although this could quite possibly be a short-lived affair, I feel the weight of Naeem's memory.

I sit up and take Luke's hand, my heart beating faster as I steel myself. 'You know I worked at refugee camps for a few years. Well, one day, some kids were going for a joyride in someone's minivan. I don't think they were trying to hurt anybody. They were just angry and restless. All these kids getting some vague form of education in these crappy demountables, it would drive anyone mad.'

Luke's touch remains, but he's still, attentive.

'The kids used to wander around. I mean, they were living in the desert, and it was a bit like no-man's land sometimes. The Wild West,' I say with a smile. 'So they behaved like outlaws. Not all of them. But some of them hated what was happening to them. They knew they'd be given a rough deal.'

Luke is silent, but he gently squeezes my arm.

'One afternoon, I heard some commotion. I had no idea what was wrong. The doctor I was with went to investigate, then suddenly...'

The explosion ripped everything apart. I remember how it lit up the space around me, how it sounded, the way time froze, like I was watching it happen in a film, not standing in it. The shape of the world around me bent in unimaginable ways, the frequency of sound shifting until it felt like there was nothing to be heard, and nothing to be felt.

'There was an explosion. It was pretty bad. It happened in winter... Everything was slippery and snowy. It was so cold. The kids ... They'd veered into a truck carrying oxygen tanks for the hospital. It was an accident.'

There were two of them, I was later told.

'Have you ever seen an explosion?' I ask Luke.

He nods once. 'Quite a few, but not too close.' We lock eyes. His hand on my shoulder gives another gentle squeeze. 'How many died?'

'Eight people. Including the two kids.'

'Fucking hell.'

'I never went back after that.'

Everything had changed forever.

***

Luke parks his car outside my apartment building. I feel the need to be polite, so I invite him in. Luke almost snort-laughs. 'I wouldn't do that to you. I recognise a fellow hermit when I see one. I'll see you tomorrow at work.'

He moves in for a kiss, his hand caressing my cheek while he does so. An excited burn rushes through my body and I have to stop him. My forehead meets his with a soft bump and I smile.

Luke waits until I'm safely inside the building, taking off once I give him a final wave.

I am still smiling as I trudge my way up the stairs. My mind is bursting with the events of the last day, my stomach churning in excitement. The burn is familiar, but while there is uncertainty there, it opens up into a field of possibilities rather than one burdened by an immediate dead end. This, I realise, is what hope feels like; a rising storm after a drought. Scary, but in a good way.

When I reach the final step, my smile dissolves as I take in the silhouette of a man seated on the floor outside the door to my apartment. My initial fright gives way to a deeper worry that I am hallucinating. I would know his figure anywhere, but I feel his presence like it's a quantifiable essence. The scent of aftershave reaches me before the man looks up and meets my gaze.

It's Khaled.

His energy is different – he wears his pain. But it is him, in the flesh, and I am in disbelief.

atonement

Chapter 24

The things we do. How we affect each other.

Khaled looks out of place in my kitchen. The shape of him is the same. But he is haunted. It's not his presence that worries me, it's his spirit, the air of sorrow that hangs off him. He is antsy, wandering around like a tourist of the ordinary, his hands fisted at his sides as he traverses the kitchen.

I'm still in my clothes from the day before, stirring a pot of Lebanese coffee at the stove. The scent begins to restore me after the shock of finding my ex-husband at my doorstep. I close my eyes as I think of Luke.

'What's this?' Khaled says in Arabic. He's holding up the napkin with Kat's list of experiences for The Experiment, which I had stuck to the fridge door with a magnet.

'It's just something funny my co-workers came up with,' I reply, also in Arabic.

Khaled is reading it, his eyes slowly following Kat's scrawl down the napkin.

'Slow dance with a man,' he reads, his voice low. His mouth forms a sardonic smile.

My stomach aches as I remember slow dancing with Luke. He would have driven home with a smile on his face.

Khaled returns the list to the fridge, tapping the magnet against it so that the napkin is upside down.

'It was just a bit of fun.' I fix my attention on the pot of coffee. It starts to boil furiously, so I turn down the heat and stir it into submission.

'Where do you work?' Khaled asks.

'At a patisserie cafe and chocolate studio.'

'I see,' he says.

'I like it there. I'm learning a lot.'

Khaled studies me from across the kitchen table. 'You have changed a lot,' he says. 'I almost didn't recognise you.'

'Same.'

'Your hair. You cut it.'

We're both quiet, and I look away. The sound of my spoon against the metal pot is a clunky soundtrack.

I hear the scrape of a chair being pulled out. When I turn around, Khaled is seated, his fingers tracing patterns on the table, his eyes dark.

I switch off the stove, place the pot on a silver tray then locate small coffee cups and saucers. I dig out a small jar of sugar. It feels like a strange offering for this meeting point between two competing worlds. Khaled has only just swept back into my life, but it's startling how much becomes clear. I have, as he put it, changed so much.

'Do you have somewhere to stay?' I say as I search for something sweet. I find a packet of biscuits, rip it open and slide out the tray. I don't bother plating them up.

'I missed you,' he says.

'There are hotels in the city. I can help you book a room.'

'So that's it?'

I pour the coffee, my hand steady. 'We're divorced, Khaled. It's over. I don't understand why you're here.' I regret being so abrupt when I see how he bristles at my words.

He takes the cup of coffee I offer him. 'You wanted the signed papers, didn't you? Not just my words?' He pauses. 'And I have questions.'

He is calm, but this is Khaled's version of serenity. As always, it's about being in control.

'My brother is dead.'

His blunt words rush through me like fire and I wince. But I minimise my reaction. 'I know. I was there.'

'Exactly.'

'*Allah yirhamo.*'

'I'm getting married again.'

I crack a wry smile. I can't help it. '*Mabrook.*'

Khaled is unimpressed. 'Is that it?'

'What would you like me to say? I hope she's everything I wasn't.'

'That won't be hard.'

'Well, for once we're in agreement,' I say, rising from my seat, the coffee and biscuits untouched.

'How could you just leave like that?'

I close my eyes and try to centre myself. Khaled getting married does not surprise me. It's been eight months since my departure. I am not even concerned. He's not like me. I doubt he's laid it all bare and inspected the damage, or turned inward.

I give him my full attention. My eyes on him, I stand tall. 'Can we stop pretending, Khaled?'

'Yes. I want you to tell me the truth.'

'You are not my husband anymore. You divorced me by text, remember?'

'I was angry. It doesn't count.'

'It always counts, Khaled.'

I hear the door open and a few seconds later, Lara calls out to me. She looks startled as she steps into the kitchen. 'Oh. Sorry, am I interrupting?' She looks at Khaled then at me. 'Who's this?'

'I'm her husband,' he says in English.

Lara manages to see the humour in it. 'Not anymore. Did Sahar invite you here?'

'He's just leaving,' I say. I meet Khaled's gaze, fearless but frustrated. 'You have to go. We can talk tomorrow.'

I lead him out, but he stops at the front door.

'I wish you hadn't shown up the way you did,' I say, my arms crossed.

Khaled takes a moment. 'How did I show up, Sahar?'

'Like a storm.'

I close the door and rejoin Lara in the kitchen. She looks worried. 'Bloody hell.'

Then I collapse into the dining chair and exhale several shaky breaths. My hands grip the dining table and I try to clear the mental scenery crowding my mind. Khaled in various stages of grief, never friendly, sometimes needy.

Lara approaches me. 'Are you OK, babe?'

'I think so.' I try to steady my breathing but my entire body is shaking, a shadow of overwhelm hanging above me.

'Should we call the police?'

'He's not dangerous, Lara. Just angry and embarrassed ... and grieving.'

Then I see it: an envelope Khaled has left me. I drag it over to me and inspect its contents. They're in Arabic, but I can read the language well enough to see that they are divorce papers, and Khaled is yet to sign them.

Lara grows impatient. 'Just sign the papers and tell him to bugger off.'

'What if he doesn't sign them?'

'Then we'll find someone who can help you make him.'

'He came all the way from Amman to do something he could have done by mail.'

Lara shrugs. 'People get funny about being the loser in these situations.'

I nod, more settled. 'I had sex with Luke.'

Lara's response is delayed. 'I swear, sometimes I wish I was a drinker.' Then she studies me long and hard. 'OK. Out with it. Every last dirty detail. No more fucking breadcrumbs. What happened?'

'I just told you.'

'Not with Luke. In Jordan. The scars. You haven't told me about the scars.'

'I know. OK.' I lift my eyes to meet Lara's, her face etched in worry.

I already know that I can't give Khaled what he wants: some kind of twisted victory, no matter how bittersweet. We have both lost something irretrievable. Our marriage bombed, but really, it's Naeem's ghost that haunts us both.

Jordan

The seventh year

The refugee camp is bitingly cold, a storm is threatening, and a pregnant woman is bleeding. I am Naeem's assistant for the day, and despite the tense atmosphere, he has been playful up until this point and his presence dims my anxiety. We trudge through deep snow to reach a prefab that would fail to keep a family warm. Outside, we find a little boy waiting, his hands knotted together. Naeem gives him a lollipop and the boy tries to smile.

Inside, a young couple are seated on a thin burgundy mattress, a white sheet across the woman's legs in a nod to propriety. She is on her back, moaning, her feet kicking at the straw mats covering the floor, one hand on her belly. She lets out a piercing scream. Even in the near darkness of the room, I can see the agony on her face. Her husband bends over her in panic.

Naeem's voice drops as he offers her reassuring words. '*Ya sitti,*' he says as a sign of respect, then tries to usher away her terrified husband. Naeem appears calm, but I read the panic in his tightly held body. 'Sahar, we need the ambulance,' he tells me in English. 'Go now.'

I run out of the prefab, my mind stained with the image of the woman, her face drained of colour as she bled onto the mattress, reddening the white sheet. Lost in thought, I trip and fall, my foot collapsing sideways. I yell out in pain but keep going, spurred on by the image of the blood spotting the straw mats like a trail to hell.

Ten minutes later, the woman is being transported to the clinic. Naeem travels with her, and I retreat to his private room. Two hours later, when Naeem returns, I'm stationed on a cot, my knees folded up to my chest, my arms wrapped tightly around them. I am shaking, that woman's nightmare a painful reminder of my own miscarriages. I am still wearing my wet shoes and my clothing clings to my skin. My headscarf sits loosely around my head. Naeem assesses me from the door.

'Take off your shoes,' he says, coming towards me.

I remove my hiking boots and strip off my socks. My ankle throbs. I rub it and Naeem takes hold of my foot to inspect the damage. 'You're swollen,' he says.

He wraps an icepack around my ankle then sits beside me on a plastic chair, the kind that belongs on a patio on a hot summer's day. He rubs his face as though he is trying to scrub the day away. We are both in shock, but I hate to see him in so much pain.

'I don't know why God lets people suffer like this.'

Naeem almost chuckles. 'Do you want a drink?'

I decline, but watch, my body slowly starting to settle, as Naeem rummages around in a steel cabinet. He emerges with a small bottle of dark liquid with no label on it. 'It can help with the shock.'

I decline again with a slow shake of my head. 'I don't want any. You have it.'

He unscrews the cap quickly then drinks straight from the bottle. 'You know, if you stay here, people will talk. I'm not taking patients right now,' he says.

I remain seated, my eyes fixed on the wall, my mind in a place I didn't know existed and I want to laugh. As if I could be worried about what people would say amid such tragedy. Up close, I've witnessed the loss of a wife and mother. I am an ungrateful person to think I ever had it hard as a child.

'I don't care what people say.'

Naeem's eyes pour into mine. A gentle ache rises and expands in my stomach. But he makes no move towards me. I feel unsettled. The cord that runs between Naeem and me is suddenly frayed.

'Why are you doing this?' I say. 'Do I mean so little to you that you can change your mind all the time?'

Naeem's demeanour shifts, and he breaks out of his sullen mood to come closer. He drops into the seat again, his hand searching out my knee. He squeezes it before his head lands between my knees. I run my fingers through his thick, curly hair.

We sit like that for a while, silently unpacking the mess around us and between us.

Eventually, we separate and Naeem removes the icepack. He walks over to the bin, then tosses it inside. It lands with a thud.

My body feels heavy, but I wait for him to turn around. When he does, my face is placid as I search for connection in his eyes; the same eyes that have searched mine so many times.

Naeem hesitates. 'You should get going before they block the roads.'

I scramble off the cot, but as I sweep past him, he takes hold of my arm.

'I'm still a man. I don't think we should be alone anymore. Someone could walk in at any time.'

I nod. 'I wish I'd never met you,' I say.

I go to leave but Naeem's response is instant. He pulls me back and draws me to him. Then he holds on tight as if for the last time.

We kiss, standing there like two lovers lost. It is intense, and timeless. Then we hear the commotion. The crescendo of chaos is jarring; it's a mixture of things – horns blaring, people shouting, a smash. With it, a feeling of immediate panic.

We break apart, dazed. Naeem heads to the door.

The room lights up. There is no sound as the shockwave rips through me. Then everything stops. It is, for a few moments, transcendent. I am powerless, but completely surrendered. Then it becomes real. There is sound again, and it is terrifying in its mass of screams, sirens and invocations. My eyes struggle to stay open amid the chaos. Panic spreads through my body, but I can't move.

I don't know how long it takes me to remember where I am, and who is with me, but as some point I think of Naeem and search for him. I see no one. Then the world turns black.

I wake up in an ambulance. It takes me a while to become fully conscious, but then I remember everything, relive it quietly in my mind. My body awakens to the terror, even though I'm so tired, the flesh around my shoulder ripped open, blood down my side. I can't tell what blood is mine. It feels as if it's my life that has been blown apart, everything I worked so hard to hide blasted into view.

I have no power over karmic punishment.

Chapter 25

Perhaps there is no such thing as good or bad luck. Just good or bad days.

At work the next day, I immediately seek out Luke. I find him in the pantry and I'm relieved because we're alone but for a new junior in the kitchen.

Luke's entire body changes when he sees me. His tense expression softens into a smile. 'Hey.'

I move closer and pull him towards me.

'Are you OK?' he says.

I lean in, suddenly hyper aware of the fragility of our connection, barely constructed. In a moment, Khaled could collapse it all.

No. I am the destroyer. Everything I have kept hidden, once in view, will demolish all that I have built.

I don't respond, but find myself resting my forehead against Luke's. He places a hand to the back of my head then kisses me on my crown.

'What's wrong?' He steps away, resting his hands on my forearms, like he's trying to keep me steady. 'Sahar.'

'I have to tell you something.'

Luke waits but I give him nothing. 'I'm guessing it's not something good?'

'I just don't know where to start.'

Luke is trying to stay neutral; I can see this in the way he studies me, how he stays close, his hands still on me. I move in and give him a hug.

'I'd ask if you're breaking up with me, but this isn't generally how people do it,' he says, trying to lighten the mood. He cracks a smile then brushes away some stray hairs from my face.

'Do you consider me your girlfriend?' I say, knowing this is hardly the point.

'You can tell me anything,' he says. 'But I don't think we should be talking about this in the pantry.'

'After work at your place, then?'

'OK.' Luke hesitates then kisses the top of my head. 'Get back to work,' he says in a mock-stern tone, but I can see he is worried, his body tense as he returns to his task, his face no longer lit up by a smile.

***

I'm on edge all day. I make mistakes with every task I undertake. I stare at my bag, because it contains my phone: the one link Khaled always has to me. Last night I sent him out of the apartment, but I have no idea where he landed.

Khaled's call comes at midday, just as I'm binning a botched tray of maple-glazed cinnamon scrolls. They are my recipe. I know how to make them by heart. They are burnt and bitter.

I escape out onto the street to take the call.

'I'm at a serviced apartment,' Khaled says matter-of-factly, and I realise he had planned ahead. I forgot how wily he can be.

'I'm busy, Khaled.'

The sooner I see him, the quicker he'll leave. I know this, and yet I want to delay proceedings. To cling to normality. Pretend that when I go into the bakery, I can be carefree, share flirtatious looks with Luke, and where my biggest problem will be Kat's disapproval.

'Sahar.'

'Fine. We'll meet tomorrow. I'll message you the details.'

Then I hang up and consider how and where I can end this once and for all.

***

After work, Luke and I share a tense trip in his car back to his apartment, during which I try to formulate my explanation. What do I tell him? What do I owe him? How do I face him again once he has the truth?

I look over and he meets my gaze with a half-hearted smile. He places a hand on my knee and squeezes it, then returns his hand to the steering wheel.

When we reach his apartment, Luke switches on the lights then heads straight to the fridge. He offers to get me a drink. 'I can make you tea, but I'm going to need a beer.'

'I'm fine,' I say. The nerves are crawling through my body, and I don't want to draw this out. I take a seat on the couch and wait. Behind me I can hear Luke's movements in the kitchen. There's the sound of a beer bottle cap being released, a cupboard door being swung open followed by the flip of a rubbish bin lid.

Then he's beside me, taking a seat on the couch but allowing for some distance. He looks so different now that we've been together, and I want to forget I ever said anything and slide into his arms instead. I have never had a Luke before. Only a Khaled and a Naeem. Nothing and too much.

'Would it help if I ask questions?' he says, but his tone has a hint of frustration to it.

'I don't know.'

'What are you afraid of?'

'You won't look at me the same way after I tell you this.'

'Why don't you let me be the judge of that?'

I swallow my nerves and take a deep breath. 'Everything I told you about my time in Jordan is true. But I was in an unhappy marriage. I couldn't have children. I stayed busy by working. And I loved my work.' I turn to face Luke properly. 'The person who got me the job was my brother-in-law.'

I stop. Time seems to dissolve before I steady myself. I don't know how long I sit there, waiting for the moment where it feels safe to release the truth.

'We cared about each other. We didn't have an affair exactly ... but I loved him.' I force myself to look up.

Luke's gaze is focused on something on the floor as he takes in the information.

I feel tears threaten to spill out, but I finally let myself say the words I've been holding onto for so long. 'He died in that explosion.'

'OK,' Luke finally says, like he understands. 'OK.'

'I didn't want to tell you because I'm ashamed, and also because it's in the past. But I think I needed to. And because ... my ex-husband showed up last night.'

Luke's eyes widen but he lets me continue.

'He wants something. I can't bring his brother back, and he and I don't like each other. But he's not going to leave until he's satisfied.'

Luke exhales. As he makes a move, I expect him to get up, but then he surprises me by abandoning his beer bottle and taking my hand. 'Sahar, we're still new here. I don't know when the right time is to talk about something like this. Maybe you didn't need to tell me.'

I flinch. 'I understand.'

'What do you understand?'

'We're new, so better to end it now, right?'

Luke chuckles. 'That's not what I said.'

'You didn't need to, Luke. I can see it in your face.' I release his grip.

He lets out an exasperated sigh. 'Sahar, you've just told me I'm competing with a ghost. I need a minute.'

'You're not competing with him. You're just you.'

Luke smiles. 'But he's still in your head. Still inside you. Right?'

'I'm sorry, Luke. I swear, you weren't an answer to a problem.'

'I don't want you to be sorry. I just want you to be OK. Do you need help with your ex?' Luke is still here, making space for me. His hands find mine again.

'No. I know him. He'll tire himself out. I should go,' I say, scrambling out of my seat.

'You don't have to,' Luke says. He sweeps past me before I can reach the door. 'Stay.'

'After all that?'

But then Luke's hands, warm and soft, are brushing away the hair from my face, and his unwavering gaze remains on me. 'I told you, Sahar. It's a lot to take in, but I wasn't telling you to go.'

Relief fills me up and I move into his arms. Soon enough, his lips are on mine, his hands sweeping down my body.

***

I wake to a dark room, a sliver of moonlight casting a silvery glow through the bedroom window. I'm beside Luke in his bed. I check my phone. It's late, almost eleven.

I have three messages from Khaled. I worry that he's been by the apartment, but my fears are assuaged when I see I have no messages from Lara.

Like a thief, I get out of bed and slip into my clothes. Thankfully, Luke doesn't stir.

At the door to the bedroom, I take one last look at him then I quietly gather the rest of my things from the living room and carefully open the front door.

I am not going to drown myself in regret, but I have no business being here, trying to stop the inevitable destruction.

The facade built in haste will crumble quickly. But I can stop it from hurting Luke.

***

I come into work extra early on Monday and head straight to Maggie's office by appointment.

Maggie indicates for me to sit, but I stay where I am, arms crossed.

'Sahar, what is it?' she says, kind but also curious.

'I need a couple of days off, Maggie.'

'I see. Including today?'

I nod. 'Yes. There's something I need to handle and I think it's going to cause some issues if I'm at work.'

The idea of Khaled turning up here fills my mind, but it's not an unrealistic possibility. I can see it happening; an ordinary day in the bakery, and he appears at the door of the kitchen, ready to disrupt my life.

'Just a couple of days. I'm sorry, Maggie, I'm—'

'In recovery. I know.' She maintains her steady gaze, her eyes warm, concerned. 'Are you in any sort of danger?'

'No. I don't think so.'

This hardly appeases Maggie. She clasps her hands together on her desk. 'Take longer, Sahar. Even if you think you don't need it. Take the week at least.' With a sigh, she rises from her seat to come towards me. She envelopes me in a hug and it's too much. The loving act threatens to set me off, but I can't detach and I begin to sob quietly in her arms. It feels like minutes have elapsed when I finally extricate myself.

Maggie places her hands on my shoulders. 'You came in here all those months ago ready to turn everything upside down. You'll have that fire again, Sahar. You'll see.'

'Thank you, Maggie.'

'I want you to check in with me. And we're going to check in with you.'

***

I leave Maggie's office red-eyed and emotional. In the kitchen, Kat, Inez and Luke are gathered at his counter. The moment I appear, Kat and Inez make their way towards me.

'Fucken hell,' Kat murmurs, pulling me into a rough embrace.

'You're not leaving, are you?' Inez says, and I shake my head.

'I just need to sort some things out,' I say. I look up and see Luke watching me, his face full of confusion.

When they release me, Luke steps forward. 'Can I talk to you alone?'

I farewell Inez and Kat and follow Luke out of the kitchen. He leads me to the chocolate studio. It feels strange to be here with him. Our entire relationship was built in this space. It's the first place I ever saw him, the first time I watched him at work and fell in love with his abilities.

I feel numb, unsure what to say. But then Luke pulls me in for a hug and it's not asking anything of me. I can sense it in the way he holds me. Tears spring to my eyes again, and I feel safe but also guilty. I had Luke under false pretences. He has every right to hate me, but instead, he's taking care of me.

I pull away.

He looks down at me. 'Why did you leave like that?'

'Because I shouldn't have stayed. I was just confusing things more.'

'Don't I get a say in that?' When I don't respond, he lowers his voice. 'Don't go.'

'I'm sorry, Luke. I have to sort this out.'

Luke shakes his head. 'Let me help you. You don't have to do this alone.'

But I do. When I don't respond, Luke moves away. 'I guess I'll see you when you're back, then.'

I nod. My mind sweeps longingly to our recent union, our bodies entwined.

For a stretched-out moment, my past is buried. I can't bear to leave him like this, so I move towards Luke and he wraps his arms around me.

'I'm so sorry,' I tell him.

'Me too.'

I start to walk away, Luke's hand still attached to my arm. Eventually he has to let go, but the look on his face almost makes me change my mind.

The moment I leave the bakery, I feel like I can finally breathe. My departure felt like a goodbye. It wasn't. I can't imagine not returning. Everything I have worked so hard to achieve, and now Khaled's presence has threatened to shatter it all.

It is not an illusion, I tell myself. All of this, no matter how quickly I tried to put it together, means something.

I walk down King Street and dial Leo.

Chapter 26

Control on the way down.

It's approaching sunset, and the sky is a glorious watercolour of orange and pink. Khaled is waiting for me outside Musicale. He's dressed well for the occasion: tailored pants and a dress shirt. He looks like a young Arab bachelor, the type Dina used to make fun of when we frequented Abdoun to smoke shisha and spy on her latest love interest.

I feel a pang of remorse for the loss of my relationship with her. The possibility that she exists in the world hating me physically hurts. But I understand why she hasn't made contact. She was always the one who saw the truth of things, and I hope that even now, amid tragedy and loss, she can spiral to the heart of what has transpired.

'We couldn't do this at your place?' Khaled is speaking in Arabic again. His English is strong, almost American because of his education, but he carries more weight speaking his mother tongue.

I remember now. This is what he did when we were married: pushed me to speak in English so that he could improve, but when he was unhappy, I had to learn his language.

I reply in English. 'There's no way I'm going to be alone with you, Khaled.'

His eyes light up in anger. 'Have I ever laid a hand on you?'

'I'm not worried you'll get violent.'

'What then?' he says in contained fury.

I don't answer, waiting for his emotions to fizzle out. I trail past him and knock on the door. I provide the password, and the door swings open.

'You OK?' Leo gives me a cautious smile.

I nod. 'Thank you for letting me use the space.'

'I'll be out of your way, but on standby.' He gives me a look and I nod again. Really, I want to hug him, but Khaled will think I'm only doing it to provoke him.

'Come on,' I say, and Khaled follows me in, Leo maintaining some distance behind us.

The room is empty and dimly lit. Instruments and microphone stands line the stage. I lead Khaled to a small table in the middle of the room. Out of the corner of my eye, I see Leo signal to me then disappear into the kitchen.

Khaled is unimpressed. 'I come all the way here and this is where you bring me? So you're a drinker now?'

'I'm not. But you're one to talk.'

He chuckles. 'I forgot how smart you are.' He drapes an arm around the back of the seat. He is a good-looking man, dripping in the kind of confidence most people only dream of having. 'Can we at least get a drink, then?' He looks to the bar.

'What are you doing here, Khaled?'

'You know what I want.'

'I have no idea.'

His eyes bright, Khaled cracks a smile like he knows a secret, then leans towards me. 'I used to think there was no way you were really so innocent. No one's that sheltered. Now I know you're a good actress.'

'OK, Khaled.'

'Do you think I'm stupid?'

'I think you're a lot of things. But you're not stupid. Just selective.'

'Meaning?'

'Ignorance is bliss.'

'I wasn't ignorant. Did you fuck him?'

My breath catches in my throat. I raise my head to face Khaled, to look him in the eyes. 'I didn't sleep with him. But I did love him.'

Khaled sucks in a breath. His eyes grow dark. 'You were still acting like a slut. What do you think people are saying about you? What do you think they're saying about him? Who comes out looking the best, do you think?'

'I can only imagine what people must be saying about you, Khaled.'

Khaled's voice is a furious whisper, but it's getting louder. 'Do you really think he loved you? You were a novelty to him. Magda spat him out when she saw what he was. A dreamer. Some big-shot doctor who wanted to save the world.'

'You're upset. I understand. But I wasn't the right wife for you,' I say, my own anger now rising. 'You didn't even care about me. Why did you let me come? Why did you make me stay? You're so fucking proud!'

Khaled tries to stare me down, but long-held resentment is boiling within me, and my words are finally tumbling free.

'Do you think I was happy? Do you think I enjoyed being ignored by you? The only time you looked at me was when you wanted to fuck me.'

'God damn that mouth of yours, Sahar.'

'I would curse the day I met you. The only thing that stops me is that if I hadn't met you, I wouldn't have met your brother.'

Khaled jolts and knocks over the vase in the centre of the table. He's breathing deeply, but I'm not afraid of him. It's not Leo's hulking presence, nor the comfort of an empty, forgiving space. It's the removal of the mask, at last. I no longer need to pretend. I have grown too much to go back.

Still. I know my part in this, and I train my gaze on Khaled. 'If Naeem could still be alive and the price was that I never get to see him again, I swear to God I would want him to be alive. I'm not going to make excuses for what happened between us. It wasn't right, but I couldn't stop it.'

A few tears unexpectedly but rapidly spill from my eyes. Khaled's anger dies down. Now he is morose.

'I'm sorry for my part,' I tell him. 'I never intended to make trouble for you or your family.'

Khaled's energy slowly thins out – it's not soft, but the edges of his emotions are now blunt instead of sharp and ready to cut into me. He plays with the overturned vase, his eyes downcast. I wait for the next onslaught, but instead he breaks down into tears.

I don't know what to do. But as I watch him sobbing, his body shaking, his breath coming short and sharp, I realise I have to do something. The release is painful. It physically hurts. I know from experience.

I move my seat closer to him and tentatively extend a hand towards him.

Khaled grabs my hand, then turns and leans into me, and I find myself allowing it. I can barely contain him in my arms.

'He's gone,' Khaled sputters.

I close my eyes, the tears spilling freely down my cheeks. Khaled and I, finally in connection, linked by the spirit of someone we both loved.

***

Afterwards, we sit at the bar where Khaled drinks his sorrow. I stick to water.

We occupy tall stools beside one another at the counter in an oddly comfortable silence. Both of us are emptied out, the past finally exhumed.

I feel lighter. Not good. Not happy. My sorrow runs deep and in different directions, but this moment with Khaled feels like a cosmic correction. At the very least, a necessity.

'What made you ask for me in the first place?' I say to him. 'It's obvious I'm not your type.'

Khaled smiles into his brandy. 'The woman I loved found someone else. So I did too.' He meets my eyes. 'I found someone who was the complete opposite of her.'

'Right.' I let out a short laugh. 'So I was a consolation prize.'

He shakes his head. 'When I saw you at the wedding, you looked beautiful. And you were respectable and polite. I wasn't expecting the person who arrived a year later.'

'I didn't think I'd be living in Amman for eight years. Call it even.'

'I told myself that we'd be the same in real life as we were on the phone. But it's harder to hide when you're in front of someone.'

I raise an eyebrow. 'Hide what? Your lack of interest?'

Khaled stares ahead, contemplative. 'Hide who you are and what you want.'

Energy doesn't lie.

We're not looking at each other. We both face a wall of wine and spirits. Behind the shelves is a mirror, but the wooden slats obscure our reflections in the dark. We look like monsters.

I hear Khaled take a gulp of his drink then place the glass down.

'Do you think if I'd been more confident, you would have loved me?' I ask this despite not caring about the answer. Perhaps I just want to feel better about how things unfolded. A simple affirmation that I didn't stand a chance.

Now he looks at me and I turn to face him. I hold his gaze.

'I don't know,' he says. 'I don't know why you said yes to me.'

'I didn't think about it. I prayed *istikhara* then pushed ahead.'

'Did you do it wrong?' Khaled says, and even I have to smile at that.

But then, I met Naeem.

'I always thought you should have been with someone like Magda,' I say.

Khaled's eyes darken a little. 'My brother didn't know what he had.'

These small confirmations are what I need to finally sever my cords to the past. I didn't imagine my awful marriage. I didn't transform Khaled in my mind into someone he wasn't as an excuse. Even now, as I look at him – unkempt but attractive, confident and strong – I understand the reasons for my initial choice. I felt powerless in life, so I said yes to someone who seemed all-powerful. Strangely, it is an aura that remains despite his heartbreak and vulnerability.

'I liked your hair long,' he says.

'I know. But I didn't cut it because of you.'

***

The night spirals into some strange forgiveness process. After assuring Leo that I am safe, Khaled and I walk down King Street together. We end up at a park with a graveyard that appears haunting in the orange glow of the streetlamps, our breath puffing in the chilly night air. The sky above seems the darkest kind of black, but the moon, sitting among a thin sprinkling of stars, offers a faint light.

We sit on a concrete slab and stare at the graves. Khaled is tipsy, but it hasn't made him mean. If anything, he seems subdued.

'My father visits Naeem every day,' he says.

I think of my visits to my parents' graves, how much I unload each time I go; how I seek to communicate with their spirits in a concealed realm. Was I visiting Naeem, too, in those moments? Not for the first time, I wonder if they are witnesses to my indiscretions. Do the dead see all, and if they can, do they care? What would Naeem think of my time with Luke? Does he feel easily replaced or betrayed?

Khaled pulls out a packet of cigarettes and extends it to me. We make eye contact and I sense it's a meaningful offer. I take a cigarette and he lights it up for me, then does the same for himself.

I bum-puff, not wanting to inhale the smoke.

'My mother is on medication,' he says.

I close my eyes. 'It will get easier.'

'She'll get distracted when things start moving again.'

'Like when you get married.'

Khaled shrugs. 'And Dina. She's getting too old to do what she does. She makes everyone nervous. They'll scare her into getting married. It's not fun being a spinster in an Arab country.'

'If anyone can manage it, it's Dina.'

'I don't think she cares. She's a closed book. Opens up when she pleases.'

'Does she hate me?'

'No one hates you, Sahar. They don't even know what really happened.'

I look up, startled. 'How is that possible?'

'I told them we're divorced because I ended it. I want kids and all that.'

'But I never said goodbye to them.'

'They put it down to you being too shy and embarrassed to face them.'

'They must know there's more.'

'Maybe. But they're in a hole. They don't care.'

We drop into silence, smoking, sore, strangely connected.

***

Khaled leaves the next day. Outside his serviced apartment, we stand apart, the energy between us transformed even if it's not warm. At least it's real. It feels better this way.

He hands me the signed divorce papers. 'I have something else for you,' he says, pulling out a paper bag from his backpack.

I hold the parcel in my hands and detect immediately that it's a book.

'I had to clean up Naeem's things,' Khaled says. 'I found this. It had your name in it a couple of times.'

Tears spring to my eyes as I rip open the bag to find a battered copy of Naeem's Mahmoud Darwish book in Arabic, complete with notes in the margins. I struggle to hide my shock and pain. The meaning to this gift, so layered and complex.

'Thank you,' I say, trying to keep myself steady. I wonder if, despite the anger and the meanness, Khaled came here not to punish me. He knew, like me, that no new beginning would be whole without this complex but necessary excavation. He thought he was right, in the same way I have justified my place in events. But perhaps now, instead of regret there is acceptance. There is relief. I'm grateful that we had a chance to inspect the remains of our story. I have reached a point that I cannot return from: acceptance that Naeem is gone for good, and with him, some part of myself.

'Your family were good to me. I'm glad you told them you divorced me on your own.'

Khaled nods slowly, his eyes examining me.

'I'll tell them something more truthful. That we both want to start again. And that you're where you belong. You were never at home in Amman.'

I exhale and look up to see Khaled watching me, disappointment drawing down his features.

I'm surprised by the flood of emotions that follow. Tears continue to spill out of my eyes, but I wipe them away, my face stiff with the effort not to cry.

'I hope you get your new beginning,' I tell him. 'It's possible.'

I know it was for me.

***

That night, I go to trapeze alone for the first time. I don't overthink it. I simply do. I can manage the pikes with a level of ease, and I can shimmy my way onto the bar without assistance. It's only when I'm up there that the reality of what just transpired dawns on me, and for a moment, I lose my grip and I think I'm about to fall.

recovery

Chapter 27

My road winds and curves ahead, and I experience vertigo, unsettled yet so alive to the feeling.

I'm grateful that Maggie insisted I take time off. I would be useless in the bakery. I feel ungrounded, restless, a bit lost. At home, I lie on the couch and inspect Naeem's book, trace the handwriting, breathe in the pages, yearning for any hint of the *oud* that he used to wear.

Mahmoud Darwish was like Naeem's guide to life, a passport to another world of possibility that fuelled his hunger for a just, meaningful existence.

I finally look at Naeem's photo, the only one I have, hidden away in a random folder on my phone. The American journalist who took it favoured candid shots. He captured Naeem's essence, even from a distance: his smile and warmth as he tended to a male patient; the way his whole body seemed to expand with awareness because he had a purpose.

Sometimes I think that Naeem was an illusion – an intoxicating, comforting way to survive a problematic marriage; a passionate, wild fantasy. A towering presence who kept me alive when everything inside of me was threatening to die. He was life in an arid landscape.

My phone lights up with messages throughout the day. Samira sends me a disaster report about her kids. Inez sends me a photo of something she's working on in the bakery, then one of her posing provocatively on the lyra at the academy. Kat says the least but packs her brief message with the most meaning.

I have a new idea for our wog cakes. Stop bludging and come back.

Luke does not send me a message.

Leo calls. 'Maybe it's time to get that tattoo: when it all feels shitty and the world seems mean.'

'I don't trust my judgement right now, Leo.'

'You get tired of grief, sweetheart. It wears you out. It has a point until it doesn't.'

When Lara arrives home in the early afternoon, she inspects me, still on the couch with Naeem's book, my eyes red and my body sore. 'I was waiting for this to happen,' she says. 'I'll let you wallow for a bit, but I'm watching.'

I take another day off. My phone goes silent and I'm grateful for the peace. Outside, the sky is a dark grey, and the wind is blowing through the trees, creating a natural soundtrack that is both punishing and comforting at once. I pass the day doing very little but listening to music and snacking on chocolate. I flip through a tarot guidebook from a deck of Lara's, and relive my evenings with Luke.

I am in my pyjamas and thick woollen socks, ready to settle in for a night of more of the same, when Samira arrives with two large pizzas and a surplus of energy.

'Enough,' she says, and Lara agrees.

Ten minutes later, Inez and Kat arrive with a box from Maggie's.

'*Habib,*' says Kat, inspecting my appearance.

Inez ushers me towards the bathroom. 'I bought you a bath bomb. Lara said you have a tub.'

'You can't come out for at least fifteen minutes,' Lara yells from the kitchen.

Inez draws a bath and I watch, quiet and a little frustrated at the forced interruption.

'It's nice of you to come by, but I do take showers.'

Inez unwraps a colourful bath bomb – bright pink and blue with glitter – then tosses it in. 'My grandmother told me no problem feels the same after a proper bath.'

I undress, watching as the ball starts to fizz, the colour inking its ways across the surface of the water. The room fills with steam and sound, and a zesty aroma stings my nose.

Inez helps me out of my shirt then dumps it on the floor. I strip off the rest of my clothing, not at all worried about my modesty.

'I brought you my new cake,' Inez says, her smile bright. 'Well ... a prototype. It's a vegan chocolate and strawberry take on madeira with pink frosting. You're going to love it.'

Stepping into the bathtub, I force a smile. Inez's eyes follow me and I see her gaze trail the scars.

'Are you upset that we're here?' she asks gently.

'No,' I say. 'Just a bit embarrassed.'

She turns off the taps and suddenly it's quiet. I can hear the girls chatting and laughing in the kitchen.

'I missed you at trapeze,' she says, sitting on the toilet lid. 'Amber said you managed the pikes all by yourself last time you went in.'

Without warning, I start to cry, a gentle sobbing, staggered release of pent-up emotion. 'I'm sorry,' I tell her. 'I feel like I've let everyone down. But it's like something took the wind out of me.'

Inez fixes me with a sympathetic look. 'You did such a good job of keeping your grief below the surface, you had no idea how it showed.'

'I was just trying to get on with things.'

I think of Maggie sitting me down early on in my time with her, lecturing me on the dangers of staying so busy you don't have time to think.

'We've all been there in different ways,' says Inez. '*Not* that I'm trying to minimise your grief. I know you went through something big. But we've all got sorrows and regrets. We've all had to say goodbye to things we've lost before we were ready to.'

'I feel so stupid.'

'You're not stupid. Just stubborn.' Inez softens. 'Even now, you're focused on how it looks. Just allow it, Sahar.'

'I can't. It hurts too much. It physically hurts.'

'You're not alone, honey. This is aftershock. You're coming back down to Earth. But you've come a long way.'

I nod. 'I think too much.'

'Well, I don't think you of all people are going to be able to quieten the mind. But you have to be careful about painting over the cracks you know are there. It doesn't fix the problem.'

I take in her words, studying the soapy neon bathwater. There's something more I need to know. 'How's Luke? I'm assuming he wasn't invited tonight.'

Inez gives me a strange look, then rearranges her expression to something more neutral. 'I don't know, same old Luke. Always busy at work. But he's more distant than usual. And no, he wasn't invited. Kat and I reached out to your friends.'

Before she can tell me anything more, Kat pops her head in. 'Just checking in. We all think it's a bit weird that Inez is watching you have a bath. Just saying.'

Kat's deadpan expression is enough to break me out of my moment of sorrow, and despite the tears marking my face, I shake with laughter.

Inez reaches an arm around me and kisses me on the cheek. 'I could do much worse, thank you very much.'

***

We have dinner together. I'm the meeting point between two sets of friends, who in strange ways seem to mirror each other. Inez and Samira are warm and dedicated, full of life, and spurred on by their rich imaginations. Lara and Kat are the truth-tellers, the rebellious ones who are fiercely loyal and passionate about everything.

'I have to say, I was a bit put out that you had friends besides Samira and me,' Lara says. 'But then they kept checking in on you and they brought dessert, so they must be all right.'

I smile, a bit sheepish. 'I'm sorry I've been such a drag.'

Lara crosses her arms and fixes me with a stern look. 'I'm not bloody surprised you're having a moment. How do you get better if you pretend nothing's wrong?'

'I wasn't pretending. I was trying to move forward.'

Lara lightens her stance. 'Look ... Do what you have to do, but my wedding's in two weeks and I still need your help so that it's not crap.'

'You know you don't even need to ask,' I say.

'I clearly do. Also, since you've become an expert in chocolate, I was hoping you could do bonbonnières. Samira would buy sugared almonds for sure.'

'Well, excuse me for trying to inject some tradition into your special day!' Samira says in a miffed tone.

'I'll do make-up!' Inez says with a little clap, like she's calling out an answer on a game show. 'I mean, if you need someone.'

Lara studies Inez's make-up. 'I don't have any hair and make-up booked. So if you can make me look like you, then yes, please.'

Inez and I look at Kat, who momentarily feigns innocence, then she sighs. 'Ah fucken hell. Fine. If you need someone to do your hair, I can help you out.'

Lara beams. 'I was just asking for bonbons, but sure.' Then she looks at me. 'And Sahar is making my cake,' she says a little fiercely, like the fate of the world depends on it.

I'm still sorting through the wreckage, but as I look around the room, I realise something profound. My friends are here. And there it is: a glimpse of my true foundation, the thing that holds me in place no matter the weather.

Chapter 28

Belief does not disappear, it changes shape.

The next day, I wake up feeling revived. I'm keen to get moving again, to return to the things I abandoned in haste. The gym. Trapeze. My chocolate tarot box. Luke.

I'm not sure where I stand with Luke, or how things will be when I return to work next week. I'm tempted to find out, but instead I reorientate my focus onto what I need right now: to take advantage of this small but significant opportunity to finally declutter both my belongings at my parents' house, and the possessions I have with me.

I start with the apartment. I don't have much, but I discover Kat's original list for The Experiment. There, at the bottom, like it was an afterthought, in Kat's messy handwriting are the words: 'Learn how to swim', beside it an illustration of a mermaid.

***

My parents' house sits on a quiet suburban street in south Sydney. We're close to the beach here, but despite its sundrenched streets and palm trees, it doesn't quite have a seaside feel to it. It's old-school Sydney: multicultural, populated, not poor but not dripping in wealth either.

Still, I can see that newly renovated houses pocket the street. There are more cars, and they are shinier. The worn-out migrant experience I was raised in has been spun into something less definitive. I wonder if any Arabs occupy the area at all now.

The house looks different, but in the grey light of the afternoon sun it's clear that some things remain intact: the cracked white paint, the rusted mailbox, the peeling house number. I brace myself, with Lara and Samira standing either side of me. Empty of its inhabitants, the house strangely appears smaller, deprived of stories to fill its rooms, bereft of energy to keep it humming.

Inside, it's not as musty as I thought it would be, but the air is stale, and with the blinds half-drawn, dust blankets the space in a haze of particles. There are no ghosts here, but it feels haunted. There's a heaviness in the air. If I could light it up to show hidden worlds, what invisible beings would appear?

We lift the blinds and throw open the windows in every room.

The living room appears as I last saw it – off-white leather couches, a wooden coffee table, framed Islamic calligraphy on the walls. Then I notice the television is gone, and something's not quite right in my mother's crockery buffet. There are pieces missing, but it looks deliberate.

I ache. The pain is physical. I wasn't expecting it to strike me with such force, but a quiet urgency builds with each step I take. I touch the walls, reach out for my mother's scent, search for a memento of my father. The emotions don't produce tears; instead, they feel stuck, lodged somewhere between the crown of my head and my heart. Despite our challenges, I was safe and protected here. I was loved, even if it didn't feel loving all the time.

'This place is giving me the heebie-jeebies,' Lara says, wrapping her arms around herself.

In the bedrooms, I find several boxes neatly stacked but with no markings to indicate what's inside. Our lives, shuttered and farewelled without ceremony.

In the kitchen, with its large adjacent dining space, are more boxes. I stem the melancholy crowding my senses. I hear the sound of memories – laughter and women speaking over each other. The sounds of joy and belonging.

I use my key to rip open a box and gasp when I realise these are my things, carefully packed as though they have been awaiting my return. I flip open the lids to reveal cake tins of different sizes and an assortment of baking tools, all packaged in plastic. I remember wrapping the items before I left for Jordan, but the boxes must be from my mother. I thought she'd given away all my things as I'd instructed.

'Wow,' says Lara, coming up beside me. She crouches down to sit next to me on the tiles. 'Hoorah for hoarder mums.'

Mama was always an efficient woman, so this neat hoarding takes me by surprise.

I scramble to my old bedroom. A *dua* for a happy home, which I printed out and placed on the door to my room, remains stuck there, its edges browned, the black print bleeding into a faded yellow background. I touch it and a half-smile forms. It's like navigating an abandoned place, its residents having left in haste. A museum of a past life.

Inside, there are only a few boxes stacked on top of my double bed. In the wardrobe, I find a few of my old *abayat,* the ones I left behind thinking my stay in Jordan would be temporary. Running my fingers across them, I close my eyes in memory. I had seen marriage as a graduation in piety, and had fully intended to dress more conservatively.

I open my eyes and pull one of the robes out. There's mould on the shoulder pads, the result of years of neglect.

Samira and Lara crowd the doorway. 'I have to clean all of this out,' I tell them, already pulling at the dresses and throwing them onto the bed.

Lara removes an *abaya* from my hands and replaces it carefully in the wardrobe. 'Why don't we just take this one step at a time?'

I sense grief in the air, an anguish that haunts us all, but I can take it. It will feel odd clearing out these things, like I'm completely erasing that old version of myself in the process. I'll hold her up against my body and see how she fits. I already know she's too small for me in every way.

***

Together with Lara and Samira, I search through the boxes in the kitchen to see what can be salvaged. I want to create a home kitchen when I move into a new apartment. I have cherished my time with Lara, but I'm looking forward to having my own space for the first time in my life.

My business inventory is wedged between my library of books and trinkets from my younger years: things

Mama later packed up but without any order to them. I am misty-eyed but I do not cry.

Lara rises noisily from her spot and gently squeezes my shoulder as she goes in search of her phone. 'Music. We need music.'

'And chocolate,' says Samira, reaching over to her bag. 'I brought Snickers.'

We murmur between ourselves as we continue the stocktake, occasionally stopping to add items into one of three piles: cake tins and baking trays; decorating tools; miscellaneous. My book of recipes is intact, even though the pages are yellowed around the edges. Beneath it are books filled with orders I carried out for customers, with notes in the margins.

Occasionally, we find some clothing or pyjamas that have lost their elasticity, faded items from a glory box my mother assembled for me before I was even engaged. Lara gasps at a small box containing over-the-top lingerie that I didn't know even existed. I add a pile for rubbish.

Two hours in, Samira goes to answer the door. As always, pizza.

'Hot, hot, hot,' Samira yelps, dropping the boxes onto the counter. 'Ah crap, we don't have plates.'

'I'm sure we do somewhere.'

I find some in the cupboard and give them a quick rinse. Then we fashion a space on the floor of the kitchen, using a rug as protection against the cold tiles. The dining table, so central to our catch-ups in the kitchen when we were young, is noticeably missing.

'You know, when I said I wanted to do something special pre-wedding, this wasn't exactly what I had in mind,' Lara says. She rips out a slice of pizza and throws it onto a plate. 'I probably shouldn't be eating this, but honestly, I don't think it'll make a difference at this point.'

'Are we waxing you as per tradition?' Samira jokes.

'Has someone given you the talk about what to expect on your wedding night?' I say.

'Shut the fuck up,' Lara says, but she's happy.

Life is a spiral. We revisit the same things, but from a higher perspective. Ten or so years ago, we sat in my mother's kitchen helping Samira work through a romantic dilemma – she thought she had lost Menem when Hakeem showed interest and she blinked.

Her situation was different to mine. But there's an emotional symmetry to the moment when Lara prods me for information about Luke.

'We haven't spoken,' I say. 'I'm not sure what it's going to be like when I go back to work.'

Lara bites her lip. 'I'm sorry, babe.'

I sigh. 'I can't be mad at him. I'm the one who walked away.'

'What happened?' Samira queries. She knows of Luke, but it's Lara I spend the most time with and confide in about men.

'I told him the truth,' I say. 'That my sort-of-ex-husband showed up to confront me about Naeem. But you know, it was after we'd slept together.'

'You slept with Luke?' Samira whips her head around to face me.

'Not the important point right now, Samira,' says Lara, but she bites back a smile. Then she gives me a sly look. 'I didn't ask before because you seemed really upset, but how was it?'

'Lara!' Samira shakes her head as she pulls out another slice of pizza. 'Are we really having this conversation?'

'I'm just curious. I mean, your husband was the worst.' Then Lara remembers herself. 'Sorry. That wasn't cool.'

'Well, you know...' I play with my food. 'He was different. In a good way. It helped that we actually like each other.'

Samira's eyes widen, her mouth full. 'Oh my God. Are we comparing our sex lives now? Is that what we're doing?'

'We're not comparing,' says Lara. 'Gawd. Did he faint when he saw your boobs?'

'No, but he stayed there a while.'

'I give up,' Samira laments.

Then my smile fades. 'Is it awful that I live like the past never happened? I never mourned Naeem. I never honoured him outside of my mind. I feel like I cheated him out of being mourned properly because I had to pretend nothing had happened.'

'You were in that explosion, too,' says Samira, her face drawn.

'It's going to sound crazy, but when I think about it, all I can see is what the explosion did to him. Like it didn't really happen to me; I watched it happen to someone else.'

Lara and Samira are both quiet.

'I know they're ugly, but I like my scars. I swear, if I didn't have them, I worry I'd find a way to forget.'

'Can you understand Luke's perspective, then?' Lara says. 'How does he compete with that?'

'He can't.'

'He's not supposed to,' Samira says. 'Do you think you had one chance at love and now it's over?'

'Luke isn't really an option right now,' I say. 'Honestly, I think I should move on.'

'But you really like him, don't you?' Lara says, leaning in closer.

'I do. But this is what happens when I try to do normal.'

'Babe, this *is* normal. Even Samira's love-life was crap before she got over herself.'

'Hey!' Samira kicks Lara in the leg.

Lara continues, unperturbed. 'I mean, her story was definitely more romantic comedy than drama. But still. She had hiccups.'

Samira shrugs her agreement. 'True. Menem stopped speaking to me for a while, remember? I mean, he's Muslim but he was always untraditional, so I think I did his head in with my insecurities. Luke probably has no idea what a Muslim woman has to deal with. This is easy for him.'

Lara nods. 'And it probably doesn't help that he's intense like you.' She contemplates for a moment. 'I think I'm more midday movie. Sahar is "based on a true story" drama, what with refugee camps and whatnot. I'm telling you, embrace it. It's the only way.' When I don't respond, she studies me. 'You're feeling guilty, aren't you?'

I shake my head. 'Not guilty. Just ... icky.' I could have come back and slept with a man just because, but I never did. I was intimate with someone

I genuinely have feelings for. So why does it feel so bad?

'A lot is happening at once,' Lara says. 'But you haven't done anything wrong. You were getting to know someone.'

Samira clears her throat. 'While I have evidently become the Sahar of the group, and I am quietly repenting on your behalf, Lara is right. You should talk to Luke. At least then you'll have an answer. I sucked it up and it worked out pretty well.'

I warm at the memory of lying in bed with Luke, of slow dancing with him in the intoxicating haze of early attraction. The amount of trust he had earned was immense for me to be able to do all of that and not wake up in a cloud of shame. He was gentle and loving and showed a desire I had only ever seen play out in my mind.

'Enough about me,' I say. 'How are we going to celebrate Lara getting over herself?'

'Ha!' Lara abandons her pizza in order to tackle me. But it's not long before it's a group thing.

***

Two days later, I'm at the academy with Samira, preparing for one of two things I have to do before I return to Maggie's. Samira has a weighty tripod, a large shade and an impressive camera with a fancy flash. My instructor, Amber, and some of the regulars, including Inez, are with me. Samira says it will be more dramatic to have a few people present, but she is focused on me.

I stretch while Samira sets up. I can't help but be impressed as I watch her work.

When it's time, I get up and head to a trapeze swing beside Inez. 'Is here OK?' I ask, tying up my hair.

'Yes.' Samira takes a test shot then twists her mouth. 'But do you mind keeping your hair out?'

I take my place behind the swing. 'It's not very practical.'

Samira is already clicking away with a remote, making adjustments as she goes. 'But it's more photogenic.'

I leave my hair out.

Amber guides us onto our swings and I move into position. As I progress into the movements, I am pleased by the improvement in my ability. When I drop into a half-angel, I can see the expression of gentle surprise on Samira's face.

'What's this called?' Samira says, clicking away.

'A half-angel.'

Samira chuckles. 'I wonder what a full one looks like.'

***

Leo is helping me complete one of the final items of The Experiment. Tomorrow I return to work, so he insists we celebrate with dinner at an Italian restaurant he describes as Sydney's best-kept secret. 'Better than my speak-easy,' he jokes.

Afterwards, we ride back to Newtown on his motorcycle. Leo parks on the main strip outside a tattoo parlour. We remove our helmets, and he indicates the door, the frame of which is inked in black and red.

'You sure about this?' he asks.

'I think so. But I still have no idea what to get.'

'That's OK. They have books that you can flip through. Lots of pretty pictures and nice words. Just start small. How about a chest plate?'

'Very funny.'

When I don't move, Leo helps me off the bike. 'Want my advice?'

'Always.'

'Get something easy to hide. That way, if you end up hating it, you don't have to see it.'

I loosen up and shake away my nerves as Leo releases his hold. I'm not interested in a symbol, or a reminder. But I think there's a way to imprint my story with something that doesn't try to encapsulate or bind it; something that no matter how much I grow and change will always resonate.

'Do you know where you want it?' Leo asks.

I bite my lip. 'Can they tattoo over a scar?'

'Pretty sure they can.' Leo smiles his approval and reaches down to take my hand. 'Don't worry,' he says. 'It will only hurt for a minute.'

Chapter 29

I am healing my timeline.

My first day back at work and it quickly feels normal.

Inez and Kat are pleased to see me, both involving me in their creations.

Luke is polite. He acts the same way he did after he first kissed me – like nothing ever happened. It hurts, but I can't bring myself to ask him for a private chat.

Instead, I ask him if it's OK to use the chocolate studio to flex my tempering muscles.

'Of course,' he replies.

I want to say something, but my mind feels empty.

***

I use the time in the studio to make chocolates for Lara's bonbonnières. I opt for milk chocolate hearts filled with raspberry cream and dusted with a sweep of red lustre.

It doesn't take long to box them. Afterwards, I retrieve my notes for the tarot project and get to work. The Tower, card number sixteen: a building on fire and people leaping from it before it will be burnt to ash. Sudden and unexpected upheaval that ushers in the opportunity to rebuild. This one has to be dark chocolate: bitter with a sweet surprise inside – peanut brittle, or perhaps hard caramel.

I lose track of time, and before I know it Inez and Kat sweep into the studio. I check my phone and see it's five thirty.

'We're going out and we're not taking no for an answer,' says Kat.

Inez bites her lip. 'You can say no.'

I smile. 'I'd love to come.'

We end up at the bar Luke took me to the night we first kissed. Kat goes up to the counter and starts ordering.

'Hey, it's mocktail girl.'

I look up to see Aiden, the bartender who made me a special drink.

He smiles. 'I was wondering when I'd see you again.'

I feel Kat's and Inez's eyes on me.

'Shiraz, mojito and whatever she wants,' Kat says to Aiden, inclining her head towards me. 'You obviously know her order.'

Kat and Inez go in search of a table, while I wait for the drinks.

'So, what can I get you?' Aiden says.

Before I can respond, I hear a man clear his throat behind me. Without looking, I know it's Luke. I turn to face him and manage a polite smile.

Then I realise he's not alone. Beside him is his ex-girlfriend, Bianca. She's dressed casually in a strapless top and jeans, her face made up more naturally than the night I saw her at the club. Her hair is still silky and long, and her beauty is blinding. Up close, I see that she seems more ordinary in other ways. Not exactly warm, but she's no Cruella.

Luke's eyes meet mine and he nods but doesn't say anything.

I turn back to Aiden. 'Please make me something special again. But this time I'm paying.'

***

'Luke's here. With Bianca,' I say as I place the drinks down on the tall table

Kat and Inez have secured towards the back.

'Who?' says Kat, taking her drink.

I give her a look. 'Really? The woman you call Cruella.'

Kat nearly chokes on her drink. Then she looks guilty. 'We were going to tell you.'

'Tell me what?' I take a seat and study the impressive drink Aiden has made for me. It's a rainbow of lemon, raspberry and orange.

Inez and Kat exchange a look.

'Well, we weren't sure *what* to tell you,' Inez says, consoling and kind. 'We just saw him walk out of a club with her one night when we were out drinking. But I guess this confirms it.'

I force my mouth into a smile. 'It's OK. We're not together. He can see whoever he wants.' I raise my glass. 'Besides, cute bartender gave me his number.'

I glance behind me to look at Aiden. But it's impossible not to see Luke and Bianca at a table near the front, deep in conversation, their heads close together.

Chapter 30

We are not the things we do, even though they say so much about us.

It's the day before Lara's wedding, and the day of her KK. Samira drives us to the sheikh's ramshackle office in the western suburbs, where Hakeem is waiting with a friend. The sheikh is old with a thick grey beard and a majestic red turban. He reminds me of my father and I smile as he intones a brief lecture on the duties of the husband and wife, and tries to keep it light by telling Hakeem that a smart man lets his wife be right.

I have to squeeze Samira's hand as he says it; she looks ready to leap out of her seat in protest. But it doesn't irk me as deeply as it does her. Perhaps it's simply that I am not surprised. Rather, I can see the effort the sheikh is making to navigate his own murky inheritance about gender issues. Besides, all that matters to me in this moment is the outcome: we leave the office half an hour later with a newly married couple.

***

That night, Lara sleeps before Samira and I do. We're sharing my bed, but we're awake, jittery and excited because tomorrow is about more than Lara and Hakeem. We're in our pyjamas, a packet of chocolate biscuits between us, and Samira is painting my nails fire-engine red. 'For courage.'

An unspoken conversation hangs in the air between us, waiting to be expressed, and as Samira has declared, I need courage to say my fears aloud.

'Why have you never said anything to me about the way I've changed?' I finally say.

Samira doesn't respond immediately. She carefully brushes on the nail polish then uses her fingers to clean the edges.

'Well, first of all ... if you wanted to talk about it, you would. It didn't feel appropriate to push you.' She starts to apply another layer of the polish. 'Second, I wasn't surprised. You've been changing for a while now. The last couple of times I saw you, you'd already changed how you dress. You didn't seem as anxious around people. You were a bit more ... mature?' Samira lifts her gaze and bites her lip, wary of insulting me.

I concede the point. 'I'm a bit delayed.'

'Your parents were pretty hardcore. I mean, Lara and I had our struggles, but our parents were free spirits compared to yours.' She pauses. 'And third, who am I talk?'

'What?'

'You obviously see my new and not-so-improved hijab. One day, I just had this realisation that I was doing everything I was supposed to be doing, but it didn't feel like anything. It was all just action, and no thought. And then I had kids, and I started second-guessing myself about what to teach them. I want them to have God, of course. But I also want them to be outside playing, not worrying about hellfire.' Samira exhales, her breath trembling. 'I will never tell my daughter that something is *ayb* or that she can only do something when she's married.

Never. And I also know that the world won't end because I'm not the perfect *muslima*.'

'Did you ever want to take off your headscarf?'

My mother, when women would abandon the headscarf: *It's the beginning of the end.* Samira, in her turban, is playing with the boundaries of faith.

Samira shrugs. 'Kind of. But then I just changed how I wore it. I think it keeps me on the line. And, honestly, it doesn't bother me.' She pauses, inspecting my nails, then she blows on them. 'But I hate it when people use my headscarf to prop up my work. I think that's partly what made me change how I wore it. I didn't want to become a poster girl for diversity, like "I can haz talent as a hijabi"?' she says in a mocking tone and we chuckle. 'I don't want to be special because I look different.'

I feel tears unexpectedly prick at my eyes. 'Samira, you are so talented. Don't ever let anyone make you doubt that. You would not get hired because you tick a box.'

But I think about my own wobbly introduction to Maggie's business, and how I thought I was a diversity hire. And yet, I knew I was capable. I've doubted many things in my life, but not my ability in the kitchen. Instead, I was fuelled by my stubborn refusal to accept a junior status.

Samira places my hands carefully down and looks up at me with a misty-eyed smile.

'These quick nail polishes are amazing. My turn.'

I hold up the bottles and do a little dance with them. 'Which one?'

She selects a light pink, and I take the bottle and twist open the lid, forcing down the wave of emotion that Samira's confession has unleashed.

Samira looks deep in thought. 'Sahar, you know I'm proud of you for being so brave and not staying in a bad marriage. I'm glad you're living your life more fully now. But make room for love,' she says, her eyes flickering over me. 'Don't worry about the clichés and all that "I am enough" stuff. You are, but you're allowed to worry about not being enough, too. That's how we get to know ourselves. Our relationships help us grow and change. It's kind of beautiful.'

My history of love trails behind me, increasingly distant and obscure.

'I don't know, Samira. I don't think I'm built for intimate relationships. I don't even understand myself sometimes.'

Samira is watching me paint her nails. 'You know how I knew Menem was good for me?' She looks up and I stop. 'It's how easy it was to be with him. I could just be myself. I didn't have to modify my behaviour or worry that I offended him. If he didn't message me back straight away, I never worried that he was playing games.'

I apply the finishing touches to the first coat as we contemplate. Then I blow on Samira's nails, and kiss her hands. She laughs.

'It's the same with God,' she says, withdrawing her hands. 'If your whole relationship is spent thinking you've screwed up, it's never going to feel good.'

The simplicity of this truth hits me hard.

'Just talk to Him,' Samira continues. 'Say things out loud. Find out what you want to know. I still pray, but I don't beat myself up if I miss one. And I don't feel like I have to make *wudu* just to connect.'

'Sometimes I forget how complicated religion can get,' I say. 'Everyone tells you how simple it is, before throwing a hundred rules at you. It's exhausting.'

'That's why I loved Hajjeh Noura. She kept it simple.'

Our favourite Islamic teacher. That sweet, young woman who wore a hijab but not elaborately, who played basketball with us in an *abaya* and headscarf. She was accessible and exuded a warmth that wrapped around you like a warm blanket.

Hajjeh Noura wasn't married. I remember how the girls felt sorry for her, wondered if her beauty was not enough. But I saw it clearly: she didn't care. 'One day, you will understand love,' she told us.

'I should pay her a visit,' I say. 'How is she?'

Samira's face falls. She hesitates. 'I thought you knew.'

'Knew what?'

'She passed away. *Allah yirhama.*'

'What?'

'A few years ago. Cancer. I think it was stomach; it was really sudden and brutal. She got treatment, but it was incurable.'

I abandon the nail polish in shock. I try to make sense of it, but it feels like I've been hit in the head. Hajjeh Noura, a woman who spent her life trying to make sense of her spiritual inheritance, who was never offended when her more pious and religiously strict students judged her mystical habits.

My nose tingles and tears drop out of my eyes. When I look up, Samira is wiping away tears, too.

'She was so young,' I say.

Samira nods. 'And so beautiful. Inside and out.' She takes my hands in hers. 'She died well. She was loved and she was not afraid. There's truth under the layers, Sahar. That's what you need to find. The things you still hold to be true.'

I remember the last time I saw Hajjeh Noura. I wonder now if she knew of her diagnosis then. She was pallid, a little tired, but she was focused entirely on me. It was my second or third visit back to Sydney after my marriage. I had met Naeem, who was gaining influence as my faith weakened.

'God doesn't stop existing just because you don't know what to believe,' Hajjeh Noura told me, her voice and eyes soft as she held me in her gaze. There was no judgement, just compassion.

'What if I don't want to be how I was before?' I told her in response.

'I don't think you're meant to be, *habibti*. Find the way you want to be. Find the in-between parts hidden in life and hold them up to the light. But don't punish yourself. Find peace – however that comes, find peace. That is true liberation.'

***

The next morning, I am the first to wake up. I rouse Samira then head to Lara's bedroom. Kat and Inez are due to arrive any minute to do hair and make-up.

'Five more minutes,' Lara drawls.

'You're getting married, get up!'

I drag her out of bed, but she flops back onto the mattress. I get a shower going and return to find her asleep again.

'Lara! I'll make you a coffee, come on.'

Lara grumbles her way to the shower and I set about making an Arab breakfast.

Inez arrives ten minutes later looking like she stepped out of a 1960s fashion catalogue. 'How's the bride?' she says.

'Still waking up.'

Kat soon follows, her eyes red, but she has coffees for everyone. 'Now, where's the one who's chucking her life away?'

***

The wedding is a simple affair. Lara has invited her bandmates and some of Hakeem's friends. I think they are mainly coworkers, but Lara mentioned something about sparring partners at the gym he frequents. Inez and Kat are last-minute additions, clearly having bonded with my childhood friends while I untangled myself from Khaled.

How they all banded together to catch me.

We're the adults today. Samira's parents are absent, as is Lara's cousin Zahra, and her family. 'I'm tired of the *wajib* bullshit,' Lara said, when Samira told her that people would get offended. 'Hakeem doesn't have anyone here, and my parents are overseas. Who would your parents sit with? Just don't tell them it's a wedding. It's a lunch, which is true.'

I admired her for taking the stance. At forty, we're finally learning to make choices that feel right rather than being tied down by obligation.

The luncheon is at a bistro that overlooks the harbour. Hakeem and Lara have rented out a private space, and it's perfectly intimate. The long table has small place cards with our names on them, the bonbonnières I made resting beside each one with a sticker documenting the event and date.

Kat and Inez delivered the cake in the morning, and Lara starts to cry when she sees it. It has thick off-white buttercream icing and a trail of red roses cascading from top to bottom. Surrounding the roses on top are two different types of keyboard – musical and computer. The musician and the geek.

'You've always understood me,' Lara says, pulling me in for a hug.

She is radiant and predictably beautiful. Lara will always be that to me: the beauty with a heart and a sharp tongue – authentic and loyal. I struggled with what to buy her as a gift. The cake would not be enough. Eventually, I settled on money, like a true Arab. I don't want to decide for her what she and Hakeem need the most.

As Arabic music starts to pound through the speakers, I am reminded of Samira's wedding years ago and the person I was back then: a quiet, anxious observer who had to be seated near the exit and refused to dance because it was a mixed event.

Lara wastes no time taking to the centre of the small crowd, joining hands with Samira while their husbands look on. Then suddenly, she is in front of me, taking my hands and pulling me out of the seat.

And I don't resist. This time, I am going to dance.

Chapter 31

I want to find the in-between parts hidden in life and hold them up to the light.

I got lucky with my apartment search, finding a one-bedder two floors down in the same building as Lara's apartment. I had considered moving to my parents' home, but it made no practical sense. Here, I am walking distance from work. Here, I can carve out a space free of lifelong anchors and memories. Besides, I have come to know Newtown, its backstreets and regular haunts. I have friends here. Workmates.

Lara and Hakeem come by at midday to finish the move out of her apartment. Lara gifts me everything in her kitchen and gives me free rein on anything else I need.

After lunch, Lara hands me her deck of tarot cards and the thick book of interpretations. 'I could never get the hang of it,' she says. 'But I know they speak to you. So why don't you have these and you can be my reader going forward?' She laughs as she bundles them into my arms. 'Besides, my friend Angela tells me your first deck should always be gifted to you.'

When we're done, we stand in the empty apartment. I swallow my emotion. This is where new life was breathed into me when I first returned to Sydney.

The realisation feels like too much. I know Lara is negotiating similar thoughts, because she won't look at me and is pressing her lips together in that way you do when you're trying not to cry.

'I'll take that last one,' she says, pointing to a small cardboard box resting by the door.

I watch her leave, then the tears settle in my eyes. I have obviously become a crier, and I am not happy about it.

'Thank you,' I say to Hakeem.

We begin moving towards the door. 'It's nothing,' he says. 'You did very well to get the place downstairs. Are you happy with it?'

'It's perfect.'

'You're welcome anytime at ours. You know that, right?'

'I know.'

As we enter the hallway, I take one last sweeping look around and hold the view in a mental embrace. This apartment is filled with so many histories, and so many to come. I wonder how many love stories it will see, how much despair, how many new beginnings and small joys. I have never lived in a home the same way as I did in Lara's little Newtown apartment.

***

Later that night, Inez and Kat come by with dinner – proper, old-school calzone stuffed with cheese and beef for me, salami for Kat, and vegetarian for Inez.

'Love what you've done with the place,' Kat says, stepping around boxes. There aren't many of them; the benefit of a busy life is that I haven't accumulated unnecessary stuff. But I need a couch. The bed I slept in at Lara's will do for now, but I need to look at creating a bedroom, too. The thought excites me, even with the nerves about having to make design decisions. I've always just fitted myself into the space I was in – from my parents' home to a husband's, then to Lara's apartment. I've never had to think about what I like.

I make space for us on the living room floor, pushing boxes aside, then spread out the 'wog mat' Lara let me take during the move.

We eat and murmur conversation. Kat tells us about the trip she's planning to the Greek Islands at the edge of the European summer with some friends. 'Three months and I'm outta here. I'm counting it down.'

Then Inez carefully extracts some pamphlets out of her bag. She extends them towards us, beaming. 'My burlesque show. You have to come.'

We grab the pamphlets. I'm in awe and Kat looks like a proud mother.

'It's at Musicale?' I give her a sly look. 'I think Leo will be there.'

Kat stares at Inez. 'Fucken hell. You don't shit where you eat. Didn't this one just learn that?' She indicates towards me.

'I have no regrets,' I say – a revelation that even I find a bit startling.

'I didn't pick the venue,' Inez says, although her cheeks have gone pink. 'I'm actually kind of hoping he won't be there. It's not like I'm not already freaking out.'

'You don't have to take your tits out, do you?' says Kat, ever the diplomat.

This kicks Inez into life. 'You are the worst.' She chuckles. 'I don't have to, no, but I might.' She kisses Kat on the head, then looks at me. 'The more important question is, do I invite Luke? I feel bad leaving him out.'

'Of course. Invite him,' I say quickly.

'I doubt he'll go now he's hooked up with Cruella,' Kat says. 'She probably keeps tabs on his every movement.'

My stomach sinks at this reminder, but I try to hide my disappointment. Inez gives Kat a forbidding look and shakes her head.

I stay focused on my food, but then Kat lets out a sigh and I wince.

'Do you want to talk about it?' she says.

'Not really.'

'You should talk to him,' Inez says.

'I don't know what to say. Luke has moved on. And I should now, too.'

There's an awkward silence that Kat splinters a few seconds later.

'It's not like being a lesbian is much easier.'

'But the sex is better,' Inez and I chorus, and we all laugh.

Then Inez clears her throat and locks eyes with me, a question in her expression. I know what she's asking and I nod. It's time.

'So, Kat,' Inez begins, 'there's something else Sahar and I have to tell you.'

Kat is immediately alarmed. 'What's wrong?'

'I did the list you drew up for me,' I say. 'Inez is going to perform burlesque. Now it's your turn to do something.'

Kat shakes her head. 'I told you. There's nothing I haven't tried.'

Inez is starting to look genuinely nervous. 'Maggie and I called the producer from the food channel and they're interested in doing a story on the cafe and its social media popularity,' she says in a rush.

'Right,' says Kat. 'Well, good for you. You'll be great.'

'No. They want *you.* And they've agreed to go no frills.'

'Meaning?'

'Meaning no make-up, just the basic TV foundation and touch-ups so that you don't look sweaty; that sort of thing.'

Kat's response surprises me. I can detect some resistance, but she isn't swearing at us or batting the idea down.

'What if I fuck it up?'

'It's not possible,' I say, and I mean it.

'Fucken hell, I can't leave you two alone,' Kat says, and we smile like idiots.

Kat is still processing the trickery. 'If I'm being dragged into this, we've also got to get Luke, the little fucker.'

Chapter 32

Chocolate is not just a flavour. It's a feeling.

The next morning at work, it's just Inez, Kat and me. No juniors, no Luke. We're puzzled, but Maggie comes in a few minutes past six to announce that Luke has called in sick.

'I think we can all agree that this is unusual,' she says, 'but he assures me that he's OK.'

'He's human, after all,' Kat says with a snicker.

'Inez, you're in charge,' Maggie says. 'Sahar, you wanted to see me?'

I grab the prototype of tarot chocolates from under my bench and the deck of cards Lara gifted me, and follow Maggie into her office.

'OK, miss,' Maggie says, shimmying into her seat. 'What do you want to show me?'

My hands tremble as I pass her the rectangular black box with a red ribbon.

Maggie unties the ribbon with a flourish and leans back to take in the selection. She inspects the tray of multi-flavoured decorated chocolates, then glances up at me.

'What am I looking at?'

'Each chocolate represents a tarot card,' I say. 'More specifically, the twenty-two cards in the Major Arcana.'

Maggie winces. 'English, please.'

'OK.' I produce Lara's deck and open the box, but the cards are stuck, so I have to wrestle them out. 'Sorry.'

Maggie waits, more patient and curious now, her fingers splayed across her cheek.

I forage for the majors and fan them out across the bench. 'The Major Arcana represent the big milestones in life. The Fool,' I say, holding up the card, 'sets out on a journey to liberation. The World...' I hold up the card, which shows a naked woman wrapped only in a garland of leaves, surrounded by symbols of her liberation. 'This is the end of the journey. Completion and wholeness. In between, we have the big things we are confronted with when we live fully: love, separation, hope, and, of course, fulfilment. If you're lucky, an authentic life.' I take a breath. 'Each chocolate is one of these cards. But they're not made to look like them; I have designed each one to taste like the meaning of the card.'

I have Maggie's attention. 'OK, you've got me interested. But it sounds like a lot of work.'

'It is, and I know I need to revise it. The chocolates take a long time to produce, so I will need to modify them, and perhaps offer them individually across a period of time, rather than as a box set. Then there could be a highly priced box for a special occasion. But what do you think of the basic idea?'

Maggie studies the tray. 'May I?'

I nod. 'I made a few of each.'

Maggie selects one randomly and cuts it open. She nods, impressed. 'Nicely filled,' she says, taking in the thick ganache centre. She bites into it. 'Chilli. Which one is this?'

'The Devil.'

Maggie looks surprised. 'Aren't you clever?'

'You like it?'

'Sahar, this is fabulous.'

I sit in the moment, moved by Maggie's approval.

'I had my cards read once,' Maggie says. 'She was a relative of a relative. An old Italian woman who stopped halfway to have a ciggie.' Maggie cackles. 'She read my cup, too.'

'And?'

'I don't remember all the details, but she did tell me I would get married and I did. I just would've liked her to have warned me about the divorce, too.'

We laugh and I point to the cards. 'The Devil symbolises bondage but also marriage.'

'Sounds about right.' Maggie bites into a white chocolate square. 'How do I know which is which?'

'We'll have it on the box. But that one is The Star. Wishes fulfilled.'

'Popping candy inside. Super clever.' Next, Maggie plucks out a heart-shaped piece and cuts it open. It oozes a pink filling.

'The Lovers.'

Maggie lets out a long, contented sigh. 'There it is. You finally found your voice.'

'What's my voice?'

'Chocolate as life. You like mysterious things. You're a feeler. It's a good voice to have. It means you'll connect with people, not just their tastebuds.'

'Thank you, Maggie.'

'This is very good, Sahar. You paid attention. You're not as different as you thought you were, right? No crying.'

But I can't stop it. My eyes brim with tears and Maggie rises from her seat and pulls me close. 'You're doing just fine.'

When we separate, I wipe away a tear and clear my throat. 'There's something else I wanted to run by you. It's not fully formed in my head yet.'

Maggie listens as she covers the chocolate box and ties the ribbon.

'I haven't figured out exactly how it would work, but how would you feel about introducing a charitable initiative? Or involvement in a community program? Something to contribute to the community.'

Maggie lets out a tiny sigh as she studies me. I don't know what to make of her response because she is inspecting me like I have chocolate on my face.

'That sounds like a very good idea, Sahar.' She remains quietly intense for a few more seconds, then abandons the box and takes my hands. 'I'm very glad that I took you to that improv theatre and made you face your worst fears.'

'What, making an idiot of myself in front of other people?'

'Raising your voice.' Maggie smiles. 'Maybe we should arrange another team-building day. How do you feel about singing?'

'Oh God no, please.'

'I think Luke would love it.' Then her expression grows serious as she notices my response. 'I know you don't see me a lot, but I see a lot more than you think. There's something between you two, yes?'

'Not anymore.'

'I don't want to micromanage your personal lives. You're adults. But you have to see him every day and we're not a big team here.'

'I know.'

'Do I need to have a word with him?'

'No. We're fine. Honestly.'

When I leave Maggie's office, it occurs to me that ordinary joy comes in being true to what you're curious about. Even with The Experiment coming to an end, I never sought out what truly interests me. And sometimes, you have to go back to the beginning.

***

I return to my bench in an inflated mood and get to work on my cake for the day – a peaches-and-cream sponge. I lose myself in the work, and I've just finished a batch of cakes when Kat ushers in Samira.

I look up in surprise. 'What are you doing here? Is everything OK?'

Samira lingers at the doorway, a bit shy to enter. In her arms is a large white box tied with a red ribbon.

'It's OK, come in,' Kat says.

'I wanted to surprise you, but I couldn't wait.' Samira holds the box aloft. 'Is there somewhere clean I can put this down?'

I sweep the debris off my counter and give it a quick wipe down. Samira carefully manoeuvres the package onto the counter.

'Open it,' she says, stepping back and lacing her hands together, her smile more brilliant than the sun.

'What is it?'

'Just open it.'

I untie the ribbon and lift the lid of the box. Inside, resting on some tissue paper, is a framed black-and-white photograph of me doing a half-angel. The rest of the class are in it, too, but they're out of focus. Only I am clear. The lines of my body are tight, my hair hanging down.

I look at it in awe, unable to speak.

'Please tell me you like it,' Samira says.

I turn to Samira and embrace her like it's the last time I'm going to see her. When we break apart, I see that she too is emotional.

'OK, you like it.' She brushes her forehead and says, 'Phew,' then she wipes away the tears spilling from her eyes.

'It's beautiful,' I say.

'So beautiful,' says Inez, coming to a stop beside Kat.

'Wicked,' says Kat, lifting it up.

Maggie joins us, her eyes switching between the frame and me. 'This is you.'

I nod. 'I know, I find it hard to believe, too. My friend Samira took it.'

Maggie analyses Samira, who is still swimming in pride – she knows I'm floored.

'Could you take photos of us? Make it look like we know what we're doing?' Maggie asks.

Samira laughs. 'I would love to.'

A few minutes later, I am preparing to walk Samira out when Kat calls out, 'Give her some tarts.'

'Want some treats?' I say.

Samira grins. 'Like that's even a question.'

I package up some caramel and fruit tarts then lead her out.

When we reach her car, Samira places the box inside then turns to face me, taking my hands in hers. 'Sahar, are you in love with Luke?'

I look away. 'I don't know. Luke is different. It doesn't feel the same with him as how I felt with Naeem. What I had with Naeem was real, but ... it was a connection I had no say in. With Luke, I had a say in it.'

Samira ponders this. 'You should tell Luke how you feel. It can't get worse, right?'

'Of course it can. We work together. But when he's not there, it's never the same.'

'I understand.'

I think she does. Or wants to, which is the same thing.

'I love you so much, Samira.'

'Stop it. No one is dying here.'

But I can see that we're both drowning in some emotion we didn't realise was there.

Samira pulls me close. 'I hate what you went through, Sahar, but I'm so glad you came back. It's not as lonely, you know?'

'I know. I'm glad too.'

Samira swoops into her car before we can dissolve into another round of shared tears. I wave as she drives off, then head back into the kitchen.

Maggie makes a beeline for me. 'I wasn't kidding about your friend. Can you get her in to take photos of us? I think we've got our team.'

'Of course.'

But as I look around me, I know we don't. Luke is not here, and our team is incomplete.

***

After work, I make my way to Luke's apartment. I am uncertain about what I will say to him, assuming he's even home, and that he's alone. This is not my final step to liberation or a happy ending. It's a necessary step I have to take, because he is a gap I had not anticipated, but one I don't wish to fill with something or someone else. I have a right to this – to getting to know someone on my terms – without needing it to mean something before it can show me what it wants to be.

I press the buzzer and wait, a box of my tarot chocolates in hand. There are brushstrokes of orange in the sunset sky, and I wonder how, even when the worst things happen, so much remains beautiful.

'Yep,' Luke's voice comes through the intercom.

'It's me. Sahar.'

After a pause, the door buzzes open, and I take a nervy ride in the lift up to Luke's floor. When I arrive, he's at the door, waiting for me.

'Can I come in?' I ask.

He stares back at me, and I think he is going to turn me away. But then he shrugs and steps aside, indicating for me to enter.

I walk inside.

Luke brushes past me and heads to the kitchen, where a pot boils away on the stove. As usual, music is filling the space, but Luke turns it down then returns to the kitchen bench.

'I was hoping you'd be home,' I begin nervously. 'I want to apologise. And to explain. If you'll let me.'

Luke stays focused on his food preparation. He chops into carrots, the sound dull and sharp.

I am uncomfortable, ready to flee, but I force out the words. 'I'm not going to make excuses or try to change the story. I know I messed up. And I am so deeply sorry.'

Luke's focus is still heavily on the vegetables.

'I wasn't trying to hurt you. But I was a mess, and I needed to sort things out.'

As Luke chops away, I lose patience. 'Will you at least listen to me?'

He lets out a sigh and abandons his knife. 'You're sorry, you feel better, we're all good.'

'You slept with your ex!'

'You went to Leo!'

There's silence as we both take in each other's words.

'There's nothing between me and Leo,' I say carefully.

Luke shakes his head. 'I told you I would be there if you needed me. Instead you slept with me, snuck out, then went to Leo.'

Technically, all true. In facts, however, not essence. Regardless, it doesn't sound very good.

'Luke, I didn't want to involve you. All Leo did was give me a safe space to talk to my ex-husband.'

And, well, he helped me get a tattoo, but this is hardly the time to mention that.

Luke abandons the food. He places his hands against the bench, looking genuinely upset. 'I was already involved, Sahar. We slept together. I was just trying to catch my breath.'

'I'm sorry. I couldn't bear to hurt you so—'

'So you went and decided for me.'

'It was easy to go to Leo. He's a friend. You're not.'

Luke can't look at me.

'Luke.'

He remains silent.

'That's all?'

'By the way, I didn't sleep with Bianca. I couldn't. It wouldn't have been fair to her.'

'You were at the bar together.'

'We both had things to say.'

The revelation should make me feel better, but knowing he's unattached and still rejecting me is much worse.

'I'm back at work tomorrow,' he says. 'It'll be weird for a while, but eventually, it will go back to normal. It's no big deal.'

Luke's dismissal splits me open. My time with him was ephemeral. Intimate in ways beyond the physical. As I contemplate the rigidity in his body, I realise that he is more fully formed in my eyes than Khaled and even Naeem. He has greater dimension. With him, I got to try out how it feels to build a connection, not simply get handed one. In some ways, I already knew him before we became intimate. Naeem was a genuine, inexplicable connection, but one that had nowhere to go. I have landed in the place I was taught to avoid my whole life; the place our mothers warned us about when it comes to men and their gaze. In all of the lessons on how to behave, we were never taught to examine the emotional outcome.

I try to orientate myself, my face aflame. Then I remember the box of my Major Arcana chocolates, and place it on the counter. 'I hope you like them.'

I start to walk away, then stop and turn around, but Luke is back to his work.

'You know, it was a big deal to me, Luke,' I say quietly, my voice steady. 'I have only ever been with one other person. And I felt more connected to you in a few months than I did in eight years with him.'

Overcome by emotion, I turn around and continue walking towards the door. I'm halfway across the room when I feel a hand on my shoulder and I stop. I'm shaking as I turn around to face Luke, who pulls me towards him.

'I'm sorry,' he says. He meets my gaze, cups my face in his hands, using his thumb to rub my cheek. 'I'm so sorry,' he repeats, his mouth searching for mine. 'I have so much to learn.'

Chapter 33

I don't always know how the pieces come to fit together, only that when you're in the right place, eventually they must.

The following day, Luke is at my apartment. We spent the previous night together – an evening talking, reviving our connection.

In my small living room, Luke holds up a frame and inspects it. 'Your folks?'

It's a series of black-and-white photos of my parents in their youth, smiling because life was yet to fill them up with ideas and ambiguities.

'Yes. Before they got super religious.'

Luke studies it, and I watch him. He lingers. 'It must be hard with them both gone.'

'It is. I kind of feel like I said goodbye to them on bad terms.'

'You had a fight?'

'No. We were just ... disconnected. I don't think we ever understood each other.'

'They were your parents. Join the club.'

Luke replaces the frame, which takes central place on the multi-coloured runner spread out on my small wooden buffet. I found it at a furniture shop one afternoon after work. It's light brown, worn out in a few places, but also full of character. It carries silent histories.

Luke continues along the shelf. Next, a family photo taken in Palestine when I was eight or nine. We're neatly positioned in front of a backdrop of a painted rainforest.

Luke smiles. 'Cute.'

Then, a photo of Salim and Naila on their wedding day, both of them looking content, almost relieved. Beside that a compilation of photos of their children from a few years ago. I still owe them their special cakes.

I wrap my arms around Luke from behind. I'm excited to share this with him. I have never collected visible memories, but I've always noticed it in other people's spaces. This table, packed with the people I love, is proof of my fullness.

Luke has moved on to the photos of my girls: Lara and Samira, taken on the morning of Lara's wedding. I wrestled with which one to frame. I almost chose one where Lara was dolled up as a dreamy bride, her hair long with a slight wave, but I liked this one, taken by Inez. We're assembled in the kitchen, a pot of Arabic coffee in the centre of the table, all three of us happy but unkempt and yet to be made up. The real us.

'This one definitely brings out your natural glow,' Luke jokes, and I mock-smack him on the arm. He laughs then moves on to a photo of the three of us from our university years.

'Oh crap, no,' I say, but Luke has raised the frame too high for me to reach it.

'You've got it on display,' he protests.

'I need to ease you in with that one!'

Luke lowers the photo to examine it properly. He scrunches his eyes, bringing the image closer. 'This can't be you,' he says.

'I was a late bloomer.'

Luke gives me a strange look. 'I'm not insulting you. I genuinely can't believe this is you.'

I shrug. 'I look different.' The girl in that photo feels like a phantom limb. I can never really shake her, no matter how irrelevant she is to the person I have become.

'It's not even that. Just ... something is missing. She's not a force like you are.' Luke stares at the image a while longer, then he smiles and replaces it. He's about to move on when he catches my subdued expression. 'Did I upset you?'

'No. I just wasn't expecting that reaction.'

Luke smiles. He kisses me then moves on to the last item: The Experiment list, framed.

'Bloody hell.' He grins. 'That day. Jesus. Fucking improv.'

'I think that's the first day I felt like we could get along.'

'*You* tried to make an escape.'

I wince. 'I did, and I failed.'

'You get points for trying.'

'Is that when you first liked me?'

'No. I think it was the day of your audition, when you tried to school Maggie on a better way to make panna cotta.'

I shake with laughter, but my face is burning from embarrassment. 'Was it that bad?'

'The panna cotta?'

'No, what I did.'

'It wasn't great, but you made a good dessert, so you got away with it.'

'Thank God.'

There's one more frame I have to find a home for: the one Samira took of me on the trapeze. I pick it up off the floor. 'What do you think? Where should it go?'

I scan the small space, hugging the large frame, wondering if it's ridiculous to put myself on display. But then I look at it and I don't just see myself, I see what Samira saw that day. I see what I am finally ready to show others. And there's something else, something that plucks away at my thoughts until eventually it lands: the photo reminds me of The Hanged Man card that Inez saw in my reading. Feeling stuck, but using the delay to see the world from a new perspective. I break into a stupid grin at this gentle synchronicity.

'How about above the couch?' Luke suggests. 'It's still on display, but you're not constantly looking at it.'

We use a plastic hook to secure it in place then settle onto the couch. Luke relaxes against the arm of the seat, while I sit cross-legged, facing him. He reaches for my hands, holding them in his, a bit fidgety.

'Anything left on the list?' he says.

'Swimming lessons.'

'Want me to teach you?'

'No. I'd like to do that one on my own, if that's OK.'

'Of course.'

'But speaking of the list,' I say, 'Inez is doing burlesque, and Kat is doing a TV segment. You didn't do anything. Just saying.'

Luke smiles. 'Maybe I did do something.'

'Really?' I say, dubious.

Luke is silent, but his eyes are still on me.

'It can't involve chocolate,' I say.

He shifts in the seat, bringing his head in closer to mine. 'I think it can involve chocolate a little bit.'

My stomach burns. This intimacy – still new, so thrilling.

He kisses me. 'What if I fell in love?'

A warmth fills me. 'Luke. Come on. You're not that much younger than me. What about Bianca? I'm sure there were others before her.'

'I've been attracted to a lot of women. I think I've even thought I was in love. But no one got into my head the way you did. No one made me think about myself the way you did.'

I kiss him, and as usual, his hands go to my face and mine to his shoulders. When we separate, he studies me, one hand touching my hair.

'You're not allowed to tell Kat that that was my thing.'

'I wouldn't do that to you.'

We sit in silence for a few seconds, his expression unclear, but then I wonder if he's waiting for me to address his big admission. I smile.

'I love you, Luke. Would you believe me if I told you I've never said that to anyone before?'

Luke exhales. His eyes on me, he reaches out to take hold of my hands. He lifts them to his mouth and kisses them, his hands still wrapped around mine. 'I do recall you saying you've never even been on a date.'

'You know what's funny? Everyone else seemed to see it before we did,' I say.

'That happens.'

I take in his blue eyes, his smile, the ease with which he sits in my apartment.

'I have no idea how to introduce you to my brother. But I think you should meet him.'

Chapter 34

Control on the way up.

It's a sunny afternoon as we gather in the small laneway behind the chocolate studio, where the walls are graffitied in red, blue and green. Today, Kat is making her TV debut. But first, we're having our photographs taken as a team: Maggie, Luke, Kat, Inez and me.

Maggie wants to adjust our appearances, but Samira intervenes. 'It's better for everyone to look exactly as they do on a normal day.'

'I'll button up my whites, Boss, don't worry,' says Kat and Maggie stares her down.

We're all in our whites, our caps on, looking like baker surgeons. But Maggie is dressed in her usual attire: a skirt and a knit top, some chunky jewellery and her lips painted bright red.

'You all look just fine,' Samira says, giving us a final scan. She has already set up her equipment. In front of the graffiti wall, she places a couple of plastic milk crates about a metre apart and directs Maggie to sit on one, and Maggie makes a face.

We naturally find our positions. Luke touches my arm as he brushes past me to stand beside Inez, who takes the second crate. Kat stands to her left, and I stand on the end beside Maggie.

'Just talk among yourselves,' Samira says. 'I need to do some test shots.'

It's not long before we're in full flight: Kat is mocking Luke for not knowing how to smile, Inez is playing the diplomat and Maggie is expressing her dismay at everyone's behaviour. Luke does smile, though, lifting his gaze to me more than once. Soon, everyone is in high spirits, and we forget that Samira is there, recording the camaraderie.

'OK, we're done with this lot,' she says, detaching the camera.

'That's it?' says Maggie.

Samira smiles and brings the camera over to Maggie. She displays a series of photos, all of them natural, candid – the kind of images you could happily place on the wall of a cafe to show who is at work behind the scenes. A group of people laughing together, gazes filled with meaning. Maggie gets misty-eyed. 'That's my family,' she says. 'You got them.'

We cheer because it feels like a celebration. Kat hops over to Maggie and smacks a kiss on her cheek.

'Next, we do individuals inside,' Samira tells us.

As the rest of the group wander back to the kitchen, I help Samira pack up.

I swing the tripod bag over my shoulder and she carries a similar one, the camera around her neck. We each take a crate.

'So, how's it going with the hot baker?' Samira says, giving me a furtive look.

'We're dating, I guess.'

'O-M-G, Sahar,' she says with an exaggerated American accent. 'You, like, totally have a boyfriend.'

'We're not teenagers.'

'But you like him. You think he'll convert?'

'Oh God, Samira. Don't start.'

But when I look over, she's laughing. 'I'm sorry. I just find your life very exciting.'

'I don't know about that.'

'Look, remember what you told me about Menem? It wasn't on him to give me my faith. Same thing applies here. You do you and all that.'

We reach the kitchen and Samira slows down. 'I'll take this,' she says, grabbing hold of the tripod. 'By the way, Lara confirmed: dinner this Saturday at her house.'

'Can we have something besides pizza?'

'Why would you even say that?'

Samira disappears into the kitchen ahead of me just as I spot Leo crossing the street. He sees me and gestures for me to wait.

'Hey,' he says when he reaches me. 'How's the weather today?'

'Sunny, no chance of rain.'

'Why aren't you inside making lots of sweets so that I can make more money?'

'Funny. It's school-picture day. Want your photograph taken?'

'I don't want to break the lens.' Leo indicates to the doorway. 'Have you showed off the tatt yet? I'm sure they'll be impressed.'

'Not yet.'

Only Luke has seen it, but I keep this to myself.

***

Inside, Samira is already taking photos. Right now, she's capturing Kat, who's assembling a lime-coloured jelly mousse square.

We all take turns, even Maggie, who dons her chef's whites to deliver her signature dish: the chocolate dome sprinkled with gold lustre. I see a different side to her as she works: she's in the zone and it's a striking image. I wonder if she misses the hands-on work.

Samira also captures the juniors prepping – which they would usually do in the morning. Luke does his lemon drizzle cakes then dashes off to the chocolate studio to start prepping for the next shoot. Samira moves on to Inez, who is working on a vegan doughnut with thick vanilla icing and rose petals.

I would have liked to be in the chocolate studio, but I quickly forget this as I deep-dive into one of my fancy 'wog cakes', the creation I came up with while working with Kat. I forget that Samira is there, finding comfort in the waves of the process.

When I'm finished, I help Samira bundle up her equipment to take over to the chocolate studio, where she will photograph Luke. But then Luke pops his head into the kitchen and calls out my name.

'Sahar,' he says. 'You're coming too.'

'I've already been photographed.'

Luke rolls his eyes. 'Please? For me? You're more photogenic than I am anyway.'

I glance around and meet Kat's look and she shrugs. 'Go on,' she says, cracking a smile that seems as close to a stamp of approval as I might get.

In the studio, Luke is playing instrumental music and I am quietly pleased that I recognise the artist: Explosions in the Sky. The mood is mellow as I put on my apron and get to work.

Luke has already melted the milk chocolate buds, a batch large enough for two people to work on from either side of the bench. We quickly find our flow, and as always, I find comfort in the sounds of metal scraping against marble – a peaceful fight. Catharsis.

Samira is clicking away, but she wants photos of us making actual chocolates. 'Maggie wants lots of options for the website.'

'There's going to be a website?' I say.

Luke nods. 'She's come around to it. But I'm in charge of making it happen.'

'That's great,' I say, my smile wide. This is no small thing. This is Luke's vision coming to life.

He smiles back. 'OK, let's keep it simple. Which tarot card should we make? Has to be milk chocolate, obviously.'

'You don't want to do something more generic?' I indicate to the shelf heaving with moulds for everything from hearts to seahorses.

'It should be something different. We need to show we're special.'

I ponder the options. Some are too complicated, and don't use milk chocolate. For a moment, I consider The Chariot, the card of movement and progress. Cherry-filled triangular milk chocolates – red, energetic, bursting with flavour, directional, with a light spray of gold on the top because the journey leads to success. But what about Temperance? Chewy caramel in a thin circle, an indent down the middle, one side sprinkled with sea salt. The card of balance, of patience and weighing up options. Sweet and salty all at once.

But then the answer lands. I smile.

'The World.'

A milk chocolate dome that contains random flavours – caramel or mint, strawberry or orange cream – because liberation does not look the same to everyone. No matter the contents, it will be delightful, refreshing and rewarding. The outside is sprayed with silver and gold.

Luke and I temper the chocolate next to each other. Then we make the domes, taking on the same tasks in sync. We pour the tempered chocolate in, standing side by side. I know how to do this quickly and easily now, but Luke is still faster than me, so he gradually slows his pace. We tap the moulds against the bench then tip out the excess into the bowl of chocolate. I become mesmerised by the process, and once again forget that Samira is there, documenting our movements.

I glance at Luke and he meets my gaze. He gives me a look that I now recognise as contentment and I tighten my lips to stop myself from smiling stupidly.

When it's time to fill the chocolates, we complete each one precisely, tap the trays then pour chocolate over the moulds.

We all take a break while the chocolates set. Samira dutifully photographs them and Luke boxes them up for her as a gift. She tries to pretend she doesn't want them, but her wide-eyed look of delight betrays her. Chocolate is not just chocolate, after all. It's a feeling.

Chapter 35

We think darkness is what transforms us. But what of the things we see in the light?

It's Saturday night, and Samira, Lara and I are at Hakeem's father's house – Hakeem's inheritance. Hakeem never sold it, and with Lara, he has painstakingly restored it. It looks modern, with wooden floorboards, and bright white paint on the walls.

Lara takes us on a tour, showing us their handiwork: an elegant bedroom out of a catalogue; a spare room that is both an office and storage closet. The living room is spacious, with wide couches, a circular coffee table and a large television. Samira's photo of Lara onstage sits above it, and opposite, by the main window, is the painting of the striking Arab woman she had on the wall in Newtown.

The bathroom is my favourite room: black-and-white art-deco tiles, with a vintage bathtub. It gets me thinking again about my parents' house, which still sits unused and unrented. Neglected.

The pizza is delivered by a fatigued-looking man in a scratched-up helmet.

'Will you help me clean out Mum and Dad's place?' I ask them as we sit down to eat. 'I think it's time.'

'Of course we will,' says Samira.

'I think I'm going to ask Luke to help, too,' I say. 'And Salim.' Now it's my turn to wince. The thought of the two of them meeting tightens my stomach.

Hakeem enters the kitchen and Lara immediately moves towards him. 'I'm leaving now,' he says and gives her a peck on the mouth. 'Bye, ladies.'

Lara follows him out, and Samira and I lean over to the window to spy on them.

'Damn it, we can't see anything,' she whispers.

We laugh, and Samira thrusts open the second pizza box, assessing its look. 'Hot, hot, hot,' she says as she plates a slice of pizza. 'So ... Are you going to explain the tattoo?'

'How did you see it?'

'It's peeking out above your jeans.'

'Do you have super sight?'

'What's next? Are you going to join a motorcycle gang?'

We hear the door slam, then a moment later, Lara sweeps back in and drops into her seat. 'Are you asking her about the tattoo?'

'OK, I'm wearing a longer top next time.'

'I think it's awesome,' Lara says. 'What does it say?'

I stand up, turn around and pull aside my top, lowering my jeans a little. They scramble out of their seats to study it.

It's small and looks like a spider web, the words tightly coiled in a spiral.

'My Arabic sucks,' Lara says. 'Please translate.'

'*Famaa ana fil-wujuudi ghayri,*' I say. 'I am no one in existence but myself.'

'I like it,' says Samira. 'You got that from Hajjeh Noura, right?'

'Who got it from Ibn 'Arabi.' I smile as I remember how little time I gave to Sufi teachings years ago. How Hajjeh Noura had to conceal her love of the mystery. How it beckons to me now with its boundless potential.

'Who's that?' says Lara, her focus more on the hot sauce she wants to pour on top of her pizza.

'He was a Sufi mystic.'

'I'm just glad you didn't get a butterfly,' says Samira. 'They're so clichéd.'

'What's wrong with a butterfly?' says Lara. 'Have you ever seen what they go through to look like that? It's fucking torture. I saw it on a documentary once.'

We give her an enquiring look.

'Fine, it was a clip on Facebook, but same diff. They have to squeeze out of the cocoon and it almost kills them.'

I smile at the poetry of her observation. So much of my life has been spent stubbornly refusing to emerge from the cocoon because it was too painful.

I select a piece of pizza and carefully orientate it on my plate. 'What tattoo would you get?' I say to them.

'A musical note for Lara,' says Samira, chuckling as she bites into her pizza.

Lara hooks an eyebrow, offended. 'Please. I wouldn't be so obvious. A sword piercing a heart. Very red, and very big. That's me.'

Samira and I concede that this is very Lara.

'What about you, Samira?' I say.

'I'd probably get a quote. Or something to do with my kids and Menem. Like their birth dates.'

'That's nice,' says Lara. 'Meaningful.'

'Well, I have another proposal for you, and it's not getting tattoos,' I say. I put aside my pizza and brace myself. Lara stops mid-bite and Samira waits, curious. 'The Experiment's done. But I'm going to do a new one.'

'Oh God,' says Samira, but Lara's eyes light up.

'Are you going to do burlesque like Inez?'

I actually laugh out loud. 'Ah no. That will never happen. Ever.'

'It could happen,' Lara says, looking genuinely disappointed.

'Sorry. My ambitions are far more modest than that. This list is going to be an ongoing one. There's no expiry date or specific goal in mind. And I was wondering ... what would you think of doing some things with me? It doesn't have to be something you couldn't do because your parents or the community said no. If something comes up and you like it, it goes on the list.'

Samira straightens up, like she's being called to action. 'I love it. We can put it in an online doc. Count me in.'

'Lara?'

'Of course. What's first on the list?'

'Well, for me it's swimming lessons.'

'I want to try trapeze with you,' says Samira. 'What you did scared the crap out of me. I liked it.'

'I want to go on a holiday with you both,' says Lara. 'I'm always on the road with people I like but don't love like you guys. We should've done Europe together when we were single and our boobs were still perky.'

Samira shakes her head. 'I have never had perky boobs.'

'Me either,' I sigh. 'But they look good when I'm flat on my back.'

We have a proper laugh and Lara jumps up, returning a few moments later with a laptop, a bit breathless with excitement. 'OK, so where are we going?'

'Somewhere not too far,' Samira says. 'I can't do that to Menem and the kids. It's been ages since we went away together.'

'I don't mind so long as it's somewhere with mountains or ocean, or both,' I say. In Jordan, I developed a love for nature, its extraordinary capacity for beauty, destruction and repair. I loved to hear the sound of my hiking boots against the hard earth. I was in awe of the natural world that withstood so much, and saw everything without judgement.

'Too easy,' Lara says, typing away. Samira goes to sit next to her, offering more suggestions, and I watch, peaceful.

Even with our differences, when I look at Samira and Lara, I see myself, my history, present and future intertwined. It occurs to me that a cycle is complete. Like in the Major Arcana, I restarted life in Sydney as The Fool, setting out on an adventure, unsure of the terrain, but so desperate for change I couldn't look down, unpacking groceries and grief in Lara's small kitchen in Newtown.

How far we've come. Lara's new kitchen is larger, but we are the same in the essentials – just lighter – about to start a new journey and take on new adventures.

I will be a fool again, I think, rising from my seat to join my friends. But this time will be different. This time, while I am not fearless, I am no longer afraid.

Sahar's Soundtrack

1. You Won't Find Me – Narrow Skies
2. The Sun – Charlz
3. Killing Me – Luke Sital-Singh
4. The Chain – Fleetwood Mac
5. Dear Miss Lonelyhearts – Cold War Kids
6. Mended – Vera Blue
7. Hands of Time – Groove Armada
8. Burn – Ray LaMontagne
9. Feel It (In the Air Tonight) – Naturally 7
10. I Wasted You – Flora Cash
11. Forest Fires – Axel Flovent
12. Swim Good – Frank Ocean
13. Clean – Taylor Swift
14. Bring It on Home to Me – Sam Cooke
15. Waves – Dean Lewis
16. We Stayed Up All Night – Tourist (feat. Ardyn)
17. Mad World – Gary Jules
18. I Love It – Icona Pop (feat. Charli XCX)
19. Electrical – Eves the Behaviour
20. Silence – Marshmellow (feat. Khalid)

21. Halo – Beyoncé
22. Dancing on My Own – Callum Scott
23. I Should Live in Salt – The National
24. Come See About Me – Nicki Minaj
25. Never Let Me Go – Florence and the Machine
26. Your Hand in Mine – Explosions in the Sky
27. Chicago – Sufjan Stevens
28. By Your Side – Sade
29. Lightning Crashes – Live
30. The One That Got Away – The Civil Wars
31. Leads Me Back – Sarah Blasko
32. Dance Monkey – Tones and I
33. Ether – We Are All Astronauts
34. Unchained Melody – The Righteous Brothers
35. When Doves Cry – Prince
36. Freedom – Beyoncé (feat. Kendrick Lamar)
37. Drumming Song – Florence and the Machine
38. Bad Love – RY X
39. We Were in Love – Ta-Ku
40. Bird – Bedouine

41. Want to Want Me – Jason Derulo
42. I Will Wait – Mumford and Sons
43. Little Talks – Of Monsters and Men
44. Who Knew – P!nk
45. Last Request – Paolo Nutini
46. I'm Jim Morrison, I'm Dead – Mogwai
47. Hotline Bling – Drake
48. All We Do – Oh Wonder
49. Renegades – X Ambassadors
50. Flesh and Bone – Keaton Henson

Acknowledgements

These characters have been with me for more than a decade, and I'm so gratified that I was able to journey with them across three books. This story has been significant for so many reasons, not the least because it signalled a new way of writing novels for me. Sahar doesn't have the kind of sense of humour that Samira and Lara have, and writing her story has been a profound experience – one that I will always treasure.

With that being said, I have to say it was all possible because my agent, Tara Wynne at Curtis Brown, truly heard me when I told her that not only did I need to write Sahar's story, but that I wanted to revisit my previous novels in the process. Thank you, Tara, for not only aligning this book with the right people, but also for helping to revive the ones that came before it.

Which brings me to the other instrumental players in this book's development. First, my gratitude to Lex Hirst at Pantera Press, who saw and understood early on my vision for this story and threw her full support behind it. Thank you also to Lucy Bell, editor extraordinaire, whose passion for the novel made the editing process a rewarding one. Your keen eye, insights and perspectives were invaluable. Alex Nahlous, you are a wizard. Thank you for a masterful proofread. My gratitude to Alison Green for your support from the start, as well as the rest of the Pantera Press team who so enthusiastically backed this book.

Thank you to Rebecca Knights of Coco Chocolate for taking the time to instruct me on the ins and outs of running a chocolate business, and to Josh Magee from Improv Theatre Sydney for the games suggestions.

The Copyright Agency provided me with funding support at a crucial time, for which I am very grateful – you are an unvaluable organisation to Australian creators.

Thank you to the Hillarys of Ed Hillary IP Ltd for permission to use the Sir Edmund Hillary quote, and to the Joseph Campbell Foundation for the guidance on quoting Joseph Campbell.

As always, I give thanks to my husband and test reader, Chris Larsen – your support is everything. Thank you also to my family and close friends, who no longer blink when I announce that I'm writing a book.

Book Club Questions

1. What was your first impression of Lara, Samira and Sahar's relationship? Has it changed at all?
2. What role does food play in Sahar's life?
3. What does Maggie's diversity plaque represent? Why is it significant?
4. Why does Leo help Sahar?
5. How did Sahar's life in Jordan change her?
6. Why do you think Sahar struggles to share her story with Lara and Samira?
7. Sahar describes an instant connection to Naeem and wonders if they were linked in another time. How would you explain their connection?
8. How has Sahar changed from the beginning of The Experiment?
9. Agree or disagree: *Chocolate is not just chocolate, after all. It's a feeling.*

10.   If you were to create a chocolate tarot card, what flavour would it be?

11.   What experiences would be on your experiment list?

12.   What do you think the future holds for Luke and Sahar?

If you enjoyed
The Things We See in the Light,
try these other wonderful stories
by Amal Awad

Available as eBooks and print on demand in November.

About the author

Amal Awad is a journalist, screenwriter, author and performer. She has contributed to *ELLE, Frankie, Meanjin, Going Down Swinging, Daily Life, Sheilas,* SBS Life and Junkee. She has also produced and presented for ABC Radio National and has held senior editorial roles at numerous trade publications.

As a public speaker, Amal appears at schools, universities and writers' festivals around Australia. She presents workshops on storytelling and creativity, has been a regular panellist on ABC TV's *The Drum* and was a TEDx Macquarie speaker in 2019. As a screenwriter, Amal has worked on several film and television projects and is in development on more. She has also directed short films, a pursuit she continues alongside writing and performing.

Amal is the author of *Courting Samira*, *This Is How You Get Better* and *The Things We See in the Light* as well as the non-fiction books *The Incidental Muslim, Beyond Veiled Clichés: The Real Lives of Arab Women, Fridays with my Folks: Stories on Ageing, Illness and Life*, and *In My Past Life I Was Cleopatra*. She has also contributed to the anthologies *Growing Up Muslim in Australia: Coming of Age* and *Some Girls Do ... (My Life as a Teenager)*.

Back Cover Material

'Awad brings her trademark intelligence and insight to this big-hearted story of a woman building a new life – a cross-cultural delight'
TONI JORDAN

In the cafe, I watch as a woman takes a photo of her plate – an impressive, glossy lime-coloured dessert with shards of chocolate perched on top. I want to feel that ease and confidence, too. Like this is my city again, and I know my way around it.

Eight years ago, Sahar pursued her happily ever after when she married Khaled and followed him to Jordan, leaving behind her family, her friends and a thriving cake business. But married life didn't go as planned and, haunted by secrets, Sahar has returned home to Sydney without telling her husband.

With the help of her childhood friends, Sahar hits the reset button on her life. She takes a job at a local patisserie run by Maggie, a strong but kind manager who guides Sahar in sweets and life.

But as she tentatively gets to know her colleagues, Sahar faces a whole new set of challenges. There's Kat and Inez, who are determined that Sahar try new experiences. Then there's Luke, a talented chocolatier and a bundle of contradictions.

As Sahar embraces the new, she reinvents herself, trying things once forbidden to her. But just when she is finally starting to find her feet, her past finds its way back to her.

**'A story of growth and change – from cocoon to butterfly'
SASHA WASLEY**

**'Full of flavour … warm, emotive and uplifting'
KANEANA MAY**

www.ingramcontent.com/pod-product-compliance
Lightning Source LLC
Chambersburg PA
CBHW012003120726
47902CB00015B/2116